Zane pressed another fervent kiss on my mouth.

My body instantly ignited with lust again, and when he pulled away, I tried to keep him there with my lips, my head following his as he took a step back. "We don't have time."

"What do you mean?"

He lit another cigarette, his hands twitching as he devoured me with his eyes, sucking heavily on the cigarette as if that could replace my mouth on his. "It's Caleb," he explained, his voice short and terse. "The queen sent him as a spy, not because she expects me to need help. This is yet another test for me, the misbehaving protégé. She's putting you in my reach and has forbidden me to touch you. And Caleb will be her lapdog that will report back to her."

"Oh." Words failed in my throat, and disappointment crashed through me. "So we can't . . . be together?"

He shook his head, silent. The only sound was the sizzle of the cigarette paper. A long moment passed between us. "I thought it would be enough just to be in your presence again, but . . ." He gave me a rueful look from under a floppy lock of hair, and my heart melted all over again. "You're very hard to resist."

That made my legs weak with desire. "But you just kissed me."

His eyes grew hot as he stared at me. "Oh, I plan on kissing you and touching you every time he turns his back. You have my word on that."

Turn the page for rave reviews of The Succubus Diaries . . .

My Fair Succubi is also available as an eBook

Everybody loves these fun and sexy books from Jill Myles!

SUCCUBI LIKE IT HOT

"One hell of a ride. Myles's creation has a wicked sense of humor . . . good characters and plenty of sizzling sex."

—*Romantic Times*

"Weaves steamy scenes with humor and an intricate and interesting plotline, so the book is an excellent choice to dive into on a chilly night."

—Fresh Fiction

"Jill Myles expertly turns her paranormal romance into a cleverly enjoyable story filled with passionate encounters and unanticipated predicaments. . . . *Succubi Like It Hot* will tickle your funny bone and leave you grinning continuously."

—Single Titles

"Jill Myles has a fun and engaging writing style . . . ."

—Bitten by Books (5 Tombstones)

"Sexy and exciting. . . . I can't wait to read more of Jackie's adventures."

—Night Owl Reviews (4.5 stars)

GENTLEMEN PREFER SUCCUBI

"Sustains an extraordinary, confectionary appeal. . . . Myles's sexy, wacky humor is definitely something to watch."

—*Publishers Weekly*

"Jill Myles just wowed me! Don't miss this book!"

—*New York Times* bestselling author Kresley Cole

"Engaging. . . . A fun, sexy romp that you'll hate to put down."

—*Romantic Times*

"Hysterical and sexy. . . . An excellent combination of chick-lit, paranormal romance, and mystery."

—Fresh Fiction

"Appealing characters, passionate desires plus interesting original ideas . . . all interwoven to construct an outstanding paranormal tale."

—Single Titles

"Awesome. . . . Thanks to Ms. Myles for giving paranormal romance readers a new series to become addicted to."

—Fallen Angels (5 Angels; Recommended Read)

"Witty, sexy, and wickedly fun. Jill Myles is a captivating new voice, and I can't wait to see what she writes next."

—*New York Times* bestselling author Ilona Andrews

"A fabulous roller-coaster ride filled with sex, adventure, humor, and just enough darkness to keep the reader guessing. Hot, delicious, and witty, the hottest new star in the genre has just landed."

—*USA Today* bestselling author Kathryn Smith

"A lavish confection of a book, its deliciousness frosted by dark-winged angels and vampires with bite . . . supernaturally sensational."

—National bestselling author Ann Aguirre

"Deliciously sexy and fun. . . . With stiletto-sharp humor and two heroes to die for, *Gentlemen Prefer Succubi* is a temptation no reader should resist."

—National bestselling author Meljean Brook

"You can't read one page any more than you can eat just one potato chip. Jill Myles is inventive, addictive, and wickedly entertaining."

—Award-winning author Charlene Teglia

ALSO BY JILL MYLES

Gentlemen Prefer Succubi

Succubi Like It Hot

Available from Pocket Books

My Fair Succubi

The Succubus Diaries

Jill Myles

Pocket **Star** Books

New York   London   Toronto   Sydney

Pocket Star Books
A Division of Simon & Schuster, Inc.
1230 Avenue of the Americas
New York, NY 10020

This book is a work of fiction. Names, characters, places, and incidents either are products of the author's imagination or are used fictitiously. Any resemblance to actual events or locales or persons, living or dead, is entirely coincidental.

First Pocket Star Books paperback edition January 2011

POCKET STAR BOOKS and colophon are registered trademarks of Simon & Schuster, Inc.

For information about special discounts for bulk purchases, please contact Simon & Schuster Special Sales at 1-866-506-1949 or business@simonandschuster.com.

The Simon & Schuster Speakers Bureau can bring authors to your live event. For more information or to book an event contact the Simon & Schuster Speakers Bureau at 866-248-3049 or visit our website at www.simonspeakers.com.

Interior design by Julie Adams
Cover illustration by Shane Rebenschied

Manufactured in the United States of America

10 9 8 7 6 5 4 3 2 1

ISBN 978-1-5011-0454-1

For Meljean Brook. Because when I grow up, I want to be you. Or, you know, just write like you.

Thank you for being such a good friend.

Acknowledgments

Behind every clean, polished, exciting finished book is a sloppy, disorganized manuscript that takes a lot of work. It's no surprise that I have a hardworking team on my side that I am thoroughly grateful to be working with. Major thanks to my editor, Micki Nuding, who doesn't seem to mind my "Choose Your Own Adventure" style plot synopses or the fact that I really like exclamation marks. Thanks to my editor's assistant, Danielle Rose Poiesz, who always has time in the day for my questions, no matter how irrelevant. And a big thank-you to my copyeditor, Patty Romanowski, who has eagle eyes when it comes to continuity. Thank goodness you do, or else my characters would run around naked and their eyes would change colors on every page (I am not kidding). Also, a special thanks to my agent, Holly Root, because she is everything that is good and hardworking, and never seems to mind that I sometimes email her in LOLcat. Professionalism, I haz it.

A big thank-you to my husband, who tirelessly does the dishes when I'm on a deadline, always has time for brainstorming, and is the most supportive person a girl could ask for. You're my secret co-writer, plotter, motivational coach, and artistic sounding board all at once. I'm a lucky, lucky girl to have you.

A special heartfelt thanks to the crew that I email on a regular basis—Ilona Andrews, Rae Carson, Gretchen McNeil, Kasey Mackenzie, Michelle Rowen, Jane Litte, Vernieda Vergara, and far too many others to count. You guys keep me sane (ish).

Also, a big thank-you to everyone that has messaged me through Facebook, Goodreads, Twitter, Livejournal, or simply taken the time out to write me an email about how much you liked the books. I read every single one of them and every time it makes my day. So thank you, thank you, thank you from the bottom of my heart. I never realized what a blessing an audience can be. You guys rock, and I sincerely hope you enjoy this book.

CHAPTER ONE

At Fred's subtle touch, my breath caught in my throat.

A small moan of delight escaped me, and I clutched at his sleeve. "Do it again," I whispered.

He moved his fingers over the spot once more, his breath coming hard with excitement. I had to bite my lip to keep from crying out with sheer pleasure.

"What do you think?" he murmured huskily in my ear.

Oh God, I was in danger of losing control if he didn't stop.

"Jackie?"

"Classic Puuc," I said with a gasp.

"Do you think so?" He touched the monitor again and zoomed in on the area in question.

Good archaeology was better than the best orgasm. My fingers spasmed against his sleeve in excitement. "Oh my God! Stop! Stop right there! Look!"

Fred froze the cursor and turned the monitor to me.

I stared at the blocky red shape on the screen of the radar equipment with utter delight. "Definite classic Puuc! Look," I said, pointing at the edge of the red blob with my fingernail. "Thick, heavy veneer stone with a clean edge. These lighter spots around the side suggest doorways cut into the rock. I bet if we dug it up, we'd find a stone relief to rival that of Chichén Itza." I leaned over the monitor, my heart slamming in my chest. "Can we pan out to the rest of the jungle?"

Fred leaned over me, plastering his groin against my backside. My co-archaeologist was the possessor of one raging boner. Bad idea to lean over the table.

"Jackie," he murmured in my ear. "Forget about the dig for a moment. I need to talk to you."

I clamped my thighs together tightly, trying to rid myself of the unwanted feelings of pleasure. Despite the fact that I didn't want Fred in the slightest, my cursed succubus body reacted to his touch. I shoved my elbow backward, hard, trying to gut him. "Get off of me," I said, squirming away.

"We're finally alone," Fred said. "I wanted to tell you how I feel." His young face was alight with desire, his dirty brown ponytail damp with sweat. "No one's around."

That had an alarming ring to it. I turned and glanced around and, sure enough, the local workers that we hired to help out around the dig were nowhere to be seen. None of the university team was around, either. That was odd. All the guys at the site were normally so taken with my looks that I couldn't shake them, no matter what I did. I had an adoring admirer or two following me at all times, even to the port-a-potty.

It really sucked to be supernaturally beautiful.

Fred moved toward me again and caught my hands. "I've been holding back for months now, waiting for the right moment." His hands were sweaty, and a droplet of sweat rolled down his nose and splashed onto my arm. Gross.

"And you think now is a good time? It's ninety-five degrees in the shade, Fred, and we're in the jungle. I haven't showered in four days—and it smells like you haven't showered for longer." I wrinkled my nose and tried to jerk my hand away again. Where did everyone go? The deserted grounds should have been crawling with archaeologists.

It gave me the willies.

Fred pressed a fervent kiss to my hand. "You're so beautiful, Jackie."

Sigh. "Duh."

Of course I was beautiful. I was a succubus. We were cursed to have our faces and bodies remolded into that of a man's ideal fantasy. To think I'd once complained about how mousy my old looks were. I never realized how damned inconvenient it would be to be gorgeous.

"I've never met anyone like you." He continued to kiss my knuckles, pressing moist lips against them.

I doubted this dork met a lot of women, period, much less a succubus. Fred was the type of guy who probably got picked last in gym class and owned a vast library of Dungeons and Dragons books. Not exactly a ladies' man.

"Fred," I began. "You do realize that Noah's going to kick your ass if he sees this." It was a bluff, of course.

Noah—my beautiful Serim lover—might glare sternly at Fred or throw some money around to have Fred removed from camp, but I doubted he'd actually get physical with the guy.

Noah was too elegant for that sort of thing.

But my suitor was shaking his head with passion. "He's busy right now. And this might be my only chance to show you how I feel."

I frowned at that. "What do you mean, 'only chance'?" We were all going to be on this dig for at least another two months.

More of his sweat dripped onto my arms, and I struggled again to break his grip. Why oh why weren't succubi gifted with super-strength? No one needed it more than a hot immortal girl. Men were compelled to fall in love with my new face, and I'd have happily traded beauty for the ability to punch the hell out of Fred at the moment.

So I used the only other weapon I had available—I pretended to faint, going limp in his arms.

As expected, Fred released my hands to catch me as I went down, and I slapped my open palm against his forehead.

It worked. He collapsed.

I didn't hit him hard, of course. I doubted I could hit him hard enough to leave a bruise. But his mind shut off with the touch of my hand to his forehead, and he went down for the count.

There was one perk to being a succubus, at least.

I could shut down his mind and put him into a deep, dreamless sleep, and then pick through his memories if I wanted to. Not the most handy skill, depending on the situation, and I tried not to use it much, since it tended to backfire in rather spectacular ways. But desperate times call for desperate moves.

I didn't let him stay unconscious long. Kneeling beside his prostrate body, I touched his forehead to wake him up again, then patted his hand as if I were worried. "Fred? Fred? Are you all right?"

His eyes fluttered open slowly and focused on me. "What . . . what happened?"

I put on my best concerned expression and squeezed his hand, maybe a little too roughly. "You were leaning in to kiss me, and you passed out," I lied.

Fred sat up, cradling his head in his free hand. "I did?"

"You did." I helped him to his feet, then dusted off his shirt. "Fred, I'm not sure but . . . I think you should go see a doctor." Step one: lay the trap.

He gave me a confused look. "Why?"

I made my eyes go wide. "Well, you *do* know that if you pass out when you get an erection, that's an early warning sign of extremely high blood pressure. And you're far too young to have that sort of thing happen to you."

Brushing the sweaty, long hair off his forehead, Fred stared ahead blankly. "I've never done that before." His hand went to his wrist, as if checking his pulse.

"Of course not," I said sweetly, taking him by the elbow and pointing him toward the Jeep. "I'm sure it's nothing to be worried about." Step two: play to the ego. "You're a healthy, strong man. It's probably nothing. But just to be safe, don't you think you should head into Mérida and get yourself checked out?"

"But . . . the survey equipment . . . the dig . . ."

"There's nothing that can't wait until the crew returns later tonight." I pulled my keys out of my pocket and placed them in his hand. "Why don't you take my Jeep? Go to town, spend the night in air-conditioning, get checked out by the doctor, and come back in a few days. I'll explain everything to Mr. Gideon."

"Everything?" Fred swallowed hard.

I took pity on him. "Almost everything." I shook my finger at him. "And as long as the rest never happens again, it'll remain our secret."

Sorta. I planned on complaining long and hard to Mr. Gideon.

In a daze, Fred climbed into the Jeep and started the engine. I tried not to smile too cheerfully as the Jeep disappeared down the dirt road into the jungle. My problem neatly disposed of, I raced back to the GPR equipment to get another glimpse of those red blobs. To think that we had found another set of outlying buildings! We could expand on the dig, perhaps get another grant from the university . . . my mind raced at the thought.

To my disappointment, Fred's fall had jostled the computer, and the screen was dark. I tapped the monitor twice before glancing down and seeing the plug hanging out of the socket. A quick replugging showed that

I needed a password to reboot the system, a password I didn't have. I sighed in disgust. So much for that. And without someone to help me move the surface antenna, I couldn't do any further radar scans until the others returned.

Disgruntled, I packed up the equipment I could and went in search of the rest of the crew. We'd decided to set up in the least thickly forested portion of the ancient grounds of Yuxmal, and workers had cleared even more area to set up the tent city that had been our home for the past few months. A very empty tent city. It was midday, so unless everyone had ran off for an impromptu siesta, the campsite was truly deserted.

What the heck was going on?

The tent I shared with Noah was at the edge of camp, near the base of a massive stone pyramid—the discovery that had started the dig itself. As I approached our tent, I could hear the generator humming and the sound of rotating fans buzzing. I paused outside. The door flap was down, which seemed like a bad idea given the heat and humidity. Inside, I heard a muffled curse.

Noah was here, at least. I put aside my odd foreboding about the camp's emptiness and ran my long fingernails along the weatherproofed canvas, the sound that passed for a knock in a tent city. "Knock knock."

"Don't come in," Noah barked.

I frowned at the tent wall. "What do you mean, don't come in?" I lifted the flap and entered anyhow.

My jaw dropped. Noah was clad in nothing but boxer

shorts, and beads of sweat trailed down his flat, golden abs. The large folding table that filled the middle of the tent was covered with a paper tablecloth that fluttered in the wake of the rotating fans set at each corner of the tent. Two place settings decorated the table, along with a large covered dish. A row of pale candles was lined up in front of Noah, who held a box of matches in his hand.

"What is all this?" I asked.

"A surprise. Or it was." He scowled.

I let the flap slide shut behind me and fanned my hand at my face. In the heat, with the humidity, no number of rotating fans could make the tent feel like less of a sauna. It seemed awfully odd to have an elegant dinner set up in the tent, but it looked like that was Noah's plan. I was torn between thinking he was sweet or totally mad. "Where did everyone at camp go?"

"They went to town. Paid vacation day. A vacation day that I paid for," he said irritably as he pulled another match out of the box. "Fred was supposed to keep you busy for another hour."

I snorted and moved to the far end of the table, where a chair was set out. "If by 'keep me busy' you mean try to molest me, I'd say he finished early."

Noah ran the match along the side of the box, and a small flame flared to life. He leaned toward the closest candle, and the match abruptly sputtered, then blew out, from the breeze of the fan. He swore again and pulled out another match.

Well, now. Noah seemed a little crankier than usual,

but I blamed it on the bright blue in his eyes. The closer we got to the full moon, the more moody he became as the curse came over him and his need for sex rose.

Of course, the sight of those blue eyes and that delicious, bare sweaty chest gave me another idea—a rather naughty one. I moved to his side, my finger tracing one runnel of sweat down his chest. I dipped my finger in the damp bead and met his eyes, then tasted the droplet, a blatant suggestion if there ever was one.

"Not now, Jackie," he said impatiently.

With a sigh, I dropped my hands, returned to the far side of the table, and sat down so I wouldn't be tempted to touch him again. Another symptom of the full-moon curse—Noah was completely and utterly uninterested in sex for the days preceding the full moon, upon which we'd stay in the tent the entire day and have sex until he passed out. I gave him a bright smile. "When are you due, so we can get back to normal and I can get laid?"

He pulled out another match, glaring at it with all the hatred in the world. "The moon is full in two days."

Well, thank God for that. I did a little fast math in my head. We'd had sex yesterday morning and I would be due tomorrow morning. If I had to wait another day after that I'd be miserable as hell, but I wouldn't die from it. An overdue succubus was an exceedingly horny one, so I'd have to avoid the other men in the camp for the day, or I'd have the men trailing me like I was the Pied Piper of Hamlin. "That day can't get here soon enough," I murmured. Just the thought of not having sex for another two days made me crave it, and I crossed my legs under the table.

Noah looked over at me, a hint of a frown marring the line of his eyebrows. The scent of sulfur grew strong in the small tent as he tried to light another match.

"Don't worry about the candles," I said. "They're giving me a headache."

His jaw was set in a stubborn line that I recognized about once a month. "Fine." He put down the matches and placed the candles back in an orderly row along the table. "What were you saying about Fred?"

I glanced at the covered tray, my mouth watering as I wondered what was underneath. Was it someone's birthday? My taste buds gave a little thrill at the thought of birthday cake and ice cream, though no ice cream would survive this heat. Maybe chocolate, to take the edge off my desire. Noah knew that I loved to eat. "Fred confessed undying love for me," I said, distracted by the tray and my rumbling stomach. It had been a few hours since I'd eaten breakfast, and lunch sounded rather tasty now. "Though I promised him that I wouldn't say anything to Mr. Gideon." I gave Noah a pointed look. "Consider yourself out of the know, Mr. Gideon. And don't worry. I used my Suck powers to draw him off and convinced him to visit town."

Noah gave a little shake of his head. "Jackie, we've had this conversation before. You need to be careful around the men at camp."

My jaw dropped. Careful?

Careful?

Me?

Steamed, I grabbed a steak knife off the table. With my other hand, I took off my dirty baseball cap and shook down one of my long, bright red braids. I held the braid out from my head at a straight angle and in fast, jerky motions I sawed at the base of my braid and hacked the entire thing off, then tossed it down on the table.

Noah rolled his eyes at my dramatic show.

"Watch," I said, crossing my arms over my chest.

Sure enough, less than a minute later, I felt the hair follicles on my scalp slither and the familiar tingling that told me my hair was growing back. I grabbed a handful of the sheared ends and watched in disgust as they grew, my hair pouring down my shoulders and over my shirt, returning to the lengthy, flame-red curls.

"Do you see this?" I jerked at my T-shirt. "I'm wearing a Led Zeppelin shirt, cargo shorts, and a baseball cap. Not exactly seductress material."

"Zane's shirt, I noticed."

Grrr. He was missing the point entirely! "What I'm trying to remind you of is that no matter what I do, I can't disguise how I look. I've shaved my head. I've worn thick glasses. I've done everything short of wearing a ski mask, and it's no use. I could go out in a trash bag and someone would still hit on me."

"Jackie—"

"You know," I went on, angrily rebraiding my "new" hair, "I thought this dig would be good for my career.

I could finally set myself up as a serious archaeologist. But it's like I'm the Hooters girl at the church social! The men leer at me constantly. Someone tries to cop a feel if I so much as bend over. And all the women on the team hate me because they think I'm blowing you just to get you to sponsor the dig."

"You *are* blowing me," he interrupted with a hint of a smile.

"Not to further my career," I bellowed. "Remember that whole 'have to have sex every two days' thing? Hello? Succubus?"

He gave me a patient look. "I wouldn't be out in the jungles of Yucatán spending a small fortune on sonar—"

"Radar—"

"Radar equipment if it wasn't for you. So they do have a point."

My eyes narrowed. "You are *so* not helping your case right now, buddy."

Noah chuckled, showing me a glimpse of the good-natured, strong protector that I usually adored. He moved to my end of the table and pulled me up into his arms. "Poor Jackie. I'm sorry this isn't turning out like you want." His warm hand stroked my braids and down my back.

My bad mood rapidly dwindled now that I was pressed against his hard, sweaty body, and I slid my hands up and down his bare, damp skin. He felt so good against me. *Really* good. It reminded me that I was due for the Itch in a short time, so I reluctantly pulled away. "Unless you want to make out on the floor, maybe we shouldn't touch."

I wanted him to protest, to kiss me senseless and prove me wrong, but all he said was "You're right," and released me. Spoilsport.

I sighed. I hated the days up to the full moon.

"I brought you a few presents from town," he said, returning to the other end of the table.

Sitting back down, I clapped my hands in delight. "Edible things?" In this part of Mexico you could get a lot of standard stuff from the big Walmart in Mérida or the local *tedejon*, but I missed the small luxuries, like Pringles or my favorite shampoo. Noah was constantly bringing me boxes of treats as a result. Last week it was foil-wrapped Ding Dongs, which I tore through in about five minutes.

Succubi weren't known for their self-control when it came to food. Hedonists for the win.

Noah smiled at my delighted expression. "Part of your present is edible, yes." He disappeared under the paper tablecloth and reappeared a moment later with a large cardboard box. The words "Pop-Tarts" was printed across the side of the box.

I squealed. "Oh my God! Pop-Tarts! A whole case!"

"I had them special ordered for you in Mérida. They're chocolate." At my second squeal of delight, he chuckled. "Try not to eat them all in one day."

I eyed the box with hungry, avid eyes. "They might last two days." Maybe three, if I paced myself. It was so hard to find chocolate Pop-Tarts in this part of Mexico.

A radar discovery and Pop-Tarts. This day just got better and better.

Noah seemed pleased, his eyes so blue they glowed in his tanned face. "I never thought I'd see a woman get so turned on over a package." His voice had dropped to a huskier octave, showing that he wasn't totally immune to my charms just yet.

Encouraged, I leaned over the table, my voice turning into a purr. "Show me your package, and I'll show you an even more turned-on woman."

His eyes flashed and I recognized the interest there, fighting the lethargy that always set over him before the full moon. "Your other present first," he said.

"Whatever floats your boat," I breathed, clamping my thighs together so they'd stop quivering with excitement.

Hot diggity, I was going to get laid today after all!

He leaned over the table, placing his hand on the dome of the silver platter. I couldn't wait to find out what was underneath. This was why he'd sent everyone away from camp to be alone with me—the reason behind the big production.

"If that's a milk shake under there, they're going to have to pry me off of you with a crowbar," I warned, my eyes glued to the tray.

He lifted the lid.

A tiny turquoise box with a bow lay in the center of the plate. It looked like . . . a ring box.

"Shit," I blurted.

CHAPTER TWO

"That's not exactly the reaction I wanted to hear."

I stared at the small box, unable to move my hand toward it. I knew—I just knew—what it contained. And the dreadful knot forming in the pit of my stomach told me that I didn't want it.

"Jackie?"

Steeling my nerves, I forced myself to reach for the box. I owed Noah that much. The exterior felt velvety and thick, the last thing that someone wanted against their skin in the middle of the jungle. My fingers were trembling (not in a good way) as I flicked the box open. And stared at the ring inside.

A small, simple band of platinum clung to the biggest damn diamond I had ever laid eyes on. The size of it blew me away, and I pulled it out of the box to make sure that I wasn't seeing things. It was the size of a large button, and stuck up from the setting like one of those candy lollipop rings. The inside of the band read "Tiffany & Co". It even felt heavy. "Jeezus, Noah!"

"It's four carats. I figured if everyone was going to

stare at you all the time, they might as well have some-thing else to fixate on."

Boy, he wasn't kidding. "It's . . . enormous."

"A guy loves to hear his woman say stuff like that," he teased.

His woman—oh God. The anxiety and stress of it all came crashing down, and I carefully put the ring back in the box. I adored Noah. Had great affection for him. Loved spending time with him. We got along very well, and he was pleasant to live with.

So why did the thought of marrying him scare the holy heck out of me? Was it that eternity was such a very, very long time to be married to someone?

Especially when you still missed your ex-boyfriend?

"Well?" he said as I toyed with the box in my hands.

I hesitated. There was no good way to put this, really. "Noah, I don't know. It's just such a big step."

"Jackie," he said patiently, "we've been living together for six months, most of that in this jungle. We work very well together. We're very fond of each other. I love you and you love me. Despite the fact that both of us are compelled to have sex on a regular basis, we've both been monogamous for the past six months. I've been monogamous since I met you." His head tilted slightly as he continued to study me with those intense blue eyes. "Why not take this a step further and commit to each other? Show our commitment to everyone? If we're mar-ried, I can protect you."

"From what?" I had to ask.

"Everything."

Even that blanket statement didn't make me leap to put the gigantic rock on my finger. I gazed at the small box and flipped it back and forth in my hands, as if one sudden move might make me change my mind or make me suddenly okay with all this.

"Noah, you're four thousand years old. I'm barely pushing twenty-seven." I needed to express myself to him, but how to do so without hurting his feelings?

"I'm prepared to spend the next four thousand with you." He made it sound like a challenge.

"What if circumstances forced me to cheat on you?" I recalled with vivid discomfort my trip to New Orleans, and my run-in with an incubus named Luc. Cursed to want sex within hours, stranded apart from Noah and Zane, I'd had no choice but to make out with Luc, and our brief rendezvous had had dire consequences.

His jaw flexed. "We'd work through that. I wouldn't hold it against you."

"I know you won't," I agreed. "It's just that . . . I'd hold it against me." I placed the ring box on the table and nudged it away. "Maybe I'm still thinking too traditionally, despite being a succubus, but . . . to me marriage means commitment. Forever commitment." The kind that scared the hell out of me now, and I pressed my hand to my chest. "Commitment to me means that I'd never desire another. And right now I don't think I could make that commitment in good faith."

I expected him to make an excuse for my nature, to

assure me that it would be all right. Noah was always so supportive.

But his jaw clenched. He stood up, glared down at me for a moment, and then turned away, moving to the back of the tent. As I sat at the table like a helpless lump, he began pulling a white shirt over his head.

I frowned at his back. "What are you doing?"

He glanced over his shoulder as he pulled the shirt down and gave a small, hard laugh as he stepped into a pair of pants. "You know, Jackie, with everything that we've gone through over the past six months, I thought we could at least be honest with each other."

"I am being honest with you," I said, bewildered.

Noah shoved his shirt into his pants, then crammed his wallet into his pocket. "No, you're not. You tell me that it's about cheating with Luc, when we both know it's about Zane."

My mouth went dry. "No, it's not."

"Oh, come on." His voice took on a cold, hard edge that I'd never heard before. "You can stand there in his shirt and tell me that with a straight face? You even smell like him."

I flushed in embarrassment. Like any other lonely ex-girlfriend, I occasionally sprayed my boyfriend's shirt with his cologne. I hadn't realized that my *current* boyfriend was quite so observant.

Guess that made me a bit of a jackass.

"Just tell me, Jackie," Noah said, approaching me. He took my hand in his and clasped it against his chest. "Tell me honestly that the reason you're saying no isn't because of Zane, and I'll let the whole thing drop."

My throat closed, and I stared up into his beautiful, hurt blue eyes. I wanted to reassure him, to go back to the easy companionship we had before, but that was gone. He wanted more, and I wasn't sure I could give him more. Even though Zane had been gone six months now, I still thought of him every time the sun went down and I was left alone.

I missed him dreadfully.

"I can't tell you that." I pulled my hand out of his. "I'm sorry, Noah. I wasn't trying to hurt you."

He leaned in and kissed my mouth softly. "Then don't refuse."

I remained silent. I couldn't say the words, even though he wanted me to say them.

Noah pulled back and studied my face. His mouth hardened and he released me, lifted the tent flap, and walked away.

I followed after him. "Where are you going?"

"To town. I need to clear my head." He didn't look back at me.

I glanced up at the sky. "It'll be dark in a few hours." Every twelve hours, the Serim were cursed to go into a deep hibernation from which they couldn't be wakened. Serim took the daytime hours, and vampires ruled the night, with a little bit of overlap between worlds. "Don't stay out too late."

Noah glanced back at me, a wealth of pain in his eyes. "Don't expect me back tonight."

He'd rather spend his vulnerable nighttime hours alone or with strangers than to be with me. That stung. I watched him go without another word of protest.

To ease my hurt feelings, I tore into the Pop-Tarts. Eating half a dozen of them made me feel better. A few more, and I'd stopped glaring long enough to get up. I was hurt, but I'd be damned if he was going to make me weep into my pillow.

I chewed angrily, my cheeks full of chocolate crumbly goodness. I'd head to town, too, except that I'd given my keys to Fred. Damn. I glanced down at the table and frowned. The ginormous ring inside the ring box made me nervous. The full sum of my worldly possessions wouldn't even be a fraction of the cost of the ring.

Stupid ring. Stupid Noah for trying to propose. I muttered a few choice words about him under my breath, then sighed. It wasn't his fault I was a mess. I scooped up the ring and moved over to the heavy safe in the corner where we kept our laptops, extra cash, and other valuables. Crouching down next to it, I flicked through the combination and cracked it open.

The interior of the safe was nerdishly neat; Noah didn't like clutter. How did he manage to live with me, a female cyclone of trash? I shoved the ring to the back of the top shelf. Then, wiping my chocolatey hand on

Zane's shirt, I reached into the safe, looking for a blank sheet of paper to leave a note.

After brushing across several legal contracts and receipts for equipment, I felt something like heavy cardboard wrapped in plastic. Puzzled, I pulled it into the light.

It was a painting, encased in a polymer bag. Thin and oblong, it wasn't more than a foot in length. My thumb skimmed over the corner, feeling heavy brushstrokes through the protective bag. An oil painting, though it was hard to make out in the light. What the heck was Noah doing with a painting in the wilds of Mexico? Suspicious of another "surprise," I went into the sunlight—and sucked in a loud breath.

What. The. Hell?

It was me. Or rather, it was me before I'd transformed into a succubus. If I was dressed like some sort of Hebrew shepherdess, hung out in fields with sheep, and carried a crook, that is. The woman in the photo was swathed in long, colorful scarves, so it was impossible to tell if we had the same pudgy body that I'd had, but the face? Same round cheeks. Same too-large features and heavy brows. Long, curly, brownish-red hair hung over her shoulder, and she was smiling with innocent delight.

Her eyes were green, the only discernable difference. My fingers touched her face in shock, and I flipped the painting over. In a strange, loopy handwriting, words were written on the back. I couldn't make them out, but I could make out a date and initials:

1506. N. G.

Who was this woman, and why was Noah painting pictures of her? I hadn't even known that Noah could paint, but those were his initials. Yet 1506 seemed like the wrong time period for her clothing. I flipped the painting over again. Definitely not Renaissance; she looked like something out of the old Hollywood biblical epics.

Of course, this didn't answer the bigger question: what was she doing with my face?

My satellite phone chose that moment to ring. Irritated at the interruption, I tucked the painting back into the safe and slammed it shut. Mr. "Innocent" Noah had a few questions to answer when he got back from town. I raced into the tent, grabbed the phone off my cot, and hit the Receive button. "Hello? Noah?"

Maybe he was ready to kiss and make up already.

"Sorry, my sweet, it's just me." Remy's cheerful voice rang out over the crackling phone.

"Remy! Hi! How's the shoot going?" The last time I'd heard from her, she was shooting a new porn movie in New Orleans—*The Big Sleazy*. She'd asked me to come visit to spend time with her and Delilah—a succubus convention of sorts. I'd declined, partially because I didn't want to know what *The Big Sleazy* was about, and partially because I was enjoying the archaeological dig.

She chuckled. "Never better."

"Glad to hear it. Did they give you a lot of, er, action shots?" I cringed at the thought. I had no idea how to make small talk about a porn flick. *Were the fluffers good? Did your costar have a big wang? Any orgies in this one?* I decided to change the subject. "How's Dee doing, anyhow?"

Remy's voice became a low rumble. "Who?"

I sat down on the edge of the cot, angling one of the fans at my face. "Dee. Delilah. Succubus? Kinda short and young? Bossy? Voodoo priestess?" When that elicited no response, I frowned against the receiver. "You're staying in her house?"

"Ah, her." Remy's voice rasped a little. "She is unimportant."

I frowned. "You sure you're okay?"

"Never better," she repeated.

That kind of gave me the creeps. "All righty."

"I called to ask you a question," Remy purred.

"Oh? What's that?" And why did I have a bad feeling about this?

Her voice dropped very low. "I was wondering if you'd scream when I held you down and sank my fangs into your pretty neck."

I swallowed. That didn't sound like my bubbly BFF. "This is Joachim, isn't it?"

Wild laughter erupted from the other end of the phone.

That *bastard*. "Joachim," I said very slowly. "How did you get hold of Remy again? What happened to the charm?" When Zane and I had parted ways, he'd given me a special charm that nullified magic, and I'd given it to Remy to help her with Joachim's possession of her. For months, she'd been fine. Now Joachim was in charge of her body again?

"That's the sad thing about necklace charms," Joachim said, clucking his tongue. "If the clasp breaks, all bets are off."

Shit, shit shit. Remy was hours of plane flight away from rescue, and I was stuck in the wilds of Yucatán. "Joachim," I said, trying a reasonable voice. "Why not leave Remy alone? She's my friend and I don't want you to hurt her."

"But I want to hurt you," she said, her voice silky. "A lot. I want to see you suffer like you've made me suffer for the past six months. Gag you. Bind you. Silence you. Won't that be fun?"

Didn't sound like it, no. "You'll have to find me first." Nothing like a good ol' bluff to steel the nerves.

"You're just outside of Mérida in Yucatán." Her angry tone changed to bored. "Did you know that I'm back in New City? I'm sitting in your room right now."

It suddenly became hard to breathe. "What? Where's Dee?"

Remy chuckled, an evil laugh. "Dee's such a stick in the mud. I left her for someplace new. And I sure like it here." The evil voice dropped into a low purr. "There's no one around to see what I do."

I swallowed hard. "Joachim, let Remy have her body back."

"Why don't you come and make me?"

"Because I'm in Mexico—"

"Then it'll be a shame if your friend dies, won't it?"

A wordless squeak escaped me and I stared blankly ahead. What could I *do*?

"See you soon, whore." Remy-Joachim hung up.

I immediately called Delilah's house. Her machine picked up so I hung up and stared at the phone. Joachim wanted me to come after him, to confront him.

This was a trap—revenge. The last time, I'd trapped him in the guest bathroom at Delilah's house, a thick line of salt across the doorway keeping him inside until I'd put the necklace on her neck and restored Remy.

It was my fault she was possessed. Remy and I had been fighting over the halo that contained his power. I lost my grip, Remy went down and absorbed the halo, drawing Joachim's madness inside her. She'd been fine at first, but he soon overtook her. And now he wanted me. Goody.

I immediately picked up the phone and dialed Noah's cell. With luck, he wouldn't have it turned off.

Noah picked up on the first ring, his voice sounding odd. "Hello?"

"Noah, we have a problem," I began.

"I know."

That made me pause. "What do you mean, you know?" A little prickle of fear went down my back.

Oddly enough, I heard a low voice talking on the other end of the line, and then Noah spoke softly. "Come out of the tent, Jackie." He sounded resigned.

The words were gentle, but my body recognized the command. Because Noah had created me, I was power-less in the face of a direct order. My legs stiffened, I began walking toward the door, and my mood went from "bad" to "destroyed" within moments. Using a command was a low, low blow.

The moment I emerged from the tent, I saw why he'd commanded me.

Noah stood between two men, his hands tied behind his back. One of the strangers held the sat phone to Noah's ear and removed it at the sight of me. Both of them were the biggest dudes I'd ever seen. Noah was a little over six feet tall, and both men towered over him. Their shoulders were frighteningly broad, and both wore strange white robes.

One stepped toward me. He had beautifully dark eyes under slashing eyebrows, high cheekbones under buff-colored skin, and a long, silky mane of black hair that was pulled in a straight ponytail. He looked beautiful. And disapproving.

He frowned at the sight of me, as if he'd never seen someone like me before. "You are the succubus?"

Good lord, he even talked loud. "That's me." My gaze turned back to Noah. "What's going on?"

I wasn't panicking yet.

Noah didn't seem frightened, but I was confused by the expression on his face. He seemed . . . sad? Chagrined?

"Succubus, you will come with us," the samurai com-manded.

I scowled and crossed my arms over my chest. I wasn't a dog to be called to heel. "Now, hold on here. I'm not going anywhere until I know who you are and how you found us in the jungle."

"Jackie," Noah said patiently. "Come."

I put my hands up like paws. "Arf arf." My feet jerked forward again, and I didn't protest when the samurai grabbed my arm. He studied my neck, then grabbed the gris-gris that hung from it and yanked it off. The cord snapped, and as I watched, he stepped on the small charm bag with a crunch. Just like that, I was without magical protection.

Great.

My eyes focused on Noah's face. "Why are you working with them, Noah? What is going on?"

"We've been summoned." He didn't sound happy at all.

"Summoned? By whom?" Who on earth could possibly summon us in the middle of the jungle?

"The Serim council. We've been placed under arrest."

CHAPTER THREE

I sat in a small, dark room, drumming my fingers. Hours had passed, and I knew instinctively that the sun had set and was getting ready to rise again. I could feel the cycle even if I couldn't see it, just as I could feel the burgeoning desire growing in my body. The Itch had swelled with every hour that passed, and right now my clothes rubbed against my sensitized skin, making my body purr. Soon I'd be drooling at the sight of any man in the immediate vicinity.

This was not good. Not good at all.

My cell had smooth walls, and I'd spent all night running my hands over them looking for a window, an outlet, anything. The only way in and out of the room was through the door, and there was no doorknob on my side. I glared at the small sliver of light under the door.

As if on cue, the door opened, and the tall warrior glided into the room.

I tensed in my corner, flexing my hands. When he moved closer, he was going down. The thought made my body flush with warmth and need. Going down would be so sexy right now—

The warrior straightened, interrupting my dirty thoughts. "Succubus, if you think to use your powers on me, be warned that the rest of your trial will go very badly."

I hesitated. "What sort of trial are you talking about?"

"I am not at liberty to speak."

Of course not. "Where's Noah?" Despite the fact that he seemed to be working with these other Serim, he had an unhappy look on his face. Not good.

"He will be present at the trial," the warrior said.

I stood up and followed him out of my cell. "So who are you?"

"I am an Enforcer."

What the heck was an Enforcer? "Gee, that's nice. But I kinda meant your name."

"I see." He sounded a little puzzled, as if he wasn't used to people addressing him. "I am called Ethan."

Didn't sound very war-like. "So what am I under arrest for, Ethan?"

His elegant brow furrowed as he looked down at me. "I do not know the details."

Er, okay. "Then why did you nab me?"

"I merely enforce the decisions of the council. I am not a member." His voice had taken on the stiff, regal tone once more, shutting me down. "Please withhold all questions until you are before the council."

I resisted the urge to give him a smart-ass salute and followed him down the dank concrete hallway. It seemed like we were in the cellars or a catacomb of some sort.

The occasional oblong fluorescent light overhead provided us with harsh, grayish-blue lighting.

A quick glance behind me (just in case I wanted to, y'know, run away) showed that the hall ended near my cell, and all the other doors lining the hallway were heavy metal and shut tight. I'd have bet money that they were locked, too.

The only way out was behind the mountain of Ethan that walked in front of me with elegant grace. He didn't even look back to see if I was following, as if it didn't even cross his mind that I would be stupid enough to try and escape.

He led me through a maze of hallways and then to an elevator. We waited in front of the double doors, as if this were a normal day at the office and Ethan wasn't wearing some goofy cultist robe and had a big honking stick at his waist.

"So what's the stick for?" I asked as we stepped into the elevator.

He gave me a puzzled look. "It's not a stick. It is a bo staff."

"Oh, well excuse me, Napoleon Dynamite." I was rapidly losing my fear of this guy, despite his hulking size and blade-eyed glare. At times he seemed . . . nice? Which was weird, considering he worked for the bad guys.

Not that the Serim were really bad, not at all. Noah and his kind had descended from Heaven thousands of years ago, giving up Paradise for the love of mortal women. But then those women had died abruptly, and the fallen angels found out the hard way that exile from Paradise was a torture all its own. Some fell to the dark side and became vampires. Those who did not called themselves the Serim chose to rule "benevolently" over humans and lived their lives in a way that they hoped would someday return them to Heaven.

It tended to make them rigidly moral and impossible to deal with. To say that I wasn't looking forward to meeting with the council was a bit like saying Joan of Arc wasn't looking forward to burning at the stake.

I was concerned for Noah, though. He'd seemed very unhappy at the sight of the two Enforcers, and even more unhappy when he'd ordered me to go with them. He seemed genuinely nervous.

After all, my Itch was due pronto, and my guards didn't seem like they'd be letting me go anytime soon. Though if they were willing . . . I squeezed my eyes shut, trying to block out the mental image of a prisoner-and-guard sandwich. Now was *not* the time.

The elevator dinged loudly, startling me out of my thoughts. Ethan nodded at me and I stepped forward into another narrow cement hallway, faded linoleum lining the floor. It reminded me of an old hospital. Down the hall, though, I could see a door with sunlight pouring through the window. I could use my powers on Ethan, send him back down the elevator, and be out of this building before he had time to say "bo staff" again.

But that wouldn't help Noah. And Noah had saved

me so many times before that I couldn't leave him here to face these jerks alone.

He needed me.

Just thinking about need made my body pulse pleasurably, reminding me that I needed him as much as he needed me.

So I sighed and said to Ethan, "Lead the way."

He led me into a long, cold room. The walls were bare, with more of the cheerful concrete motif. One lone fluorescent light hung overhead, and a row of tables and chairs was neatly arranged across from two single chairs.

"Sit," Ethan told me.

"I'm going to guess one of these lovely, inconspicuous chairs is mine, right?" I gestured at one of the loners in the middle of the floor.

His mouth tightened and he gave me a brief nod.

I sat in the chair provided, frowning. When the seats across from me filled, I'd be directly in front of the unflinching eyes of the Serim. Nervous, I ran a hand through my hair and tried to tame the curls that had slipped out of my braids. It felt like I'd been called to the principal's office.

Minutes ticked by, and we were the only ones in the room. Ethan stood behind me, a massive mile of loitering warrior. I clasped my hands and crossed my legs, moving my foot back and forth in an anxious motion. After a moment, I decided bravado was the best tactic and tilted my head back to look at Ethan. "This isn't going to take long, is it? Because my plate's a little full at the moment."

First item on the agenda: find out where Remy was.

Second item on the agenda: find out who this Little Bo-Peep in the painting was.

Third item: bitch out Noah and have make-up sex.

The Enforcer stared down at me, his face smooth of emotion, then he took a step backward. I realized I'd pretty much tilted my head all the way back, putting it eye level with his crotch, and it seemed Ethan was skittish. Desire flared, unwanted and unbidden, and I clamped my thighs tightly together. Damn. The Itch was upon me.

And just to make things more annoying, the door opened and the Serim council began to file into the room.

It was hard not to be impressed by the lineup; any woman would find them breathtakingly beautiful. They were once angels, after all.

Unlike the blond Noah and Uriel, the angels before me were a variety of ethnicities, from dusky dark skin to the palest silver-blond hair. All were unearthly beautiful and ageless.

Ruining the effect were the goofy long linen robes they wore and the scowls on their faces as they regarded me. They filed in and sat down without a word.

"Where's Noah?" I asked when the door shut behind them and there was still no sight of my Serim master.

Ethan leaned in next to me. "You must not speak until spoken to."

"The same goes for you, Enforcer Ethan," one of the

Serim said, his voice clipped, beautiful, and utterly cold. My gaze went to him and focused on his long, flowing red hair and the aristocratic, pale features of his face.

"My apologies, Serim Ariel," the Enforcer said.

Well, that was a little unexpected. Ethan was huge and menacing looking. Ariel should have been scared of him, not the other way around. Still, I bit my lip to keep from smiling. Like the little mermaid Ariel? How unmasculine.

He noticed my badly hidden amusement and his mouth stiffened into a grim line.

Oops.

"Bring in Noah Gideon," Ariel said smoothly.

A door opened behind me, and I twisted in my seat. Noah looked well, if a bit lethargic and sleep-rumpled. His eyes lit with relief at the sight of me.

He came to stand behind my chair, next to Ethan, and he laid one large hand on my shoulder. A unified front. Relief swept through me, surprising in its intensity. Noah might be mad at me at the moment, and I might be worried about the painting, but we'd stick together. I put my hand on his and squeezed.

"All immortals are assembled," Ariel said, his eyes bright blue as they rested on me. "Bring in the priest."

As I stared at the unnaturally bright eyes of all the Serim, I realized that the full moon would affect all of them in the same way as Noah. Within one day, all of the Serim were going to be very, very horny. I was suddenly nervous. If they thought that having a captive succubus meant an angelic gangbang, they were in for a rude awakening.

Noah squeezed my shoulder, as if sensing my unease.

A small, dark priest entered the room with a Bible in hand, and Ariel nodded at him. "Bring the holy water. Let us begin the summoning." The two Serim flanking the far ends of the table stood from their seats and lifted heavy jars, screwing off the lids and placing each jar on the table. Then they walked to opposite corners of the room. To my surprise, they began to spill the water in the jars along the edges of the walls, murmuring under their breaths as they did so. The priest stepped forward, speaking a prayer in Latin and moving his hand in the sign of the cross as he blessed the room.

Oh no. I squeezed my eyes shut, positive I knew what was coming next. The room was being sanctified, and someone was being summoned. That could only mean one thing. I pressed my hands to my face, not sure I wanted to see who was going to show up.

Please let it not be Uriel. *Please* let it not be Uriel.

I'd had a run-in with him when I'd first been turned and hadn't known that angels liked to manipulate people with bent promises, and that Uriel was the worst of his lot.

The priest stopped speaking, and nothing happened. I squeezed one eye open slowly, just in time to see the priest exit the room again, and the Serim sat back in their chairs.

A brilliant flash of light formed in the center of the room, directly in front of me, and an angel appeared.

Not Uriel. Thank goodness.

He was, however, utterly stunning. The other Serim were specimens of all that was beautiful and fine about the human body and face, a little bit of Heaven that had sullied itself with life on the ground.

This was Heaven in its purest form. The angel was magnificent, so dazzling and perfect that my mouth went dry at the sight of him, and my heart pounded in my chest. The pleasant smell of sunlight and vanilla wafted through the room—angels were always accompanied by pleasant smells—and his bronzed skin glowed with an inner light. A cap of dark curls ringed his beautiful face, and a sweep of heavy white wings flowed over his shoulders and dripped to the ground.

I expected the Serim to drop to their knees, or bow, something to convey the awe I felt at this divine being's presence. But they did nothing. Noah's hand on my shoulder became tight, and I noticed that several of the Serim at the long table stiffened.

They might have summoned the angel, but they weren't happy to see him.

Ariel rose from his seat again. "Archangel Gabriel," he said, his voice smooth and even. "We ask that you mediate over the trial of these fallen ones."

Sky blue eyes turned to me, scrutinizing me as one would a bug or a stray cat hair on a sweater. "And in return?"

"A favor, of course," Ariel replied.

"It is done." Gabriel flexed his wings giving a slight flutter as he stood proudly.

Ariel's eyes focused—for perhaps a moment too long—on Gabriel's wings. "Thank you. We'll start with the female." His gaze drifted over to me. "You, Succubus, have been accused of dangerous, immoral behavior concerning the lives of others, crimes against your fellow immortals, and existence without authorization. This Serim council has been requested to determine the nature of your crimes and the appropriate punishment."

My jaw dropped. Were they serious? "Immoral behavior? Existence without authorization?"

"Those are the charges." Ariel seemed to be taking a little too much pleasure in this.

I felt Noah's hand tighten on my shoulder like a vise, likely telling me to be quiet. But I wasn't about to. "Don't you think that *I'm* the one that's been wronged here?"

Heck, I'd been turned without consent or prior knowledge. All it had taken was one well-timed bite from Zane and sex with Noah, and I'd been changed from my normal, dull life as a docent at the New City Art Museum to the overly breasted, lust-addicted succubus I was today. If anyone should be frustrated with how things had turned out, it should be me.

"Your accuser does not seem to agree with your assessment," Ariel said thinly.

"Who's accusing me?"

The door opened behind me again, and everyone focused on the man who slunk into the room. He was tall and lean, his brown hair long and his face leonine. For a man, he was alarmingly pretty. His eyes glittered at the sight of me, pure and deep hatred burning in them.

The last time I'd seen that man, he'd been wrapped in the arms of a very possessive demon. Which I'd called.

"Luc," I said in disgust. "It figures that you'd turn up here."

His unearthly silver eyes focused on me, and the incubus gave me an arch smile. "I'm here to see you brought to justice, Jackie. You should be destroyed for what you did to me, and I aim to see it done."

My throat went dry for a second time as he sat in the chair next to me, lounging at ease. He was completely comfortable in front of a frowning council of Serim, while I twitched like a nervous grasshopper.

"Let us begin." The Archangel Gabriel's eyes were cold as they rested on me.

Not a good sign.

The makeshift courtroom was quiet, all eyes on Luc.

"Please state how you know the succubus," Ariel ordered, sounding pleased at my reaction to Luc's presence.

"I met her in Colorado," Luc said.

"You mean you began stalking me in Colorado," I corrected. "*After* you cursed me."

"I did not curse you," Luc said in a calm voice, glancing over at me with brilliantly beautiful silver eyes. Even though he was an evil son of a bitch, he was the prettiest man I'd ever seen. His skin was a deep bronze, his hair a warm brown, his eyes a striking silver. He was also an incubus and a sorcerer, and underneath that delicious exterior, the man had a rotten heart. "I cursed a vampire named Zane."

Who had unwittingly passed the curse on to me. I opened my mouth to protest, only to freeze under the disapproving glare of the Archangel Gabriel. "Interruptions will not be tolerated, Succubus. You are not helping your cause."

Noah's hand squeezed painfully on my shoulder. Got it.

"I met Jackie in Colorado. She approached me, needing help. And so I helped her. And when she needed sex, I obliged her."

Yeah, with a bit of dry humping in a car on the side of the road. My face tinged red at the clinical way he was describing it. Noah's hand tightened even more on my shoulder. He didn't like hearing about my small "problem" with Luc, even though I'd already confessed the details long ago.

"She was crying out in my lap—"

Noah rushed across the room, grabbing Luc by the front of his shirt and hauling him into the air. "You will shut your filthy mouth–"

"Noah!" I yelped, jumping to my feet.

A hand clamped on my shoulder. One of the Enforcers pushed on my shoulder, and I sat back down, watching with horror as the Serim piled on top of my lover, separating him physically from Luc.

When had Noah gotten such a hair-trigger temper?

The two men were separated, and Ariel gave Noah a

sneering look of disdain. "Try to control yourself, Noah, or we will remove you from the proceedings."

My master's jaw clenched. He glared at Luc for a moment, then reluctantly moved back to stand over my shoulder, his hand tense as it rested on me.

"I pleasured her and made sure that she sated her needs," Luc said, looking coldly at me. "When it was my turn to take my own pleasure, she denied me and ran away. She left me aching and hurting on the roadside."

Oh please. Like he was the first man to be cock-blocked. I glanced at the row of Serim, and several of them were looking at me with disapproval and disgust. I guess it was a big crime in their eyes.

The Archangel Gabriel turned to me. "Is this true, Succubus? Did you take your pleasure from the incubus and not give him his?"

"He makes it sound like he's a prince, but that's not the case. He was going to kidnap me—"

"I did not ask for the details, Succubus," Gabriel said coldly. "I asked if it was true that you had taken your pleasure and not given him his."

"True," I gritted, my heart sinking. I could already see how this chauvinistic little trial was going to go. I was going to be skewered for my "crimes" and then judged guilty. They weren't even going to allow me a chance to defend myself.

Gabriel turned his serene gaze back to Luc. "Continue your tale."

"My master had commanded that I kidnap the succubus and bring her to a secluded cabin. I did so, but when we arrived at the cabin, she broke free from her chains and called a demon, trading her freedom for my own."

A low, disapproving murmur swept through the council.

Oh, come on. This was ridiculous! He was twisting what had truly happened. Luc had stalked me, cursed me to the point where I was dying, and then kidnapped me. The only way I could free myself was to call Mae, and I'd had no choice but to ask for her help. Now I owed the demoness a future favor in exchange for her helping me get my freedom.

It was a bum deal, but it was the only chance I'd had at the time. It was either that or let Luc rape me and sacrifice me on an altar to cast a spell and secure his own freedom from his master. But I guess he was going to omit those little details from the court.

Gabriel's cold-glass gaze turned back to me. "And is this true? Did you trade him to a demon, Succubus?"

"I traded him," I agreed. "But only because I was dying. It was the only way I could get free from him."

He turned to Luc. "And your actions were at the request of your master?"

"Yes."

The angel raised his hand, moving to his feet. "She is guilty," he declared. "I do not need to hear more."

"Wait," I yelped, coming to my feet. "You didn't hear my side of the story yet."

"Jackie," Noah said, moving in front of me to shield me. But I pushed past him.

"Don't I get to tell my side of the story? I was *cursed*," I ground out. "I was dying. He was going to *kill* me."

"There are certain rules against immortals that are sacrosanct, Succubus. You do not use another's curse against them, which you did when you took your pleasure and did not give him his." Gabriel's gaze was ice-cold. "That is not well done of you, but can be forgiven because of your youth. However, handing an immortal over to a demon for her own usage is a grave crime indeed. And if you have no moral compunctions when it comes to the lives of other immortals, you cannot remain on this plane, as you are a threat to other immortals."

Stunned, I flinched and hid behind Noah. Did that mean that they were going to destroy me? For self-preservation from a lying sack of shit like Luc?

"I ask for clemency," Noah said hoarsely. "Jackie is a new-fledged succubus. She does not know the rules of immortality."

"Youth is no excuse for carelessness," Gabriel continued.

To my surprise, Luc spoke up, his gaze sliding over to Ariel. "I ask for clemency on her behalf as well," he said with an easy smile. "I wished to bring her crimes up to the council so she may learn from them and pay a penance. In fact, I offer to take her on and teach her, if you like."

A cold chill skittered over my body. So that was his game: he wanted to get his grubby hands on me. If it was that or death, I was totally hosed. I clung to the back of Noah's shirt, frightened.

But Gabriel's cold gaze swept over Luc, emotionless. "It is not for you to decide the punishment. And this we have decided—she *will* be punished." His gaze swept over the occupants of the room. "I will return in two days. Bring your punishment suggestions at that time, and I will choose the most appropriate one."

Noah stepped forward. "I ask that I be given her punishment. She is my creation. I am responsible for her. Let me take on her fate."

No. Oh, Noah. Tears pricked my eyes. *You stupid, big, adoring lunk.*

But the angel's cold gaze swept back to him, as if seeing him for the first time. "Noahiel."

I could have sworn I saw the faintest lip curl. That wasn't a good sign.

"It is I," Noah agreed. "Jackie is under my protection. I ask that I be given her punishment."

"I am afraid that will not do," said Ariel, rising smoothly from his chair, his red hair spilling over his shoulder. "You are on trial as well, Noah Gideon. And your crime is unlawful creation: a far graver one with a rather large penance."

Ariel's mouth curved into a cold smile, and his gaze flicked over to me. "Take the succubus to her cell to await sentencing."

"I want to stay," I said, wrapping my fists in Noah's shirt like a child. Hands landed on my shoulders and waist, prying me off of my fallen angel. "Noah! Wait! Wait!"

But I was helpless as Ethan and another Enforcer dragged me out of the room and down the hall, back into the darkness.

Guilty and sentenced, and I hadn't even had the chance to defend myself.

Angels were total dicks.

CHAPTER FOUR

I was taken back to my cell and dumped there again. Ethan and the other guard had left, and I was alone. Nothing to do but sit here and . . . wait. Wait for my Itch to rise, and my blood to pound in my veins. Wait for my skin to become so sensitized that being naked was the only solution.

Wait for my fate and wait to hear what Noah's was, and if we were both doomed.

The hours passed slowly. I couldn't sleep—succubi didn't sleep—so I started braiding strands of my hair to count. Fifty strands at a time, micro-braids that took minutes to complete. When I had one hundred of them and no one had come, I started to worry that something dreadful was going wrong. When I had three hundred braids in my hair (and probably resembled a porcupine), my concern grew even more. Was anyone coming back at all? My stomach had been rumbling for hours. Were they going to starve me? I needed sex every two days to survive, but I didn't need food to live.

I stared out the window at the dark hallway, then returned to my bed, my hands sliding between my thighs and caressing the slick flesh there. My pulse was moving in a slow, languid beat that told me I was in serious need of some hot sex. Once a suck passed the line of need, we became frantic with the Itch. Any man would do, any dick would serve, and it was . . . disturbing. I didn't have that problem much, thanks to Noah (and Zane, though he was long gone), but if Noah wasn't coming back, what was going to happen to me?

Lost in thought, I almost missed the soft knock at the door.

Once it registered in my mind, I leapt up from the bed.

Ariel entered.

I frowned at him. Did I greet him? Demand to be let go? Demand to know where Noah was?

He saved me the trouble, nodding at me. His long, red hair was tied into a sleek tail down his back, and I noticed the blueness of his eyes as he stepped into my cell, then locked the door behind him.

Oh dear. This was not good. The Serim all worked off of the same clock. Right before the full moon, they had to have sex. Lots and lots of sex. A need that had been building for days, released in one amazing hours-long sexual marathon. Just thinking about it made my female parts tingle with need and my nipples tighten.

Down, girl. Down.

I moved to the far end of my cell. I didn't want to marathon with Ariel, but if he didn't leave my cell, my Itch wasn't going to leave me much of a choice.

"Hello, Jackie," Ariel said, clasping his hands behind

his back and approaching me. "I see you've been keeping busy." He cast a disapproving look at my wildly braided hair.

I shrugged, trying to seem casual. "Had to do something. Where's Noah?"

Ariel gave me a thin-lipped smile. Even the best bone structure couldn't hide the fact that he looked like he was sucking on a lemon. "Noah has been found guilty of creating a succubus and breaking the rules of the Serim. Rules that he has explicitly promised to uphold."

I shook my head. "I don't understand. He said he paid the fine and it was going to be okay." Noah had hinted that something was wrong in the past, but he'd told me that he'd fixed it, paid a penalty, and it had been taken care of.

"Ah, but that was before you broke the laws and attacked Luc Stone." Ariel moved forward, his long flowing white robe making his movements seem fluid. "And since you are an illegal creation, your crimes reflect on him as well."

"That's not fair," I said nervously.

"It is the law," Ariel said, still approaching me. "A hundred tasks of servitude—a harsh sentence."

I sucked in a breath. A hundred tasks? If they were anything like the last one I did for the Angel Uriel, he wouldn't be free of the punishment for years. Decades. "He has to serve the Serim council for a hundred tasks? What about me?"

"Your sentence is equally harsh. It is death."

I choked. "I'm sorry, did you say death? Just because someone transformed me without my knowledge and I fed a scumbag to a demon?"

He gave a shrug. "It is a harsh punishment, but that is what the council has decided for you."

I shook my head. "The Archangel Gabriel said *he* was going to decide it. Based on all the options. Weren't there supposed to be, you know, other options?"

Ariel gave me another thin smile and reached out to brush my cheek. My flesh throbbed at the touch, and I resisted the urge to lean into it. This guy was my creepy enemy.

"There is one other option that Gabriel has shown interest in. If you destroy the succubus Remy and bring the halo of power back to the Serim council, we will consider that due penance for your crimes."

"I'm not going to kill my best friend just to please you guys. Forget that." I slapped his hand away as he tried to touch me again. "It's not Remy's fault that she was possessed."

"No, it is yours. Again." Ariel's smile was cold. "You seem to be bad luck for your companions, Miss Brighton."

Understatement of the year. I swallowed hard, trying to think. "There has to be a way to extract the halo from Remy without killing her. I could do that."

"I'm sorry, but the Serim council is not interested in your friend's life." He gave another fluid shrug. "Her ties to the halo are too close to be entirely negated, and we simply cannot take the chance, even if it is removed from her. One of them must be removed from this plane. Death is the only option."

"Well, that's not an option for me, so you can forget it." I would never, ever trade my life for Remy's. Not when she'd had my back every time I needed her.

"Then it looks like death is your punishment."

Were they crazy? I pressed up against the wall. "You're going to kill me because I fed an evil incubus to a demon who was equally evil? You've got to be kidding me."

He set one hand on the wall next to my shoulder and leaned in. "Luc was not yours to torment, Succubus. His punishment is his master's choice, not yours. But do not worry. I have an alternate plan in mind for you."

Oh, I could just imagine. I didn't have to be a math genius to see the intense blue in his eyes or the erection that tented the front of his robe. "Let me guess. You want to have sex with me."

His mouth quirked slightly and his hand slid to my shoulder. I shoved it off, but he replaced it, then lowered it and squeezed my arm a little. As if . . . testing it. Weird. "Though I have to have sex with someone, I'd prefer it not be you. I'm not a fan of Noah, and the thought of you being a vampire's leavings is rather stomach turning."

Oddly enough, that insult made me feel better. "So what's the deal?"

"I need a child."

I wasn't following. "Is that some sort of code for me to dress up in pigtails and wear a bib? Because—"

He gave me a revolted look. "No. I need a *child*. I need a female immortal to bear a child for me."

I still wasn't following. "But I thought succubi were sterile?"

I didn't like the look that crossed his face or the fact that his hand stroked my arm. "Oh, but there is a way, my dear. There is definitely a way."

I shook my head at him, trying to slide away. "What do you mean? Succubi can't breed. Neither can Serim."

Which was probably a good thing, seeing as how we were all immortal and for the most part amoral.

He stroked my arm again, then tilted his head slightly. "No muscle tone, but that might be because of the succubus nature."

Was he judging me to see how fit of a mommy I'd be? Gross. "Yeah, sorry. I guess ridiculous red hair and perky boobs were higher on the list than fitness."

"No matter," he said. "I am sure the genetics will not be a factor."

"Great," I said and shoved his hand away. "But you're missing the point. Succubi can't breed."

"True. It would take . . . a miracle." He smiled at me.

Oh, I really, really did not like that smile. I swallowed hard and edged away. "When you say 'miracle,' are you thinking what I think you're thinking?"

"Those in Heaven believe the Enforcers can do more good on Earth than the Serim do. We simply take the Nephilim and raise them to be the instruments of Heaven here on Earth."

"Nephilim?" Those were supposedly the children of angels and humans. Like a lot of other things, I'd chalked it up to being more myth than real. Maybe I was wrong. "What do the angels want with children? And what does this have to do with me?"

"If you do a favor for them, it means a favor for the Serim." He gave me a cold smile. "As for what it means for you . . . all we need is for the Angel Gabriel to touch your womb as I expel my essence into it, and a miracle will happen." His hand went over to my waist and nudged the waistband of my shorts. "While it won't be the most pleasant experience, it is necessary to create the Enforcers. Don't worry." He smiled at me. "We'll take the child off your hands."

This was the most ridiculous and creepiest plan I'd ever heard. "I'm not sure I understand you correctly. You want to give me your 'essence'? And some angel's going to put his finger on my stomach and make a baby?" I gave him an incredulous look. "That is the most absurd thing I've ever heard."

Jeez, if I were a divine soldier for God, I'd have better things to do than create immortal surrogate mommies.

"Really?" Ariel's smile was cunning. "Did you not meet Ethan, then? Your guard?"

"Ethan?" I echoed, startled. "He's a succu-baby?"

"An Enforcer," Ariel corrected. "And if you breed one for us, we'll let you go afterward. No penalty. No servitude."

There was no way in hell I'd bear a kid for anyone in

the Serim, but if it would save my lover . . . "What about Noah?"

"Noah's fate is already decided. What we need to decide right now is yours."

I forced a polite smile to my face and moved farther down the wall. "While this is a thrilling offer, I'm going to pass."

"You're making a mistake."

"I'm pretty sure that I'm not," I retorted. "Now get out of my cell."

His eyes seemed to glow in the darkness, and my body tingled with anticipation. "I'll be back in a few hours to persuade you otherwise."

"Oh, I'll be here," I said flippantly to hide how hard my heart was pounding, and the fact that my voice was becoming breathy. Just his proximity turned me on incredibly, and I hated my Itch for it.

He turned and left. As soon as the door shut behind him, I grabbed the cot and dragged it in front of the door, then sat down on it to add weight. My arms hugged my knees close, and I shuddered.

As if they weren't psycho enough, they wanted me to breed a new little immortal psycho for them to raise and twist to their ways. God, how had Noah turned out so normal compared to these freaks? No wonder the angels hated the Serim.

And no wonder so many of them turned vampire. They were a hair's edge away from being evil as it was.

○ ○ ○

A knock came at the door a while later, and I yelped in surprise as my bed moved forward. I shoved back against the door. "No!"

Ethan gave me a look of surprise, pushing his way in. "Are you not hungry, Jackie Brighton? I have brought you a meal since the others have not thought to do so."

Oh, good! Ethan. I exhaled in relief, fighting the urge to hug him out of gratitude. I took the plate from his hands. Scrambled eggs, bacon, and a biscuit. Breakfast time, then. "I thought you were someone else," I muttered, then crammed the biscuit in my mouth. "Is it morning?"

"It is," he said calmly. Then to my surprise, he blushed. My body began to heat in response. "The Serim are unavailable today."

Ah. Today was curse day—the day that all the Serim had to get their rocks off. Or rather, their partner's rocks' off. The Serim curse was a unique one: they had to give their partners sexual release in order to find relief from their curse. While sex drove them, the curse wasn't lifted until the partner orgasmed, and then they were free for another month.

I suppose that was designed to keep them from living a selfish lifestyle, but I wasn't complaining. At least, not normally. Right now, though, I wouldn't have turned down an orgasm. Or three. "Are you not affected by the curse?"

"Me?" He blushed even redder and tried to give me a stern look. "You should not ask about such things."

I bit into a piece of bacon and raised an eyebrow at him. His blush was a real turn-on. So sweet. So innocent. So sexy. My breasts tightened in response. I forced those thoughts out of my mind. "Why not? I think we're all adults here."

"I am an Enforcer," he said, as if that explained everything.

"So I've heard. What exactly does that mean? Are you cursed like me?"

He gave me a slight frown, as if not comprehending. "My goal in life is to do good deeds. Is that what you refer to?"

"Uh, not exactly." I licked my fingers, then stopped, because the licking was a turn-on. I decided to try another tactic. "So who is your mom?"

Again, the strange frown. "Enforcers do not have mothers. We come from a womb, but we do not have a sentimental attachment to any females."

Riiight. "Okay." I shoved another forkful of egg into my mouth. Maybe food would make me stop thinking about sex.

"Do you have any other questions I can answer for you?" he asked, almost eagerly.

His excitement made my blood pulse, and I had to force myself not to jump on him and start rubbing myself up against his thick, muscled thigh. Mmm . . . A haze of lust slid over me. "I'm sorry, what did you say?"

"What questions can I answer for you?" Just repeating the question seemed to bring the eagerness out again.

Strange. He was kind of like a big affable nerd who didn't know how to function around girls. Living with the Serim full-time probably didn't make one the most well adjusted individual. "You got a girlfriend, Ethan?"

Again, the blush. "I do not have time for personal matters." He extended a hand, all business again. "If you are done with your plate, I will take it back to the kitchens."

I scraped the last of the egg off of the plate and placed it in his waiting hand, feeling a little better. I was even able to resist grabbing his hand and sliding it between my legs like some oversexed cougar. "Thank you. That was delicious."

His eyes glowed for a brief second, then went back to the normal black, and a faint smile curved his hard mouth. "You are welcome."

I watched as he exited, feeling a bit of loss. "Will you come back and talk to me when you're done? I'm kind of . . ." Lonely. Horny. Scared. "Bored."

Really horny. And Ethan was pretty to look at.

Ethan nodded, giving me a slight courtly bow. "If it will make you feel better, it shall be so."

"Great," I said, watching him leave with a sigh. I pressed my face against the bars of the window in the door, frustrated. I should have used my Suck powers on him. Should have tried to overwhelm him and bust out of this place. But I liked Ethan, oddly enough. He was the only one who had been decent to me since I'd gotten here.

And I was probably going to need him very shortly. The Itch pulsed hard in my thighs, and I bit down a moan. He seemed kind of virginal but he probably had working equipment, and that was enough for me.

God, to think that Noah had proposed marriage to me yesterday. I couldn't be monogamous because I was cursed to need sex far too often. What if he had a business trip? We'd be chained together at the waist for the rest of our immortal lives. Then it'd be a different kind of hell if we started to resent each other.

No, I suspected marriage was a bad idea for immortals. My best friend Remy was over four hundred years old and she hadn't married anyone. She rarely kept a long-term relationship, either. Maybe that was for the best.

Poor Remy. Possessed again. I had to help her somehow. Everyone who tried to help me just seemed to get in more and more trouble. I thought sadly of Noah, who had tried to sacrifice himself to save me. He'd said he wanted to marry me to keep me safe. Because of this? It made sense . . . but would the Serim persecute the mate of one of their own? I doubted they held any kind of sentimental feelings, but you never knew. They'd been cursed to roam the Earth because of the love of a woman. Maybe if Noah and I were in love, they'd have left us alone.

I peered down the hall again, waiting for Ethan to return, and feeling the Itch pulsing through my body. My nipples grew tight, and the flesh between my legs tingled.

My breath caught in my throat as Ariel appeared down the hall, eyes a radiant blue, a jug of holy water in his hands, and a priest at his side.

Oh shit. He was going to call an angel to make a baby on me. And I was so far gone with the Itch that I wouldn't be able to stop him.

CHAPTER FIVE

A sick frisson of excitement swept through me. Anticipation made my skin shiver, and my panties grew damp with dread. Ariel was going to screw me until I begged for release, and then he'd get me pregnant.

Though I was filled with revulsion at the thought of him touching me, my body ached with need and my head swam. My breath panted out of my lungs, my skin becoming dewy with excitement.

I was a sick, sick freak. I was well over a day overdue for my own Itch, and I could only imagine how much torment Noah was in at the moment. Because succubi needed sex so often, the Itch was a gradual pain in the ass—I could probably survive another day or two without serious repercussions. But the Serim had to fulfill their needs on the day, to the month. I had no idea what would happen to him if he left himself needing for much longer.

The thought worried me. They wouldn't let me go to Noah; were they at least letting another woman service him? And why did that leave such a bitter taste in my mouth?

I could hear water inside the jar sloshing as Ariel moved forward. Behind him, the priest followed, and Ethan. The Enforcer's expression was blank, and I clung to the hope that was coming for me.

I could sleep with Ethan, maybe, and not hate myself in the morning. Maybe.

The cell door opened despite my bed propped up against it, and I ran to the other side of the cell, pressing my flushed skin against the cool concrete wall. "What are you doing here?"

Gangbang, my sick mind said to me, making another perverted little thrill shoot through me.

No! Bad! I shook my head to clear the thought.

Ariel's eyes were the feverish almost-purple of an immortal strained beyond need. His hands tightened on the jar, and a shudder racked his body as he stared at me with heated eyes. Trying to control himself, I guessed. My fingernails dug into the concrete wall behind me for the exact same reason.

"Hold her against the wall, Ethan," Ariel said in a ragged voice. "Keep us separated until I finish."

Ethan's mouth thinned as if with disapproval, but he approached me and put his hands on my shoulders, anchoring me in place so I couldn't move or run away.

God, his hands felt good. I shuddered in ecstasy, my hips rising from the wall, trying to meet his.

He stared down at me with a distasteful look in his dark eyes, then glanced back at Ariel, frowning. "Hurry."

Well, if that wasn't a blow to the ego, I didn't know

what was. But I couldn't blame the guy; I didn't like myself much when I was like this, either. I twisted my head and pressed my cheek against the cement, closing my eyes as I tried to control my rapidly pounding pulse. I could control the Itch—a little—when I was by myself, but with a man touching me and another nearby? I was full of quickly spiraling out-of-control need. My hand slid to the waist of my shorts, needing something.

Water splashed. I opened my eyes and watched through my lashes as Ariel splashed water along every corner of the room and the priest muttered a prayer in Latin. They were turning my cell into a holy place. Sanctifying it.

All the better to fuck me with, I supposed. Ugh.

Once the water was gone, the priest exited the room. Ariel's attention focused on the ceiling. "I request the Archangel Gabriel," he said softly.

I barely had time to blink before Gabriel emerged from the shadows behind him. The angel was just as beautiful as before, too pure looking for my small, dark cell. His hair was a perfect cap of curls, the fall of his wings as lovely as before, and the drape of his simple clothing was immaculate. Just the sight of him made my body pulse with hunger.

"I am here. What is it you need?"

Ariel's violet gaze met mine, hot with need. "Leave us, Ethan."

"No, Ethan!" I grabbed his arms. "Stay. *Please* stay. Don't leave me."

Ethan looked torn, glancing at me and then to Ariel

and Gabriel. His hand twitched on my shoulder as he considered the three of us.

That small twitch was enough to send a full body shiver through me, and a small moan escaped my throat, my hips rising again.

Ethan looked stricken and released me as if I'd scalded him. With barely a glance back at me, he bowed at Gabriel and Ariel and then left the room.

Shit. I'd scared him off. Now I was here alone with these two goons.

The moment the door was shut, Ariel began to move toward me, a hint of an evil smile curving his mouth. "Do you need to sate your Itch, Succubus?"

I backed away, glancing at Gabriel. His face was emotionless as Ariel stalked me. He wouldn't help me, and he wouldn't help Ariel. He was just going to watch as Ariel used me. I shuddered.

They were supposed to be the *good* guys.

"What do you want?" I asked, though I pretty much knew at this point. I skittered to my cot, leaping over it to get away from Ariel when he reached for me. If he touched me, I didn't know that I'd be able to hold out.

"I told you what I wanted, Succubus. If you will bear a child for the angels, the Serim will remove the charges against you." He continued to stalk behind me as I circled the other side of the small cell, his movements slow and sure. The only sign of his craziness was the intensity of his blue-violet gaze, hot with need and smug with the fact that I was on the run.

"I'm not going to bear a child," I said, then yelped as he reached out and grabbed my braids. I fell to the floor, my knees and palms hitting the concrete hard. "You can't make me!"

"Can't I?" he said. Then he was kneeling over me, his hot skin pressed against mine. Revulsion filled me even as desire coursed through my body. "And how long do you think Noah can hold out before the curse destroys him? Serim are not like succubi. We cannot hold out for days at a time and let our bodies slowly deteriorate. If he goes, it will be fast, like a snuffed candle. And *you* will be responsible."

Guilt struck me, almost as palpable as the massive erection pressing against my side.

As Ariel began to run his hands all over my body, I felt the quiver of pleasure beginning at my sex and loathed it. I should have moved his hands away, should have pushed him aside as he knelt next to me and began to brush his hands against my breasts, against the crotch of my shorts. My gaze slid to the corner of the room, where Gabriel stood like a disapproving statue. He watched, dispassionate, even as I arched my neck against Ariel's lips.

Oh God, oh God. I hated myself so much, especially when a moan of pleasure escaped my lips.

"When I come inside you, Succubus, Gabriel will touch your stomach, and we will create a child, one of duty that will serve the Serim council for all eternity."

Through the haze in my mind, his words registered. "Serve eternally? Without a choice?" It sounded like

Hell. I stared up at Gabriel's impassive face, biting my lip as Ariel's fingers danced over my breasts. "I thought you were the good guys."

"We are," he breathed against my neck, biting down on the soft flesh there. My entire body shivered with a mixture of sexual response and revulsion. "But don't worry. We don't need you once the child is birthed."

A sour taste began at the back of my throat, and I locked my gaze on Gabriel as Ariel continued to molest me. "And what do *you* get out of this?"

"A deal," said Gabriel coldly.

Just like when I'd had to get the halo for the vampire queen, and in doing so, screwed over my best friend Remy. I knew what angel deals were like now.

Ariel's hand slid to my tightly clasped thighs and wrenched them apart.

I pried his hand off my thigh only to have it replaced again, like some sort of perverted octopus with eight arms. "Quit touching me," I said, though it lacked conviction. Disgusted with myself, I turned away so I wouldn't have to look at Ariel's coldly beautiful face or his long red hair.

My gaze rested on Gabriel, who looked a little revolted by the two of us writhing on the floor. I didn't want to look over at him, either. I turned to face the door, glaring at it as if it could unlock itself and save me.

A shadow moved behind the window, and my body tensed as I caught a glimpse of Ethan's frowning face. A voyeur?

No, he was holding something up. A scanner card to bypass the biometric lock on the door.

Salvation!

I glanced back at Gabriel as Ariel's hand went between my legs. My thighs were coaxed apart despite the plan I was hatching. Did Gabriel want me to breed the magic baby for the Serim? Would he try to stop me?

Then again, did I care at this point?

I planted my hand on Ariel's forehead and pushed hard with my mind, trying to disable him with my Suck powers.

For some reason, either because I had surprised him or I was getting stronger, my powers worked. Ariel's eyes slid back in his head and he fell over, falling into slumber. His cock still jutted from his robes, and it took every ounce of willpower I had not to reach for it and scratch my own Itch.

I hate you, Ariel. Hate hate hate. I repeated the mantra as I forced myself up on wobbly legs and crossed the room.

Gabriel continued to watch impassively as I headed to the door.

On the other side, Ethan paced. When I reached through the bars and waved, he rushed over, his cheeks flushing. His eyes wouldn't meet mine as he passed me the badge key through the narrow bars. "Are you well, Succubus?"

Was that some weird way of asking me if I was okay? If so, it was totally hot, thanks to the Itch, and I felt the need flare anew. I was just a mass of fireworks and nerve endings in all the most uncomfortable places. "I'm all right," I said breathily. "Can you hand me the badge and step away?"

He tilted his head at me, regarding me as if I'd just lost my mind. "I do not understand—"

"Just give it to me," I bit out, then forced myself to be calm. "Please. Look, I can't think, because you're male and hot and staring right at me and it's making my Itch crazy, so either give me the badge or open my door already."

He glanced over at me and his gaze rested on my eyes—which I'm sure were neon blue at the moment—and then blushed and hastily pressed the badge into my hand. "I will wait out here."

"Thank you." I ignored the shivers emanating from where his hand had come close to touching mine and clutched the badge so hard it bit into my palm. The lockpad scanner was almost out of reach, but with a few reckless swipes, I was able to get the badge to register. The door beeped and the bolt unhitched with a sound so wonderful, it almost made me orgasm.

I pushed at the door with excitement, relief swirling through me. Free! I could get away from Ariel—

"Wait, Jacqueline Brighton."

Uh oh. I paused at the threshold and faced Gabriel. *Bad* idea. He was so, so pretty. And he was smiling at me.

Wavering, I stepped back inside, drawn to his beauty like a really horny moth to a flame.

He beckoned to me.

I hesitated mentally even as my feet continued to move forward, my body drawn to him. "I'm not waking Ariel up," I said. "At least not until I'm safely on the other side of the bars."

"I do not care what you do with the Serim." Gabriel's voice was smooth, almost sweet. I was so close now that I could see the chiseled lines of his chest, like a perfect marble statue. His vanilla scent was almost overwhelming, mixed with a masculine tinge that made my flesh shiver with delight. I had to clasp my hands together to keep for reaching for him. Angels didn't like to be touched, I remembered that.

"So what do you want with me?"

The smile remained on his face. "I wish to make you the same deal that the Serim does, Jacqueline Brighton."

I took a step backward. "I beg your pardon?"

"Do you wish me to repeat myself?"

"You want me to have your baby? The answer is no for you, too."

A flicker of revulsion crossed his face. "You misunderstand me. I wish for you to bring the archangel's power to me."

Oh. My singing hormones couldn't help but be a little disappointed in that. "I'm not going to kill my friend just to suit your purposes," I said. "And you're a creep for even asking me that."

"I do not care if your friend lives or dies—I merely want the power currently residing in her. Find a way to remove it and bring it to me, and I shall make you a deal." His eyes gleamed with power. "Your assistance in exchange for a favor."

The fluttering in my mind was making it hard for me to think, and my skin began to itch with need. I clasped my hands tighter, quelling the need to rub up against him. "Uriel wanted the halo as well, remember? He was going to use it to eradicate the Serim."

"I do not care if the Serim live or die. My goal is a higher one. Haloes are dangerous and must be removed from the mortal plane."

"How do I know you are telling the truth and not lying to me?"

He put his hand out, palm up. An invitation for me to touch him. Greedily, I slid my hand into his, fingers flexing. Oh, his skin was so hot and wonderful against my own. I shivered with pleasure, watching as he gripped my fingers and turned my palm face up. His thumb slid across my wrist.

A burning sensation followed where his thumb had moved. I yelped and jerked my hand out of his, staring at my wrist. A small string of angelic characters had been burned into my flesh, marking me as Noah had been marked. "I give you my word, Jacqueline Brighton."

Gabriel vanished, leaving me with a stinging wrist, a confusing task, and a sleeping fallen angel with a boner at my feet.

Lovely.

I left the cell again, the lock clicked behind me, and

Ariel was safely behind bars. I could breathe a little easier, even though every muscle in my body was screaming for me to run back inside and mount him. Even unconscious, I could still get what I needed . . . theoretically. I frowned at his sleeping body curled up on the floor.

Only the succubus who had put someone to sleep could wake them. If I left and abandoned him, he'd fall into a coma. Not that this was a bad thing, but even I wasn't that cruel. I pondered it for a moment, trying to clear my head to think.

A hand touched my shoulder. "Succubus, do you think—"

I groaned and slid my hand backward, searching for his cock. With unerring accuracy, I found it and began to rub.

Ethan yelped and moved a few steps away. The fog on my brain cleared a little, and I was filled with remorse. "God, Ethan, I *told* you not to touch me."

"My apologies," he said in a strangled voice. "I am not used to being around your kind."

That was painfully obvious. I rubbed my neck, trying to will the Itch to subside. "Where is Noah being held?"

A plan was forming in my mind. Step one: find Noah and spring him. Step two: escape. Step three: shag Noah mercilessly so I could think with something other than my lady parts.

"We should not free him, Succubus," Ethan said in a disapproving voice. "He has been judged but not yet convicted. His sentence must begin first."

I gave Ethan an incredulous look. "Since my trial was a total farce, I'm not leaving him behind. And besides, I kind of *need* him—if you get what I mean." Unless Ethan was volunteering to soothe my savage beast, which, judging by his reaction to my spontaneous grope—wasn't likely. He was so pretty, though. That waterfall of black hair cascading down his back, the smooth, dark eyes with delicate epicanthal folds, the amazing cheekbones that were so high and sharp that I could probably slice food on them . . . he definitely looked edible.

Ethan noticed me staring and blanched, taking a step backward.

Okay, that did it for my libido. I had someone I was trying to be faithful to at the moment, anyhow. I shook my head to clear it. "Noah. Let's get Noah now, okay?"

Ethan nodded and gestured at the hall, relieved to have my attention focusing elsewhere. "They keep him in that wing. Apart from the others."

Poor Noah. Part of me hoped they'd brought him a woman so he could slake his desires. And part of me really, really hated the thought of him touching someone else. *Immortality sure came with a lot of baggage,* I thought with irritation. It totally messed with your head.

I started down the hall, then paused as Ethan's footsteps did not follow. I glanced backward. "Something wrong?"

He hesitated, then glanced back in the cell I'd just left. "I came to rescue you because it is the right thing to do." He was clearly torn. "But I do not know that, in good conscience, I can leave Ariel behind on the floor."

Neither could I. "After I grab Noah, we'll wake Ariel up before getting out of here. Okay?"

He nodded and seemed relieved. "I will wait here for you to return. I think I should keep my distance from the Serim." He held the badge out to me, dangling from his fingers. "You will need this in order to free him."

I plucked it from his hands. "All right. I'll be back as soon as I let Noah out."

Ethan nodded and pulled his bo staff from the sheath on his back. He rose to his full height, a frown on his serious face, and braced the stuff in front of him, guarding the cell and the sleeping Ariel.

Whatever floated his boat.

CHAPTER SIX

I clutched the badge and moved cautiously down the dark hallway. I half expected someone—Serim or otherwise—to jump out at me, hold me down, and force me to make babies with them. The Serim were nothing like I'd pictured. Noah was such a good guy that I wondered how Ariel had turned into such a full-on rat.

Then again, Zane had been a Serim once, and he'd turned his back on being merely a fallen angel to becoming a full-blown vampire. So clearly all was not hunky-dory in Serim Land.

The concrete was cold and dusty against my bare feet and I tiptoed quietly. Every cell looked identical to the one I'd been held in—the window had been knocked out and replaced with bars, and each was locked with a badge reader. I'd peered into one or two but hadn't seen Noah yet. I continued down, looking into each cell, to the end of the hall. At the last door, I peered in and saw a faint shape bent over on the side of the cot, elbows resting on his knees. His head was down in a defeated pose, and his fists were clenched.

Poor, sweet Noah. My heart fluttered at the sight

of him, so defeated. It was probably killing him that he wasn't able to protect me. I felt a surge of affection and quickly swiped the badge against the reader. Like clockwork, the red light flashed to green and the lock unbolted.

Noah didn't get up.

"Noah?" I whispered. "Noah, are you all right?"

No response. His hand clenched and then unclenched slowly, so I knew he was awake. Worry shot through me, momentarily overriding my lust. "Noah?"

"Leave me," he said in a harsh voice.

What on earth was he talking about? I stared at him, puzzled, then moved inside. The heavy door shut behind me, locking automatically, and I clutched the badge close. "Noah, are you all right? I'm here to get you out of here. We have to escape."

He shook his head slowly.

This was getting ridiculous. I moved to his side and went to touch his shoulder. "Come on, Noah."

Before I could touch it, his hand whipped out and trapped mine by the wrist. The angelic word burned into my flesh hurt like a bitch. Before I could complain, he moved forward and leaned in close to my hand. Sniffed it.

Exhaled sharply. "I smell two other men on you," he said, his voice a low growl.

What in the world? I tried to jerk my hand out of his. "Noah, I didn't sleep with anyone. You're jumping to conclusions."

He tilted his head back and finally looked at me. The

expression on his face was raw with need. His eyes were so deep a blue that they glowed in the dark, and the set of his jaw was unyielding.

"Tell me who I smell."

A command. Oh great, we were going to play this game? I tried to jerk my hand out of his as I answered. "Ariel and Ethan, probably."

His eyes darkened, his expression barely controlled.

"Don't be an ass, Noah." Oh lord, even his being batshit crazy was turning me on. I could feel my panties growing damp, felt the flesh of my sex begin to heat. "Nothing happened."

"Your scent. You took two others for your need?" He slowly raised to his feet, not releasing my wrist from his death grip. His eyes were glowing blue slits of anger. "They brought me a woman and I refused her. Refused, because I wished to stay loyal to you." His voice was hoarse with anger, brimming with barely restrained force. His eyes seemed to flash purple with hunger and need. He was beyond rational thought.

"Noah, don't do this," I said in a husky voice. *Do it, do it,* my body was screaming. My sex was wet and slick with heat, and my breath was coming in small, excited pants. We didn't have time to stop and feed our needs, yet I couldn't wait to get him alone in private. My libido was off the charts at the moment.

He stared at me with those insanely dark eyes, and leaned in and gently bit at the flesh of my palm, as if tasting me.

My knees went weak. "Noah—"

"Kneel."

Compulsion gripped me and I descended to the floor with a thump, staring up at him in a mix of confusion, dread, and sexual excitement. My hand slid up to his belt. "Noah?"

His hand caressed my cheek, but the eyes that stared into mine weren't focused in rational thought. The bluish-purple mix of wildness and emotion was impossible to resist.

I'd never seen Noah like this. Always calm, always logical and rational, never lacking control over anything in his daily life—this Noah was a stranger to me.

It excited and titillated me. My eyes were level with his cock, a tantalizing suggestion that was lost on neither of us. My hand slid down from his belt, brushing across the front of his jeans. He still wore the black polo and jeans he'd been captured in, and I found the smell of salt and sweat and man intoxicating.

His fingers brushed my cheek again, that lust-driven madness in his eyes not abating. "Put your cheek to the floor."

I blinked, startled at both the command and the pulse of desire that shot through me. Helpless to do anything but obey, I leaned forward until my cheek lay against the cold cement. Still kneeling, it made an awkward position, my rounded ass now angled high in the air.

"Noah?" I asked again, nearly writhing at the thought of him standing over me, staring at my presented ass.

The thought was delicious and I couldn't help but fixate on it. "Talk to me."

"No talking," he said harshly.

My throat locked up and no words would come out. All righty then. I wasn't in the mood for talking much anyhow, and Noah didn't seem to be, either.

His hands gripped my flesh through the shorts, palms resting on my ass cheeks. I gave a small whimper of anticipation, but he merely kneaded me through the clothing for a moment. Then he ripped at the shorts until the string-tie belt ripped in half, and pulled them down to my knees.

The breath shuddered out of me.

The sane, logical part of me thought that I should dislike the bold, almost dismissive treatment, but this new, wild, and barely controlled Noah was making me wetter than I'd ever been. It was a major turn-on to a body that was already on the edge of losing its grip on reality.

I closed my eyes and let the sensations take over me. Shivers swept over my skin as my panties swept down my legs next, pooling around my knees like my shorts. My palms pressed against the cold concrete next to my cheek, waiting. My pulse had slowed to a low throb through my overheated flesh, making each second of anticipation that much greater.

Then, when I thought I wouldn't be able to stand it any longer, I felt Noah grasp my now-bare ass, kneading it again.

My breath sucked in.

One of his thumbs slid through the seam of my sex, hot and drenched.

A startled gasp escaped me, my breath whooshing out at the sensations. With one finger, he'd just rocked my entire world. My sex clenched involuntarily, and I couldn't help but writhe against him. My hips rolled, trying to coax that finger to slide deeper, to search for the parts of me that ached so badly for it.

"Don't move," he said harshly, his own breath as ragged as the short breaths that were escaping me.

Just like that, my muscles froze in place. All wiggling ceased abruptly, and I was forced—through no will of my own—to hold in place as he ran a finger along the wet line of my sex again.

Then, nothing, for a long—too long—moment. My muscles contracted and shivered, waiting. Anticipating.

His hands touched my ass, and I felt his breath against my thighs—he was kneeling behind me. One thumb touched one side of my slick sex, the other touched the opposite side, spreading my hot flesh open for his perusal.

His mouth descended and my breath exploded, hot and keening with need. His tongue lapped at my aching, wet sex. First a hard lick, then a softer, darting one. Teasing me. Tormenting. Then another hard lick, swiping at my body before diving in to flick against my core once more.

A sob flew out of my throat at the intense pleasure.

Flick after flick, he tasted my sex with wild, urgent

need. One hand slid forward, sliding through the wet heat and finding my clit, stroking it with the pad of one thick finger. Circling it in a soft motion that was echoed by Noah's tongue. When he flicked at it again and my body quivered once more, my inner muscles contracting, his fingers slid away.

I cried out, unable to articulate words, prevented by his harsh commands. Pinned in place, helpless to tell him that I was so close to going over the edge, but not wanting him to stop, either. God, never stop.

His fingers slid over my folds again, and the urge to buck and force them into the hot, needing clench of my sex was overwhelming. But I couldn't move. It was the ultimate in frustration, locked down by his commands and needing him so badly that my entire body ached with tiny muscle spasms.

His thumb rubbed against the seam of my ass, as if contemplating my situation, and soft, gasping noises escaped involuntarily from my throat.

Then his thumb went just inside the edge of my aching, needing sex. My breath exploded again and my entire body locked up in the almost-throes of an orgasm. *So* close.

But before I could go over the edge, Noah removed his thumb. His nails scraped down the flesh of my ass, almost viciously. The sensation was so startling that it sent another shock wave of sensation through my body, and the orgasm skittered out of reach. The sound of disappointment crashed from my throat.

Torture. Long moments passed in which Noah did not touch me, and the only sound in the room was my harsh breathing mixing with his.

When my breath began to slow again, my senses grew tense, hearing and touch growing more sensitive as I tried to anticipate what would happen next. I could hear Noah's breathing, but I didn't know what he was doing, only that the warmth of his body indicated he still hovered near my body. But he wasn't touching me.

Then, something hot fanned on the vee of my sex, and my muscles clenched. The air turned from hot to cool—he was blowing on me.

That made my body ratchet up all over again, small cries beginning to erupt from my throat again. Desperately, I wanted him to touch me, to ease the ache inside of me. But all I got was the tickling tease of his breath.

When I thought I might come out of my skin from maddening frustration, Noah's large palm caressed my ass, plumping the curve of it, his fingers splaying across my skin. "You belong to me," he rasped in a harsh, wild voice. "You may fall prey to your urges, but you will know that you belong to *me*, Jackie."

His fingers dug into my ass, hard. That was the only warning I got before he sheathed himself to the hilt, burying his hard cock inside me.

It was so good and so needed and so sudden that a choked scream erupted from me, dying down as his hips rolled against mine. My legs were still cradled tight together, my cheek still pressed to the floor, so the fit was a tight one. The size of him had burned slightly as it had entered, but oh God, it was a good pain. *So* good. I gave a little gasp as he grasped my hips hard against him, pulling himself deeper into me—so deep that I felt that same shiver of pain again, and welcomed it. He was forcing my body to take him in, but I was so turned on and wet with need that I was on the edge of coming just from the one stroke. I could feel my internal muscles quivering hard, clenching around the thickness of his cock. Felt my muscles building toward the orgasm again.

Noah gave a slight thrust, more of a tease than a satisfying possession, then slid out of me again.

I nearly cried with disappointment.

"I want you to see that it is me when I take you," he ground out harshly. "On your feet."

Helpless to disobey, I quickly got to my feet, boneless and throbbing with desire.

I desperately wanted to run my hands over his gleaming skin. He'd removed his shirt, and I could see the wide expanse of golden muscles staring back at me, calling my name. *Touch meeeee. Lick meee.*

God, the need was making me crazy! My gaze slid down to his cock, gleaming with the moisture from my body, jutting hard. My mouth watered at the sight of it, and the desire began to pulse in my sex once more.

"On the bed. On your back," Noah commanded.

I sat on the edge of the bed and fell to my back, my arms still locked beside me. The position made my spine arch, jutting my breasts in the air.

Noah loomed over me. "Legs in the air," he commanded.

I obeyed, the shorts and panties that I'd nearly forgotten about sliding back down to my thighs. He ripped them off and tossed them across the floor, and then grabbed at one of my calves, his large hand sliding up to encircle my ankle. I felt something slide under my hips—the pillow. It raised my hips at an interesting angle. Noah studied my foot for a minute, then pressed his mouth to the side of it. Not a kiss, not tasting the skin. Claiming it as if he could brand me with his touch. His mouth slid farther down to my knee, then moved down the inside of my thigh. They were still pressed close together. "Separate them," he commanded. As if I *wanted* to keep him out? "And watch me. Don't take your eyes off me. Don't close them."

My breath began to catch again, the excitement reaching near fever pitch once more. My legs slid wide apart and he knelt at the cradle of my hips, his breath hovering over the curls of my sex, and he braced one hand under my hips. He glanced up at me, indigo eyes hot with emotion, and stared at me as his mouth descended on my aching, hot flesh. I felt the flick of his tongue against my clit.

Immediately, my body began to shudder with the onset of orgasm, only to have his hot mouth lift away.

"Not yet, Jackie. Don't come until I say so."

Oh God.

Again, my traitorous body stopped, and the quakes

continued to echo through my flesh, close to the edge but never quite close enough to bring me over. His mouth descended on my clit again, his eyes locked on mine. I couldn't look away. As I watched, he licked at my sex, torturously long, and slow, and my gaze was fascinated by that length of pink tongue sliding down and disappearing into the damp folds of my sex, lapping at me like a cat lapped at cream, savoring me.

The shivers of need grew to a full body quake. Noah seemed in no rush to bring me to orgasm, and the thought was terrifying as well as thrilling—how long would he keep this up? The need for sex had driven him over the edge, and *God*, I wished I could orgasm. My inner muscles clenched over and over again, but the edge always eluded me. I whimpered for the hundredth time, needing release.

Noah slid up, seating himself before me, and I could feel the hot length of his sex sliding against my own. It rubbed against my aching flesh, sliding along the slick heat and driving another sobbing breath out of my throat as I stared into Noah's possessive gaze.

When his cock slid in deep a full body gasp ripped through me. Noah grasped at my thighs, my feet braced on each shoulder, and began to slowly push forward. It embedded him deeper and deeper into my body, his face coming closer and closer to mine.

And he thrust again.

I choked on my sob. The next time, when he thrust even harder, it felt like he was so deep inside me that he was touching my core. Then again. And again. Each motion rocked us and pushed me deeper into the mattress. The muscles in my legs burned, stretched and quivering as my feet slid close to my ears. My skin felt overheated and sensitive, and my nipples brushed against my own thighs as every thrust bore Noah's weight down heavily upon me.

It was torture. It was madness.

It was so, *so* good.

His gaze roamed over my face with each thrust, wild with desire. He couldn't satisfy the Serim urge until he made me orgasm, so commanding me not to come meant that he was torturing himself as well. But still he thrust, pushing my body to the edge and never giving me the release I needed.

A new sob broke with every thrust. Every slap of his flesh against my own. Every needing, aching quiver that erupted in my body. It was an endless, delicious torment, all the while pinned down by a pair of wild eyes that were more violet than blue.

"You belong to me," Noah growled. He was pushing so deep into me that his voice was practically in my ear, my ankles almost pressed to my ears, my legs stretched wide. "You are *mine*."

He thrust again. My breath shuddered as he leaned in farther, my flesh stretched so hard that it had passed into a mixture of pleasure and pain.

My eyes remained locked into his gaze as he thrust once more, then something seemed to erupt within him.

"Come for me," he growled. "Come while you stare into my eyes."

My entire body orgasmed, my legs and muscles tensing and clenching with pleasure, my breath exploding in a shudder. Blackness swam before my eyes as he thrust again and the orgasm went on and on, continuing to spiral outward as he rolled his hips against mine. His orgasm overtook his body and I felt his shuddering last thrust inside me, felt the hot stream of his release inside, even as my hips continued to clench with need.

I might have passed out for a moment; Noah's face went fuzzy as I watched his expression contort in the pleasant agony of sex.

I panted, unable to think, to process. Unfortunately, I couldn't close my eyes and regroup, because my gaze was still locked on Noah's. As I watched him, the agonized expression on his face melted away, and the color in his eyes faded to a pale silver. And as the color changed, recognition dawned.

CHAPTER SEVEN

"Jackie?" He stared at me, uncomprehending. Then he swore, shoving off of me as if I were suddenly covered in cooties. "Jackie—what did I do? Sweetheart? Are you all right?"

I couldn't respond. Couldn't move my hands, couldn't speak up—not that I was comprehensible at the moment anyhow.

He pulled me to a sitting position but my legs still tried to raise into the air due to his command, and I shot him an irritated look.

Noah was busy running a hand down his face and feeling sorry for himself. Guilt was stamped onto his features. "I didn't realize . . . the curse must have overwhelmed me. And then I smelled them on you and . . ." He shook his head as if trying to clear it. "God, Jackie. I am so sorry. To think that I acted like that to you. Forcing you to the floor on your knees . . ."

He was making it sound like it was some sort of torture, when he'd really rocked my world. Really, *really* rocked my world. My body still quivered in the aftermath.

He gave me a look full of self-hate. "Aren't you going to say something to me?"

I tilted my head, unable to speak. A frustrated sound emerged from my throat, the only thing I could communicate.

It wasn't enough for him. "Say something to me."

Whew. "You forgot that you commanded me to be silent?" I tried to stand, but my legs kept trying to rise into the air, and my hands were still locked beside me. "Can you command me to stand like normal, please? This is starting to hurt."

"Oh. Sorry." He blinked, dazed. "Be as you normally are."

The tension in my muscles relaxed and I felt a shuddering relief roll over me. "Whew, thanks."

His jaw clenched, and he shook his head, looking away from me. "What I did to you was totally wrong. I used my power to bend you to my will."

"You did," I agreed, but it hadn't been a bad thing. Forcing me not to come until he wanted me to? Torture at the time, but freaking *genius*. I flopped back on the bed and gave my hips a happy roll.

Noah sat on the edge of the cot and buried his face in his hands. "I'm just as much of a monster as the others."

Hm. Not quite the reaction a girl wanted to see after some mind-blowing sex.

I frowned. Usually Noah was a bit of a cuddler after sex. He liked to spend time touching my skin or talking with me about business items. Trivial things, just to spend time together. Turning away from me and acting like a martyr? Not his usual bedroom MO.

"Something wrong?" I offered, glancing at the door. We really should be getting out of here, but Noah didn't seem to be in a hurry to do anything except—maybe hate himself.

He glanced over with a gaze full of hot self-loathing. "What I did to you was unconscionable. I'm no better than any of them."

Oh. He thought that forcing me into sex with him was a step closer to vampirism? Well, no. "You're still better than Ariel," I offered, reaching over to pat him on the shoulder. "He tried to rape me."

His look grew starkly horrified. "Is that why you smelled of him? And Ethan? Did he try to do the same?"

"No, Ethan's helping me escape."

Noah ran a hand down his face again, anguished. "The urge was on me so hot and heavy, I was having trouble distinguishing reality. When you get close to the end your control disappears, and you can think of nothing but your partner. When I saw you . . . I wasn't sure if you were just a fever dream. And when I smelled them on you, I was angry. Couple that with the lust and . . . I couldn't control myself." His tone was full of self-loathing. "And you suffered for it."

I patted him on the shoulder again, forcing a cheerful smile to my face. "Really, Noah, it wasn't a big deal." It was the most amazing round of sex we'd ever had, but not a huge deal. "But you know what is a big deal? Leaving here. Escaping."

"You can't. You have to wait for the council to decide your penalty, Jackie."

No, that wasn't on my agenda. "Here's the problem, Noah. They've already decided I'm guilty."

My underwear and shorts were all the way across the room. Whoops. I moved over to get them, limping a little. Definitely pulled a muscle in our sexual throwdown. "What I did wasn't the greatest thing, but it was in self-defense. Yet the Serim council has already judged me guilty, and now they've given me some crazy ultimatum—I either have to slay Remy and bring the halo back to them for disposal, or I have to agree to forfeit my body and breed an Enforcer for them."

His face grew grim. "This is why we should have married, Jackie—"

"Noah—"

"They cannot touch another man's mate. I could have protected you—"

"Noah, you're not listening to me," I said, speaking over him. "I'm not going to marry because someone wants me to bear a kid. I don't even know what an Enforcer does that is so different."

Again, Noah ran the hand down his face. "The Heavenly Host uses them to enforce their decisions. They're like hired muscle, free of the curses of Serim and succubus. And they are steadfastly loyal to the Serim and to the side of good. They're good men, but they don't realize that they do not necessarily work for good men."

"That pretty much describes Ethan to a tee," I said, thinking of the guard who had broken ranks to help me. He was enormous—his hands like mitts, and almost seven feet tall. Thanks but no thanks—I didn't want one of those shooting from my loins. "I'm still going to pass on breeding one."

He stood and crossed the room, staring at the door. "That is your sentence?" he asked me. "To either slay Remy or breed a child for them?"

"Yup. And I'm going to go with C—none of the above. Which is why we need to leave like ten minutes ago, Noah. So put on your pants, and let's go." I hopped around, trying to slide my foot into my underwear, but it kept getting caught. Damn pulled muscle. Why hadn't it healed yet?

Noah was silent behind me. As I hiked my panties up, he gave a long sigh. I heard the bed creak as he sat back down. "I can't go, Jackie. Ethan will keep you safe."

I turned around and frowned at him. "What do you mean, you can't go? I have a passkey. We can escape." I pulled my shorts on. "Ethan's going to help us."

"Jackie, I've been sentenced, just as you are. And I have dealt with the Serim before." The look he gave me was somber. "I must stay here and receive my punishment. When you escape, they will need to mete out additional punishment. I want to be here to receive it."

Sweet but misguided. "Noah, that's nice and all," I

began, spotting the passkey under the bed. I went to my knees and fished it out. "But these guys aren't going to change their minds about me. No matter how much money you fling their way, I don't think it's going to work."

He shook his head, stubborn. "Escaping is not the answer, Jackie." At my incredulous look, he added, "At least, not for me."

Shit. Shit shit shit. I went to his side, clasped his hands in mine, and tried to drag him to the door. It was like trying to drag the Rock of Gibraltar. Noah tugged me back to him and pulled me into his arms. He buried his face in my wildly braided hair, inhaling as if trying to memorize my scent.

I eyed the door. "Noah, we need to go. I'm not kidding—"

"Neither am I." His words were muffled against my chest, and his arms tightened around me. "I'm staying, but you still need to go. You need to help Remy if she is in danger."

"What about you?"

"I'll be fine. They won't destroy me." He looked at me and his mouth quirked in a half smile. "And I'm long past my childbirthing years."

I smacked his arm. "Now is not the time to be funny."

He hugged me close again. "And today shows that . . . I can't be trusted around you, Jackie. My jealousy won't allow it." Sadness crossed his face. "I'm not good for you. You have a hard road as a succubus, and I'm making it even more difficult."

Why did this sound like good-bye? A knot formed in my throat. "And what am I supposed to do when I get back home and you're not there? I still need sex, remember?"

He brushed my hair off my shoulders, regarding my face. "Find Zane. That's what you've wanted to do for a while now."

I stared at him, uncomprehending. "What are you talking about?"

"You still miss Zane. Find him. Choose him over me, if you must. But in the end, you must choose."

Oh lord. This *was* a guilt trip over the sex. "Noah," I began warningly. "You didn't hurt me. Quit playing the martyr."

His mouth thinned, clearly disbelieving. "I might not have hurt you, but I used you. Punished you with your curse. I don't like that person I became. I don't like who I am around you, sometimes."

That hurt.

I pulled out of his arms. "I see."

"You don't," he said just as calmly, pulling my hand into his again, and kissing the back of it. "But I do. And that's enough. So you are going to rescue Remy?"

"I have to." Then a thought occurred to me. "What if I bring the halo back here and offer to trade it to the Serim in exchange for your freedom? Our freedom?"

Noah's face darkened. "I don't know if that's wise, Jackie. If the Serim are sentencing you for a minor infraction simply because they want to use you, we can't trust them with Joachim's power. Look at how it has corrupted Remy. Imagine that in Ariel's hands."

He was right, Ariel would become more than a creepy rapist. He'd become a super-powered creepy rapist. I eyed the small marking on my wrist. "Gabriel offered me a deal as well." I held out my wrist so he could see the marking. "But I don't know what this means."

Noah took my hand and studied my wrist. "He has given you his word," he agreed. "This mark is proof that he has offered you truth and a message of good faith. They're rare markings. He will wear it as long as you do, until the deal has been decided or discarded." Noah held his wrist up, showing a similar tattoo I'd seen before.

"So who did you promise something to?" I couldn't help but ask.

His look became shuttered. "No one you know. It is not important."

"Well, maybe *I* think it's important—"

"Must we argue about this right now, Jackie?" Noah shook his head, a sleepy look crossing his face—a look that I'd seen plenty of times before. Nightfall must be coming soon. The Serim would all hibernate shortly. At the sight of it, my heart tripped unhappily. I wouldn't be able to take him with me after all. Not if I wanted to get away.

Tears pricked at my eyes. "We're going to see each other again, right? Promise? You're not going to just leave me out there alone?"

He got up from the bed, slowly, the onset of hibernation already affecting him. With gentle hands he pulled me close, cupping my face and turning it up to his. "I could never leave you alone, Jackie. I'm doing this for your own good—for the good of both of us. Just trust me to fix things. All right?" He pressed a soft, gentle kiss to my lips.

I kissed him back, needing him desperately. I didn't want to leave him here with the others. And I'd have no one to help my Itch when it returned in two days.

I mostly didn't want Noah out of my life, and this felt like a good-bye. So I kissed him back with all the passion and longing that I felt, until he began to pull away. I caught his lip with my own, sucking on it even as he tried to pull free.

"Jackie, you must go. This is the best time," he said softly.

I nodded, hugged him close, and then exited the cell without looking back.

I didn't entirely believe that this big separation was simply to work on the Serim council. Was Noah right? Were we not good for each other? Did Noah feel that having master powers was such a slippery slope that he needed time to regroup and mentally check himself?

It was so unfair.

I hurried down the hallway, noting that my pulled muscle seemed to have recovered, thanks to my supernatural healing ability. Ethan waited at the end of the hall outside my old cell. His face seemed to be permanently flushed and he would not look me in the eye.

"You've been gone awhile," he said in a choked voice, then dropped his gaze to the floor.

"Noah's not coming with us. It's just going to be you and me."

"I see," he said, then glanced at my eyes. He straightened with relief at the sight of their bleached color. "It was kind of him to . . . help you." The flush began to creep back over his cheeks.

"You heard that, did you?" It was sad that I couldn't even muster a hint of shame that innocent Ethan had probably heard endless minutes of bodies slapping, grunting, my sobbing cries of passion . . .

Okay, I'd managed to muster a bit of shame just thinking about it, after all. "Don't worry. You're safe from the big bad succubus for a few days."

He regarded me with a stiff expression. "If you needed help, I would have offered."

"That's sweet . . . I think," I said, then patted his hand. "Come on, we have to wake up Ariel."

We swiped the badge and entered the room. Ariel remained where I'd left him, his red-orange hair sweeping over the dusty concrete tile. I was happy to see that his "excitement" had dimmed with sleep.

I wasn't gentle when I rolled him onto his back, but he slept on, oblivious. I hesitated before touching him. Did I want to use this opportunity and get into his mind? See what he was thinking?

Ugh, not really. I already needed a shower, and reading Ariel's thoughts would only increase that need. So I slapped him on the forehead, maybe a little harder than I should have. "Wakey wakey."

He stirred immediately, eyes unfocused and blue as he came to. His hand reached for me, but I skittered away to the far side of the cell.

Ethan stepped in front of me, brandishing his bo, and I let him take charge. "Ariel," Ethan said in a somber voice. "I am leaving with the succubus. It is the right thing to do."

Ariel wobbled slowly to his feet, his eyes barely creeping open a slit. His body teetered as he struggled to fight the aftereffects of my touch and the onset of the Serim hibernation. "You . . . are . . . making a mistake . . . Ethan."

"It is the right thing to do," my bodyguard repeated. He swung out his bo staff and swept Ariel's legs, and the fallen angel went tumbling backward onto the narrow cot.

He was asleep before his body even bounced on the mattress. The sound of heavy breathing filled the air again, and his eyes stayed closed even when I went over and poked him.

"Nightfall is fast rising, and I imagine he will be most unpleasant when he awakens," Ethan said, staring down at Ariel with distaste, then back to me with an almost equal distaste. "Shall we go?"

I nodded and headed for the door. With Ethan at my side, we escaped the cell and out went into the night.

CHAPTER EIGHT

We returned to the archaeological camp. Ethan seemed to have good direction sense and we were able to make it back to Yuxmal late in the evening.

I climbed out of the Jeep. "Stay here and guard the Jeep, Ethan," I said, tossing him the keys.

He hesitated.

My heart sank. "You're not leaving me, are you?"

He straightened. "No, I will remain here for you, Jackie Brighton."

All I needed to hear. I gave him a thumbs-up and raced across camp, hitching my shorts around my waist to keep them up. Noah had broken the belt, and they tended to keep falling around my ass.

Since it was after dark and work had come to a halt, I knew where the workers would be. The scent of barbecue and the sounds of conversation came from the far end of the camp, and the portable spotlights shone on the folding tables lined up for dinner. The team liked to eat together. I wondered if they'd sent out anyone to check on Noah and me, or if they'd assumed we were off on an impromptu trip like irresponsible lovers.

I wasn't going to stop and ask. No time.

Our tent was just as we'd left it. My forgotten box of Pop-Tarts sat in the metal chair and the silver wrappings had flown all over the tent, tossed about by the breeze from the rotating fans. Our table was still set up for a romantic dinner. It was like the last two days of hell had never happened.

Couldn't think about that now. I needed my passport, ID, and some money to go back to the States. I'd leave a note for my boss, Dr. Morgan, to let him know that I had a family emergency and had to leave the dig early. The thought of leaving Yuxmal and the ruins behind broke my heart; we were just making headway on the dig.

But Remy was my best friend. I would always put her well-being before some musty ruins. She'd done the same for me time and time again, after all.

I twirled the lock on the safe and opened it, digging out my paperwork and wallet. My credit cards had a nice chunk of emergency money stashed on them, thanks to Noah. It was good to be the girlfriend of a rich guy. Seeing the ring box, I felt a new wave of guilt. I reached for it, then wavered. Should I take it? Leave it behind?

In the end I took it, shoving it into my pocket. I wouldn't wear it. But I'd feel like the biggest douche bag in the world if something happened and Noah wasn't able to get it back. Resolved, I went to shut the safe and . . . stopped.

The painting—my own face, clad in shepherdess gear—stared back at me. Oh, hell. I grabbed the painting and stuffed it into a shoulder bag. Then I added some clothes hastily, trying not to think about Noah, left in slumber back in the holding cell. *Dammit dammit dammit*. I wouldn't think about that.

I shut down the fans, penned a quick note to Dr. Morgan, and pinned it to the front of the tent. From the cluster of tents in the distance, I heard voices talking softly and saw lantern lights burning. People were still awake. I wasn't in the mood to try to explain myself to anyone so I snuck out of camp, abandoning the job I'd fought so hard for.

It was difficult to keep a regular job when you were supernatural. Something always came up; I was learning that the hard way. Remy had tried to warn me, but I hadn't listened. And now Remy was paying for my headstrong actions.

Well. No time to dwell on the past. Too much was going on right now for me to sit and mull over regrets. I fingered the gift ribbon on the ring box, thinking hard as I returned to the Jeep where Ethan waited.

"Are we ready to leave, Jackie Brighton?" he asked.

I held the red velvet ribbon out to him. "I'm ready. And you'll need this."

He took it from me with a bit of confusion on his face. "I am not understanding your reason, Jackie Brighton. Men do not wear hair ribbons—"

"Call me Jackie, and I know that men don't wear hair

ribbons." Though the thought of Ethan with his long, silky black hair in a pert red bow made me giggle. "That's for your bo. We're going to make it look like a gift, not a weapon."

"Staff," he corrected me, with an offended look. "It does not wear hair ribbons, either."

I got in on the passenger side of the Jeep and shut the door. "It needs to if it plans on going through customs."

Clearly, Ethan was not familiar with flying coach. Either the Serim flew first class or chartered their own planes. He scowled at every person who came down the aisle. "I do not like this," he murmured as a large man entered the plane and moved to the back. "This is not a defensible position in the slightest."

"Sure it is," I said, not looking up from the newest issue of *National Geographic* that I'd found in the seat back in front of me. "We're in an exit row."

"My knees are touching the seat in front of me," he whispered with something akin to horror. "How am I to leap to your defense if I am pinned in my seat?"

"Calm down," I said, flipping pages in the magazine. "It's a long flight and it'll go a lot faster if you sleep."

"I do not sleep."

Right, I kept forgetting that. I was usually the only one that didn't sleep. The plane began to roll forward on the tarmac, and Ethan's hands clutched the seat arms so tightly that I thought he was going to rip them off. "Why don't you tell me more about Enforcers?" I said.

Anything to distract him before he got an air marshal on our cases.

He gave me a frustrated look, but his hands relaxed a little. "We serve the Serim council with our lives. What more could you wish to know?"

Obviously, Ethan was still working on his social skills. "How old are you, for starters?" I would bet that he wasn't thousands of years old like Noah and the other Serim. He didn't have that weary cast to his eyes that the others did.

"I am twenty-eight."

I eyed him for a moment, curious. "So what cool stuff do Enforcers get from their parentage? Did you get super-strength?"

"I am stronger than a succubus, yes." He frowned at me as if I were asking him what color his underpants were.

"Dur. Everything is stronger than a succubus." I leaned in close as the plane tilted back and we took to the air. "Did you get the curse? You know, the two-day sex thing?"

Ethan looked scandalized. "You should not ask me such things, Jackie Brighton."

"Why not? I'm curious. Your boss wanted me to carry an Enforcer bun in my oven, the least you can do is tell me about your kind. I didn't even know you existed."

He ignored me, jaw clenched.

When the plane leveled out, he murmured, "We require good deeds."

I glanced up. He seemed a little more relaxed now, he'd lost his death grip on the arms of the seat. "I'm sorry, did you say good deeds?"

He gave me a stiff nod. "Good deeds."

"Like . . . a Boy Scout?"

He looked puzzled. "What is a Boy Scout?"

Good lord, where had they kept him for the past twenty-eight years? "Never mind. So . . . good deeds, huh? How big of a deed?"

He shrugged, clearly ill at ease with discussing the topic. "As big as it needs to be. Small deeds fuel me for a small time, larger deeds for a longer time."

Interesting. "So . . . that's why you're helping me? This is a really big good deed?"

"I am helping you because Noah Gideon asked me to assist you. Just because I require good deeds to survive does not mean I am immune to the plight of others."

So Noah had already figured out an escape route for me. I wasn't sure if I should be irritated or touched that he'd thought that far ahead.

My companion still glared down at me with a wounded look, and I gave him a meek half smile. "Sorry, Ethan. Didn't mean to make you sound like a junkie. So you owe Noah a favor, huh? What for?"

Ethan's expression went blank. "That is a private matter between Noah Gideon and myself."

Ethan had shut down; I wouldn't get any more out of him. "Well, whatever your reason, I appreciate it." I patted his hand, but when he flinched, I pulled back. "You okay?"

He nodded, his eyes wide as he stared at the flight attendant who rolled the cart down the aisle a few inches, then halted. "I am not used to so many people so close."

Yeah, about that . . . "Where did you say you grew up, again?"

"In a sanctuary. Many of the Serim have hidden from the outside world, choosing to spurn its evil, licentious ways. I am a guard there. Or I was until Ariel called me to duty." He didn't seem pleased by that.

So Ethan had grown up in some sort of monastery. Was that where he'd met and worked with Noah? "So did a lot of people live in this sanctuary?"

"Just the Serim."

"*Just* the Serim?" I raised an eyebrow. "You must have had a few chicks there at least once a month."

He gave me a stiff look. "The others went to town on regular excursions. I did not. My needs were served at home."

Not all his needs, if I wasn't missing my guess. Just what I needed to rescue my ass: an oversized, blushing virgin.

Several hours and a trip through customs later, Ethan had his beribboned staff back in hand, I had my satchel, and we were back in Wyoming. I breathed in the crisp air. In Yucatan, the temperature was constantly in the nineties. Here it was a brisk 40 degrees and breezy. Brrr!

In my shorts and T-shirt it was damned chilly, but stopping for new clothes seemed frivolous.

I rented a car and drummed my fingers impatiently on the steering wheel as we waited in traffic. It was bizarre to return home and see all the people drinking lattes and wearing springtime scarves that fluttered in the strong breeze, while I was tanned and in shorts with a very wary seven-foot virgin at my side.

At Noah's urging I'd given up my apartment six months ago, just before going on the dig. My stuff had been packed up and half sent to storage at Remy's place, with my everyday stuff moved into Noah's house. It felt weird to not have an official "home" to come back to. I turned the car onto the freeway and headed toward Remy's place on the outskirts of the city.

Wealthy, thanks to her lucrative adult film career, Remy Summore lived in a gated neighborhood on the posh side of town. I waved to the security guard at the gate as I pulled up, and he let me through. The red hair was an automatic giveaway; they always remembered me.

"Do you think the succubus we pursue will be here?" Ethan asked me, staring out the window with a stoic look on his face.

I shrugged and turned down a street. "Even if she's not, one of her servants might have an idea of where she went."

If they weren't dead.

I pulled the PT Cruiser into the driveway, frowning

at the mansion. The lawn was immaculate thanks to the lawn service, but no cars were in the driveway and no lights were on. That wasn't totally weird, given that it was past noon, but I'd expected her home to look a bit more inviting. Maybe it was just my imagination.

I parked and got out, my palms clammy. Ethel, Remy's housemaid, normally parked her little Toyota in the garage and left the door up when she was in. It let Remy know if she was in the house when Remy got home, since succubi often kept weird hours. But the garage door was down. Ethel wasn't around.

Odd.

I glanced at Ethan, who followed close behind me, his bo staff at hand. "I don't suppose you have any holy water on you, do you?"

"Not in these pants," he said quite seriously. He'd changed out of his cultist robe at my urging, but wasn't happy about it.

"Of course," I muttered.

I jiggled the doorknob. Locked. Hmm. I didn't have a key.

I knocked once, twice.

No answer.

The door had artful stained-glass windows surrounding it. We could punch through the glass and break in. It'd set the alarm off, but I knew the code and could turn it off. I eyed my small fist and Ethan's large ones. "You want to do the honors?"

He obviously wasn't following. "What do you mean?"

I gestured at the glass. "The door's locked. Break in."

"That would not be right. This is someone's house." He gave me a disapproving look.

"This is my friend's house, and I forgot my key and she's not home. Just humor me, okay? Or you're going to have to listen to me bitch if I break my hand."

"You are right, that would be tiresome." He studied the situation. "Would it be doing you a favor if I broke in?"

"Yes," I said, and took a step back in case glass flew.

I should have been more worried about splinters. His eyes flashing, Ethan put his fist through the wood door. An enormous hole was punched next to the doorknob, and he reached inside for the lock and flipped it. A moment later he opened the door.

"Thanks," I said, regarding the plate-sized hole with awe.

He shrugged and stepped inside.

I followed him, wondering why the alarm hadn't gone off. But when I got inside, I could guess why.

Remy's place was trashed.

Shredded paper lay scattered on the floor everywhere and broken glass littered the foyer, along with garbage and candy wrappers. I walked slowly, hearing the crunch of glass under my hiking boots, and peered into the living room. The flat-screen TV was smashed to pieces and hung off the wall at an angle. The fireplace mantel had been broken, and the stones were splashed with dark spots that I sincerely hoped were not blood. The couch had been destroyed, the stuffing pulled free from the leather and scattered across the room like snow. On the far side of the room, the wet bar had been demolished, the alcohol long dried into puddles staining the carpet, and the sweet smell of sugar and booze in the air. The broken glass was piled high over there.

Through the doorway I could see the kitchen, and though the lights were off, the mess was apparent. I didn't want to even think about what was left there.

"Do wild animals live inside this dwelling?" Ethan asked, his voice confused.

"You wouldn't think so," I said slowly, creeping in a few steps more. Oh, man. I didn't know what to do. I eyed the curved, panoramic staircase. The railings had been destroyed, but the marble steps seemed to be intact. "This must be Joachim's doing."

"Who is Joachim?" Ethan clutched his bo staff in a defensive pose.

"I'll tell you later. But if you see a little Turkish woman with red eyes, let me know."

Poor Remy. And where was Ethel? Not in pieces somewhere upstairs, I hoped. I sniffed the air, but nothing smelled rotten, which was good. I moved to the wet bar and ran a finger over the cracked marble counter. Dust. Just a little.

Wherever Ethel and Remy were, they hadn't been here for a few days. All of this madness had happened a while ago.

I started up the stairs. "I don't think anyone's here,

Ethan. But we should check out things before we leave."
I hitched my shorts up around my waist again.

He glanced around the shattered, trashed living room.
"I will check the rest of this floor. Should I look for anything in particular?"

"A rabid succubus. Her missing maid. A big diamond
necklace charm," I added, thinking of the necklace that
had kept Joachim at bay for the last six months. "And
holy water, if you can find it."

"You are quite obsessed with holy water," he observed.

"Trust me, it'll come in handy if we can find some." I
paused at the top of the stairs. What if Joachim was still
hiding in the house? Surely not . . . and yet . . .

I called down to Ethan, "If I scream, come and get
me, okay?"

He nodded and saluted with the bo staff.

I crept around upstairs, keeping as silent as possible
despite the broken glass and littered candy wrappers. If
Joachim was still here, I'd hear him first. When Remy
had been possessed back in New Orleans, she had
panted like a winded runner on the verge of collapse.
Constantly and loudly.

But the house was silent. I could hear Ethan moving
around downstairs, but nothing up here. I moved down
the hall cautiously, then peeked into my old room.

It was untouched.

Weird. Prickles crawled over my skin as I stepped
inside, staring around. My bed was made, the closet was
neat and the clothes hung, and the toiletries littering the

counter were as I'd left them. Boxes were stacked in one corner of the room and labeled—the stuff left from my apartment. Nice.

After putting on new clothes, I kicked the old ones under the bed and grabbed a can of hair spray, because it felt better to have a weapon, even if it was a lame one.

A quick check of the rest of the floor didn't reveal any signs of my missing friend. It was upsetting. It would have been more upsetting to find Joachim huddled in a closet, waiting to tear my throat out. But the fact that Remy had vanished really bothered me. I sat on the edge of her trashed bed and tried not to feel overwhelmed with depression. My poor friend. I'd screwed her life up good.

Something hard was irritating my butt, and I slid over, glancing down at the mattress.

Remy's gigantic diamond necklace. The one with the diamond the size of an acorn. I picked it up and fastened it around my neck. It gave a low, soothing pulse of magic, as if remembering me. I clasped it between my fingers, playing with the diamond. Zane had given me the necklace to keep me safe, and I'd given it to Remy. I tucked it under my T-shirt, hoping I could give it back to her someday.

I scanned her room one last time in the hope that something would call out to me. Her bedroom was set up similarly to my own: a mini-fridge in the corner, a TV and game console installed in the wall, and a library of movies. Since succubi didn't sleep, bedrooms were for recreational activities of all kinds.

Her cell phone lay on the nightstand, and I picked it up.

The screen was locked with a password. I thought for a moment, then entered the title of Remy's last movie.

Denied.

I tried two more movie titles, both denied.

Then I typed in 8008135—on a previous adventure, we'd come across that password and she'd laughed uproariously. The oldest calculator joke in the world: "BOOBIES." Remy loved it.

Sure enough, her phone screen lit up, displaying one last lonely battery bar on the screen. Her voicemail message was on, so I ignored my nosy feeling and clicked on the icon to listen to her messages.

The first one was from her boss. Ick. Porn director. I hit Save to cut it off before I could hear too much. Didn't want to know.

The next message was from five days ago, from our fellow succubus Delilah in New Orleans. "Remy? You there?" The voice in the message sounded worried. "Pick up, girl. You were supposed to call me to check in last night. I'm hoping you just found a hot football team and decided to make it a night, or something. So, you know, call me when you get this so I can stop worrying." She had called again three hours later, the message the same: "Remy? Call me."

I dialed Delilah, who picked up on the first ring, her high-pitched young voice practically squealing in my ear. "Remy? Oh, thank God—I was freaking out—"

"It's me," I interrupted. "Jackie."

"Oh." She sounded considerably less thrilled. The feeling was mutual. "Hi, where's Remy?"

"I don't know. I was in Mexico, and she called me. Only it wasn't her, it was Joachim. He told me to come back and face him like a man. Except he's not here, and Remy's place is trashed. She's gone."

"Oh no." Dee sounded extremely worried. "Put Noah on the phone—let me talk to him."

"He's not here."

"What do you mean, he's not there with you? Where are you? Did you dump him?"

I really, really hated the note of hope in her voice. Delilah LaFleur had a seven-hundred-year-long crush on my master, and I wasn't ready to release him to her greedy clutches just yet.

"He's stuck in Mexico right now. The Serim council arrested him."

"Arrested?" Her voice rose in an alarmed wail. "And where are you?"

"At Remy's house, trying to figure out where she's disappeared off to. Joachim has a hold on her again."

"How could you leave her alone for the past few months when you knew she was vulnerable?" Dee asked accusingly.

Like I could make Remy do something she didn't want to do? "She didn't want to go on the dig with us to Mexico. What was I supposed to do—tie her up and keep her drunk?"

"Yes."

"Not funny, Dee." I pinched the flesh between my eyebrows. Her snotty little voice could drive anyone to a headache. "It doesn't matter—what's done is done. Noah's under arrest, I'm here trying to hunt her down, and when I find her and fix her, we'll go back and get Noah."

"He's in Mexico, you say?" Her voice became thoughtful. "What part?"

"The Serim are holed up near Cancun. I don't know how long they plan on staying there, but—"

"I'll go," she cut me off. "I'll see if I can reason with them, since you didn't even try. Maybe I can persuade them to release him early."

Uneasy, jealous prickles swept over me. "What do you mean, you'll go?"

"I know a few Serim," she explained, her voice confident. "I'll go down there and see who I can persuade to look at things my way. *One* of us should be down there to help Noah out."

The rotten little opportunist. She didn't know that we'd just agreed to keep some distance for a while, but jealousy roared inside me again. I forced myself to agree. "Sounds good. Thanks, Dee."

"Keep the phone with you and I'll call back when I'm with Noah and have news."

She sounded like she was going on vacation. The phone beeped at me, signifying the battery was dying. "Okay, and you call me when he's free, all right? I want to talk to him." And make sure he didn't touch Dee's little blond jailbait ass.

"Done." She hung up.

Great. I stared down at the beeping phone with an unhappy clenching in my gut. It was either hunger, or I was really upset at Dee for maneuvering around me to save Noah. Or guilt, because I knew I should have stayed with him and I didn't.

I rubbed my stomach and glared at the phone. One more message. I sighed, holding the beeping phone up to my ear.

The message had been sent yesterday. "Remy? It's me." Zane's low, husky voice sent chills through my body, and my panties grew instantly wet.

"Sorry to call." There was a long pause on the other end of the phone, and my heart did terrible little somersaults in my chest. He sounded so . . . weary. Alone. Oh, Zane! My mind was screaming to hit the callback number, but it was daylight. He wouldn't be able to answer.

He began to speak again. "Was just wondering if Jackie got the package I sent to her. The ball is tomorrow night and . . . I just wanted to see her. But I guess you're not taking my calls, right?" The hard, cynical edge of his voice returned. "Don't suppose I can blame you for that. But at least tell Jackie I was thinking about her. That's all." He hung up.

I immediately hit the Replay button, but the screen went dark. *No!* I quickly found the charger and plugged it in, staring at the phone for a bar of juice to reappear so I could listen to the message again.

He'd called. He'd called for *me*. After saying we couldn't be together because he'd given himself up to save me, he'd called looking for me. He missed me! He hadn't forgotten me after all! I clasped my palms tightly together to keep from squealing with girlish delight. He wanted to see me despite everything. Tomorrow! No, wait. The message was left yesterday.

Tonight! And he'd mentioned a package.

I bolted out of Remy's bedroom, scouring the upstairs hallway. Package. Package. Zane had sent me a package. I ran down the stairs, tossing the can of hair spray onto the marble floor so I could pick through the wrecked living room. I grabbed couch cushions and flung them aside, stuffing flying everywhere.

Ethan rushed into the room, weapon ready, his eyes wild. As he stood in a ready stance, a piece of stuffing landed on his head. "What is it? Where is the attacker?"

"No attacker," I said. "Help me look for a package!"

The urgency in my voice compelled him forward, and he began to look inside the fireplace. "Is this package dangerous?"

"No! Well, actually, I don't know." I peered under the broken coffee table.

"Does this package have information? Will it tell us what happened here?"

"No and no." I went into the kitchen, digging through broken dishes.

Ethan trailed behind me, a confused look on his face. "Then why is this package so important, Jackie Brighton?"

I looked up and blew the bangs out of my face, frustrated. "Because it's from my ex-boyfriend."

A look of comprehension came over him as I hurried past. "We are searching for a memento from your lover?"

I ignored him and hurried outside. Trust a man with the body of an Adonis and the soul of a dweeb to not understand why it was so important to me. It was hope, wrapped up in a mysterious package. I didn't want to wait another minute to find out what was in it.

I broke into a run at the sight of the piles of mail stacked up around Remy's mailbox. Success! Sure enough, a shoebox-sized package lay on top, addressed to Jackie Brighton, care of Remy Summore. My heart slammed wildly in my throat. With my supernaturally long (and usually annoying) fingernails, I slit the brown wrapper and pulled open the box.

A red envelope lay inside over neatly folded, shimmering silver material. I stared at the material in surprise but reached for the envelope. It was sealed with black wax, and I ran my finger under it, then pulled out the card inside.

You are invited to the annual Vampire Ball to be held at the Queen's mansion. Wear appropriate clothing and leave your neck bare.

That gave me the creeps.

The date was tonight, and the card provided an

assigned time that a limo service would come to pick me up once I called the confirmation number. Go to the queen's house for a party? I *so* did not want that. But I wanted to see Zane so desperately that it hurt to think otherwise. I touched the filmy fabric in the box. *Wear appropriate clothing*, the queen's invitation said.

This was by far the stupidest idea ever. In a daze, I walked back to the trashed house, staring at the invitation.

"What is it, Jackie Brighton? What is wrong?" Ethan moved to my side and awkwardly patted my shoulder, trying to comfort me. "Is it your friend?"

"It's an invite to a party," I said slowly. "The most dangerous party in the world. And I think I'm going." I looked up at him and grabbed his shirt, my eyes wild. "Please please please, talk me out of it?"

"Your former lover will be there?"

I nodded, my throat tight. "Stupid, huh?"

Another awkward pat on the shoulder. His hands were so large, it was like being patted with a baseball glove. "Then we must go to this party."

"We?" I felt a glimmer of hope and looked up at him. He'd be hard to fit for a tuxedo, but . . . it could work. Excitement bubbled through me. "You'd get dressed up and go to this shindig with me?"

His brow furrowed. "Dressed up?"

Before he could protest, I grabbed his hand. "No takebacks—you already promised. Come on. This thing starts in a few hours, and we've got to rent you a tux."

CHAPTER NINE

Several hours later, as the sun was setting, my "date" and I sat in Remy's trashed living room and waited for our ride.

This afternoon had been a scurry of errands. We'd picked up Ethan's tux, then I'd dropped Noah's mysterious painting off at the research department of the museum with a note to one of the assistants and my phone number. They could figure out the age of the painting and, I hoped, tell me a bit more about it, because I was damn curious. Then I'd gone to the local church for supplies.

I had holy water and Remy's diamond necklace inside the small clamshell purse that had come with the dress, along with her phone and my BlackBerry. Common sense said that I should wear the necklace, but considering that a vampire had given it to me in secret, it probably wasn't a good idea to waltz into the vampire queen's lair wearing it for all to see.

The garment was more of a suggestion of a dress than an actual dress; a short, silvery miniskirt with a high slit, and two draping scarves that tied behind my neck to make the top. My entire back was left completely bare, and only an artful little chain in the front kept the two scarves from sliding under my armpits. Still, I filled out the dress far more than the designer had anticipated, and it left me almost bare to my navel.

And I was supposed to go out in public in this thing? Ethan wouldn't even look me in the eye. He'd glance over, his gaze would drop to the dress, and then he would have a blushing fit.

And then I would have a blushing fit, too.

The shoes were equally ridiculous, with little more than a spaghetti strap to anchor the four-inch heel to my foot. I'd nearly broken my neck twice already.

"Are you sure this is wise?" Ethan asked me for the tenth time in the past five minutes.

"I'm almost positive it's not," I shot back, standing as the limo pulled up. "But it's what we're doing. They might have an idea of where Remy is."

Not that it was the main reason I was going—I wanted to see Zane.

We went out, and Ethan opened the door for me, ever the gentleman. No driver got out to greet us, which pinged my radar—even more so when I slid into the limo and saw a young, attractive woman behind the driver's seat. She gave me a thumbs-up and smiled into the rear-view mirror.

Interesting.

Ethan slid in next to me, and the car took off into the sunset. I tried to follow the direction we were heading, but Ethan kept punching the buttons on the limo door, turning the radio off and on, the lighting off and on, and rolling the window up and down like a five-year-old child. By the time he caught my glare, we were out of the city and cruising onto the flat, endless highway that stretched into Wyoming for miles on end.

"Where are we going?" I asked, leaning forward to question the driver.

She only gave me another thumbs-up, then rolled up the screen. So much for that.

As I watched the sun sink into the horizon, my anxiety rose. Would Zane be happy to see me? What if this was a trap? Nervous, I twisted my hands in my lap and tried to count the mile markers.

Just when the sky was darkening to the pinkish purple shade that preceded twilight, we made a right turn off of the highway and down a long drive. A wrought-iron gate opened as we entered and tall cottonwood trees lined the sides of the road, obscuring the view from the highway. I craned my neck as the car approached our destination. A pale mansion loomed ahead of us, tall and stately, with square white columns supporting a high, arched roof. The driveway was a long circle leading up to it. Impressive, but this seemed . . . almost modest for the queen.

A line of limos crawled down the driveway. As we waited for our turn, I watched woman after gorgeous woman descend from the cars, dressed in formal, glittery gowns. My stomach clenched a little more. This was like a prom, except I had a feeling that these women were going to be eaten before the evening was up. They looked happy, though, so either they weren't aware they were heading into a vampire lair, or they knew and didn't care.

Remembering how Zane's bite brought an instant orgasm, I was betting the latter.

Our limo pulled up to the front of the house, and the driver turned and knocked on the window, then indicated that we should get out.

A little skeptical of that, I murmured a thanks and followed Ethan out of the car, tugging on the hem of my skirt.

The mansion porch was packed with people—all women, except for the man standing at my side. Some of the women were in waitstaff uniforms, tuxedo tops with tails and fishnet stockings, and high heels. The women inside were equally beautiful and equally bored looking, standing around holding wineglasses and whispering to each other.

"Looks like the vampires aren't here yet," I said to Ethan, looping my hand through the crook of his arm.

He immediately tensed, and his hands flexed as if he wanted to grab his bo staff. "This is a good thing, Jackie Brighton."

Again with the full name. His social skills needed some serious work. "Maybe we shouldn't use names for a while, Ethan—just in case." Just in case the queen had someone on the lookout for me.

My stomach chose that moment to growl, and I

glanced around the room. Sure enough, a banquet of hors d'oeuvres was laid out nearby. Caviar, giant shrimp, a dozen kinds of cheeses, fresh fruit, chocolates, and tiny sandwiches had been arrayed in a beautiful pattern, next to a table with champagne glasses. I made a bee-line for the table, noticing that the other women in the room were avoiding the food like the plague. Not this woman—I grabbed one of the tiny plates and began to fill it with food. As we waited, I ate plenty of everything on the table and washed it down with bubbly champagne.

I mean, it wasn't like I was worried I could spill it on the front of my dress. I didn't *have* a front of my dress.

As I was going back for thirds on the shrimp, a low murmur swept through the room. A moment later it began to empty, women grabbing glasses of champagne and hurrying down a hallway. Curious at their lemming-like abandonment of the party, I put my plate down and followed, dragging a reluctant Ethan with me. Ahead, women were descending down a massive staircase into a large, shadowy basement. My skin prickled.

"Perhaps this is not a wise idea," Ethan whispered as I continued to drag him forward.

"We're already in this deep," I said, but my spidey-sense was tingling, as well. I'd once likened my succubi senses to a tuning fork: when I was near another succubus, my senses tingled pleasantly. When I was in danger, they twanged unpleasantly inside me.

Right now my tuning fork was caterwauling.

The stairs descended into darkness. I shrank in close to Ethan, expecting to feel the press of dozens of women crammed against me. To my surprise, though, the women began to move apart, still murmuring and laughing amongst themselves. "This is weird," I said to Ethan, noting how my voice echoed in the darkness. "How big is this room?"

Lights flashed on and, momentarily blinded, I dropped my gaze to the floor. It was smooth and hard, like a dance floor. Odd. I squinted up at the lights overhead, staring at the vaulted ceiling.

The basement was an enormous ballroom, and we'd descended in the middle of it.

The lighting dimmed, replaced by electric candelabras that made my dress glitter in the soft light. The women around me were ditching their glasses to the waitresses and seemed to be primping in preparation of something. Despite my high heels, I was having a hard time seeing over the crowd. I craned my neck for a few moments. "Do you see anything, Ethan?"

"I see lots of women and half-naked flesh," he said in a disapproving voice.

Yeah, he wasn't going to be much help. I dragged him back to the steps and moved up a few, the better to see across the ballroom.

On the far end of the immense floor, row after row of bodies were laid out on marble slabs.

My body clenched in fright. And as I scanned the rows of figures—there must have been dozens of them—

recognition dawned and my palms began to sweat. Those were the vampires, not yet awakened from their slumber.

No wonder there were so many women here tonight without dates—they were hooking up with the vampires.

Thinking of Zane, my heart fluttered with a mixture of excitement and anxiety, and I scanned the rows of unmoving vampires, looking for a familiar dark head. It was pretty far, and the lighting was dim, so I didn't see him. That almost made it worse. Did I *want* him to be laid out with row upon row of vampires, just another evil minion to the evilest bitch in the world?

I hopped on the step, leaning on Ethan's arm as I looked again among vampires. "I don't see Zane," I worried aloud. "What does it mean if he's not here?"

My date gave a strangled sound. "Cease with the jumping, Jackie Brighton. You are in danger of losing your dress."

Oops. So I was. I went up on tippy-toe again, giving the room one last scan before giving up. "I don't see the queen, either." The large, empty throne on the far side of the room told me that the guest of honor hadn't made her appearance yet. I tugged at my skirt again, wishing it was about a foot longer and my top was wider. One wrong move and I was going to pop a boob.

"What do you wish to do, Jackie Brighton?"

I gnawed on my lip, thinking. "The rational, sane part of me says we should leave before the queen gets here."

"I agree with that rational, sane part of you. I wish it showed up more often."

I gave Ethan a wry smile and then frogged his arm. "Very funny. But we're here for a reason."

"Indeed," Ethan said in a mild voice, shifting. The rental tuxedo stretched tightly across his shoulders, the seams near to bursting. "Do the vampires know who has taken your friend? Can they help us free Noah Gideon?"

"No, and no," I said, my mood deflating a little. Jeez. Ethan needed to learn how to sugarcoat things. "That's a different set of problems. I *need* my ex-boyfriend," I said significantly. "And I need him in about a day or so, unless you're feeling romantic."

Ethan swallowed hard. "I see. Should we find him, then?"

His awkwardness was a nice change from the men I'd been encountering ever since I'd been transformed into a succubus. Usually they did nothing but stare at my breasts and try to surreptitiously grab my ass. Ethan looked as if he'd be happier if I were dressed in flannel pajamas rather than a sexy dress.

That made two of us.

At that moment, the room hushed and everyone seemed to turn at once. The vampires were rising.

As the ballroom waited breathlessly, one man arose from his bier. When Zane awoke, he did so like any other human—scratched his chest, yawned, stretched. These vampires had not gotten the same memo. One jerked awake like a drowning man, clawing to his feet, chest heaving. The next followed suit, jerking awake and crawling upright. It was bizarre to watch, and I stood there entranced as each one lurched to his feet and tried to compose himself.

The queen was still nowhere to be seen.

Then stately, classical music began. One of the vampires approached a smiling, eager woman and held his hand out. She took it without a backward look, letting him pull her into his arms and sweep her onto the dance floor. One by one, the others paired off until the dance floor was filled with vampires and their partners. Only a few women were left on the sidelines, watching the last of the waking vampires in the hope that they would find a partner themselves.

As I watched a vampire and his partner twirl past, I caught a glimpse of red eyes as he leaned in and pressed his face to the woman's neck. My blood pulsed low in my hips, sensing the desire swelling in the room.

The woman shuddered as if in intense pleasure and the vampire's arm locked around her waist, pinning her to him as they continued to dance. She missed a few steps, but no one seemed to care. On and on the vampires whirled past, and the scent of blood and the salty hint of sex began to tinge the air. As they twirled past, I could hear soft cries of pleasure as the women being bitten came to orgasm. The bizarre, roiling crowd somehow managed to move in time with the music despite being a sexual buffet.

It turned me on. Poor Ethan; this was going to be a bit much for him.

A vampire approached, glaring at Ethan as he moved

toward me, red eyes gleaming as his gaze rested on my breasts. Yipes. I grabbed Ethan and pulled him onto the dance floor. I couldn't be food if my arms were already occupied—I hoped.

"Jackie—" Ethan began to protest.

"Just dance with me," I hissed, pulling his arm around my waist and beginning to drag him around in a semblance of a waltz. Since Ethan clearly did not know how to dance, I had to lead. Unfortunately, I stepped on his foot, and he yelped. A woman's cry of pleasure resounded right after, and Ethan looked like he was going to choke on his tongue.

"Come on, choirboy," I said, circling him around. "We have to blend or this could get ugly. I don't want to be someone's midnight snack, so you need to pretend to be my date. Got it?"

"I understand," he said slowly, and his eyes flickered silver, then settled back to their normal black. A good deed fed, then. I certainly wouldn't begrudge him that.

He stepped on *my* foot and I nearly passed out. Seven foot of warrior on my teeny rhinestone-decorated toes— dear God, there was no pain quite like that. I yelped and when a vampire looked over, had to bury my face in Ethan's chest, pretending to swoon.

"Sorry," he whispered at me, shoulders stiff and awkward. "I am not familiar with romancing a woman."

"We're not romancing, we're just pretending." I pulled a little farther away from him, sensing his discomfort at having my half-naked body pressed to his. "Just dance, and we'll worry about the other stuff later."

He twirled me roughly, jerking me so hard that my neck nearly snapped. Well, at least this way I'd match the vampires' half-limp partners. Ethan took the initiative after that and twirled me around the floor, spinning so quickly that my head began to swim. The dance floor weaved back and forth. My feet tried to keep in time with Ethan's rapid turns, but we were quickly moving out of control.

I felt a subtle shift in the ballroom, the atmosphere changing. Where the room had been almost too warm for the Wyoming night, it now felt too cold. The temperature seemed to drop as we danced, and my skin began to crawl. I felt an overwhelming sensation of dread and revulsion, and I knew what that meant. As Ethan spun me past, I caught a glimpse between shoulders of the throne that we'd moved perilously close to. It was no longer empty. I saw a pair of long bare legs and a red dress, and the hors d'oeuvres I'd devoured threatened to come up. "*Stop,* Ethan," I murmured, retreat strong on my mind. "The queen's here." I wanted desperately to get away from the front of the room.

Ethan halted entirely, which wasn't what I'd had in mind. I slammed into his chest, and the couple next to us slammed into us as well.

The vampire sniffed the air, looked over at me, then hissed. "Succubus," he said, staring at my face, then down at my boobs.

Oh shit. How did he know me? I backed away, slamming into Ethan again. "Who, me?"

The vampire gazed at the dais, up at the throne, and I looked over as well.

Zane stood at the queen's side, shirtless. His wings spread behind him like a black waterfall of feathers, and black pants rode low on his hips. A cynical smile twisted his beautiful face as he scanned the room, and I noticed a rope looped around his throat. The crown prince of the vampires, every inch of him exuded power and dominance. The rope around his neck might as well have been a necklace for all that it mattered.

The queen played with the end of the tether, her midnight black gaze sweeping the crowd. Her vile mouth was pursed with distaste as, seemingly bored, she slouched on her throne. She looked like a thousand pounds of evil packed into a slender, hundred-pound body. Just the sight of her made me freeze with terror, the aura of malevolence that swam around her touching me and making my muscles lock. I had to fight the urge to run away.

This wasn't good. This wasn't good at all. Seeing that loop around Zane's neck highlighted the fact that he belonged to her—he was probably being punished for his affection toward me. He was bound to her, having exchanged his freedom for mine. Searing pain filled my chest.

I stared wordlessly at my former lover, unable to look away from that awful rope around his neck. As if sensing my gaze, Zane's cynical face turned toward me. Confusion flickered over it, and then a flicker of hope, quickly hidden. His eyes devoured me from afar, sliding over my skimpy silver dress and long, bare legs to the loose, curling hair that fell about my shoulders. His gaze fell to my hands, clasped in Ethan's, and, he finally seemed to notice my tall, muscle-bound date. His eyes narrowed to dark, red slits of anger.

Oh dear. I took a step backward, running into Ethan's chest again.

Even worse, the queen's black-eyed gaze focused on us as well. Her mouth curved into an evil smile, and she released Zane's leash, murmuring something that I couldn't hear.

Zane leapt into the audience and couples scattered, desperate to get out of his way. He stalked toward Ethan and me, the look of a predator in his eyes as I watched helplessly.

To my horror, Ethan released my hands and stood in front of me in a defensive pose, trying to protect me from the approaching vampire. "Move away, Jackie Brighton. You are in danger."

"No, Ethan, wait," I began.

Zane grabbed Ethan by his rental jacket and flung him through the air, the large Enforcer slamming into the floor and scattering people. The sound of his landing made a deafening boom, and the music stopped.

Ethan leapt to his feet and shrugged his shoulders as if unaffected by the hit, and his jacket split and fell about his arms.

I ran forward to separate the two men, nearly tripping on my ridiculous shoes as Zane grabbed the front of Ethan's shirt and lifted a fist.

Ethan pulled backward, the shirt ripping and exposing Ethan's chest, and a few women sighed with pleasure.

Zane's punch was caught midair by Ethan's meaty hand and Zane was shoved roughly to the side, flying through the air in a mess of feathers and flying limbs.

I gave a small, choked scream and punched Ethan's arm. "What are you doing?"

He automatically grabbed my hand, confusion in his face. "I am defending you, Jackie Brighton—"

A snarl sounded in the air. "Don't you fucking *touch* her." Before either of us could react, Zane dive-bombed from the air and crashed into Ethan, sending both of them skidding backward.

My hand was still trapped in Ethan's so I went crashing backward with them, my body slamming into someone else's legs. A sharp gasp erupted from my throat as my spine cracked from the hit. Ow. My knee banged on the hard marble floor, as did my shoulder.

This was going to hurt in the morning.

Someone stepped on my hair, pinning me to the floor, and my boob chose that moment to slip out of my flimsy dress. With an awkward yelp I hastily shoved it back, jerking my head to try and free it.

"Jackie, Princess," said the familiar, liquid voice that I'd daydreamed about.

The person standing on my hair was shoved away and

strong hands lifted me into the air, cradling me against a warm, bare chest. Zane held me against him as if I were a newly found treasure.

I cuddled close, closing my eyes and inhaling in his familiar scent, my heart aching with need and love. I reached up to touch his cheek, feeling the smoothness of his jaw, the soft line of his lips. He gave my thumb a small bite, his fangs scraping against my skin. I shivered.

"Are you all right, Princess?" he whispered against my hair, soft and loving and just as heartbreaking as I remembered. "Did he hurt you?"

"Just my pride," I muttered, running my hand along his neck and twisting my fingers in his hair. It was so soft, and he smelled so good. God, I'd missed him so much.

"You will release her, vampire," Ethan said in a warning voice nearby.

Oh crap. I opened my eyes and frowned at Ethan, who was taking the guardian thing quite to heart. Four vampires held him back, his arms swinging wildly as he struggled to free himself. He'd fling one off, only to have another pry his arm down. Still, it took four of them to hold him there.

Or one Zane, whom I was currently cradled against. I looked up at my former lover's possessive red eyes and touched his cheek again. "Long time no see."

"Jackie Brighton—" Ethan interrupted, but I ignored him.

A hint of a smile softened the cynical curve of Zane's mouth. "So it would seem."

Just the sight of his smile nearly broke my heart again, and I resisted the urge to burrow into his chest and pretend the world didn't exist. "Oh Zane," I whispered. "I've missed you."

He smiled down at me, fangs barely gleaming between his lips. His eyes scanned my face, resting on my lips and then studying my jaw as if he were mere breaths away from kissing—or biting—the hell out of me, and my body quivered in anticipation.

Someone clapped—slowly, mockingly. A single pair of hands. My skin began to crawl, and I knew without looking who was mocking us with her applause.

Zane's loving expression disappeared, replaced by the shuttered, cynical twist of his mouth. It hurt to see it change, but I didn't blame him.

You didn't let the queen see your vulnerabilities.

"Can you walk?" Zane murmured against my temple, looking toward the throne. "If so, I think I need to put you down."

"I'm good," I said. Though I was pretty sure I'd cracked something, succubi heal fast. He set me gently on my feet, and I hitched my dress back down from where it had crawled up my butt and adjusted my (lack of) top.

The queen lowered her hands, her eerie, entirely black eyes focused on my face. A hint of a smile curved her mouth—no teeth showing. She gestured for me to approach. Oh dear. That felt like being invited to have a seat in the spider's web. Not that I could refuse her, of course.

I warily approached the delicate woman perched on the large throne. Though the queen looked dainty in her short red dress, I knew she was anything but helpless. An ancient Egyptian who'd made a pact with a demon millennia ago, Queen Nitocris had sucked the essence out of God-knew-how-many immortals to acquire their power, and as a result, she was a little . . . frightening. She had no respect for life and was the most powerful immortal on the planet, and when she wanted something, she went after it. An aura of malevolence seemed to swell around her, as if she contained far too much evil for her skin to hold in. Just looking at her made me want to run away, screaming.

Yet here I was, mingling at her bizarre party like some sort of vampire groupie. It made my skin crawl to think that she had invited me, and I had taken the risk to see Zane again. Now, looking at her face, I wasn't sure I'd made a wise decision.

I moved forward with Zane at my elbow until I stood at the base of the dais, mere feet away from her throne.

She tilted her head, watching me with an expectant look.

CHAPTER TEN

"Kneel," Zane whispered. I dropped to my knees, grateful for the chance to hide the fact that they were nearly knocking together with fear. Zane stayed at my side, his hand on my neck, a comforting, heavy weight, and I wasn't sure if it was for support, or to keep me down.

He didn't have to worry—I was pretty much paralyzed in front of the queen. Plus, I'd probably break my neck trying to escape in my four-inch slingbacks.

The queen delicately crossed her legs and tucked them close. "So, my little succubus has returned, and without her lovely angel to protect her. Why are you here, little whore?"

"Oh, um," I stammered, "I'm looking for Remy."

The pleased, predatory look on her face diminished, the lines of her mouth hardening in a way that nearly made me wet myself with fear. "If you wish us to protect you from her, little whore, you need to learn to ask better than that."

"Well, that's a lovely offer," I began, my hands twisting in my skirt. "Except I don't really need to be protected from her just yet. I can't even find her."

"I see," the queen purred, and I felt like she was going to reach over and devour me whole. I couldn't stop the full-body tremble that took over. She moved forward on the throne, her hands clutching the sides. "Are you mocking me, whore-child? Because I can destroy you in two seconds flat—"

"No," I squeaked.

Zane's hand clenched on the back of my neck—a warning.

I shut up.

"My queen," Zane began, stepping forward and moving in front of me, probably to protect me as much as he could. His wings brushed against my face, and I shivered at the feeling of hundreds of feathers lightly brushing over my scantily clad form. The urge to clutch his leg like a small child was almost as overwhelming as the urge to run my fingers through those feathers.

"My queen, I think it is possible that Jackie does not know what has befallen the other succubus."

Uh oh. What had Remy done now? I peeked out from behind Zane's wing, trying to see the queen's expression.

Queen Nitocris stared at him, stone faced, her fingernails drumming on the large wooden arm of the throne. "Explain to her, then, Zane, if she is so very ignorant." The indulgent half smile returned to her face, and the queen's red gaze fastened on me once more. "And speak slowly so she may understand."

Lovely woman, the queen. If I weren't so insanely terrified of her, I'd have said something. As it was, I just hid behind Zane's wing like a big chicken.

To my surprise, Zane pulled me to my feet next to him, holding my hand in his. His dark eyes met mine. Gone was my cynical, playful Zane. The man standing before me was serious as could be. "Jackie, listen carefully," he said, glancing over at the queen as if seeking permission.

A command, but a minor one. I cocked my head slightly, indicating that I was listening.

"I want you to remain quiet until I am finished speaking."

It wasn't a command, but it *was* rude. He squeezed my hand, giving an almost imperceptible nod toward the queen. Right. This was for her benefit. She had to think that Zane had given me up entirely and was her creature once more, or their deal—my life and freedom in exchange for his—was forfeit.

"I invited you here because I wanted to see you," he began.

The queen cocked her head to the side, her eyes narrowed and I felt the malevolent heat of her displeasure.

"That is why you are here." His expression was guarded. "Remy disappeared from New Orleans right after you went to Mexico. I kept watch over her house for a few months, waiting to see if she would return and we could pry the essence of Joachim from her."

I didn't like the sound of that, and my face must have

shown my unhappiness, because he squeezed my hand slightly.

"Remy did not return home for many, many months. I continued to watch it, and others were dispatched to try to track her down. It seems that she was wearing a charm that blocked all traces of sorcery that could track her."

Wait. Did the queen not know about the blocking spell on the charm? I frowned up at him.

"She looks unhappy," said the queen in a dulcet voice. "Perhaps it is difficult for the poor slut to understand."

This time I squeezed Zane's hand, my mouth forming a tight, irritated smile. "I'm following," I said. "Please keep going."

"Then one day, Remy appeared back in New City," Zane continued gravely. "We sent a contingent of vampires after her, to capture and bring her to the queen."

So while I'd been fooling around in Mexico, running up and down old muddy stone pyramids, Remy had been hunted? I instantly felt like the world's worst friend.

Zane cleared his throat. "The vampires didn't return."

My attention snapped back. "What?"

"The vampires were slaughtered. We found what was left of their drained corpses the next day. Remy—or the creature inside her—had drained their essences and left nothing but the husks behind. On all five vampires. We sent seven more vampires after her, and only one was able to return. He spoke of a small woman with wild eyes and impossible strength."

That sounded like Joachim, all right. Much to my dismay.

"And now that Remy has succumbed once more, we fear that Joachim is stronger than ever." Hand squeeze. "He is ruthless and will stop at nothing to gain more power."

Hand squeeze, hand squeeze.

Zane was clearly trying to tell me something, but I wasn't reading between the lines enough. He gave me a meaningful look, but I had no clue what he was hinting at. When he squeezed my hand again I decided to repeat it back to him, trying to lead him into telling me the answer. "If she—he—has absorbed eleven vampires as well as a halo, that makes her . . . really powerful."

A painful squeeze on my hand. "Very, very powerful. And she does not intend on stopping anytime soon, from what we can tell. In fact, she has begun to hunt some of the more powerful vampires, in an effort to steal their essence and acquire even greater power for herself. Himself."

I started to piece things together. If Remy was going after the most powerful vampires, Zane wasn't safe. My hands gripped his, suddenly sweaty. As the queen's right-hand man and the second-oldest vampire, he was stronger than all the others. That also meant the queen had a big fat target on her head.

I kept my eyes lowered and glanced over at her on the throne. She sat as casually as ever, her foot moving back and forth. Only the steady drumming of her nails on the wood and the tight, insincere smile on her face showed any reaction.

Was the queen worried that Remy was coming after her?

Oh, this was really weird.

"Wow. Um, well, I don't need protection from Remy," I said, pulling my hands from Zane's. Especially not if it meant being indebted to the queen.

The queen inclined her head regally. "If you wish. Since you do not seek sanctuary with us, I will offer you a deal, whore-child."

My skin crawled. A deal? "No, wait, I don't want—"

Too late. Her grin widened, displaying rows of needle-like teeth. "You have three days to track Joachim down and remove him from the succubus and save your friend's life."

"Three days? But I don't know where he is, and I can't stop him—"

"Three days, or I will kill your friend and take the halo myself." She raised a hand and examined her nails, and then touched a fingernail to her lip, tapping it as she thought for a moment. "I find that I am quite content with the power I have here and no longer have a need for the halo. I will be pleased if you simply destroy it, and will spare you and your friend. But if the three days pass, make no mistake." Her eyes narrowed, with enmity. I could feel the malice emanating from her. "If you do not stop your friend, I will."

I swallowed hard. Some deal.

She took my silence as assent. "I see we are in agreement. As a token of my good faith, I shall loan you something of mine." She lifted her flat hand into the air, and then made a fist as if gathering something.

Zane made a choked noise and staggered, stumbling to the queen's feet and collapsing at the dais. His hands went to the rope at his throat, tearing at it.

"You are still fond of this one, are you not?" Her eyes watched me intently.

Shit. What was the answer she was looking for? If I vowed love for him, would she torture him more? If I didn't, would that piss her off? I watched Zane writhe on the ground, choking, the leash torturing him. "I . . . I think he's all right," I said, my voice carefully bland. "Nice guy."

The indulgent smile curved her mouth again. "No declarations of love for my sweet prince? Pity." She opened her hand and made a sweeping motion, as if thrusting him away. Dragged by the magic, Zane flew across the room, slamming into my legs and knocking me to the floor. I heard Ethan shout behind me and the scuffle starting again.

I picked myself up off the floor and my hands went to Zane, trying to help him.

"Zane may go with you. He is the strongest of my children, my chosen heir. He will see this done, for good or for ill," the queen said, languorously rising from her throne. Her voice was all business, at odds with her posture. "He knows his instructions and will keep in line.

And if you are not able to destroy the succubus, he will." She moved to the edge of the dais, stepping down the marble stairs on dainty, red sandals. "And I am going to give you another present to help you with your task, whore-child. This is indeed your lucky night."

"Lucky," I echoed, helping Zane sit upright as he coughed next to me, clearly drained.

"My lovely Zane shall help you track down the halo and dispose of it." Her predatory eyes focused on me again. "To ensure that he keeps his promise to me, he will bring along his keeper to make sure that he does not misbehave." She clucked her tongue at Zane and shook her head disapprovingly. "My darling vampire has been a most unruly child. And I fear that if he does not learn to obey, I shall have to destroy him and make an example out of him. I would so hate for that to happen." Her fathomless black eyes fixed on me.

"No examples," I breathed, though I didn't know what I was promising. All I knew was that Zane had to be safe from her.

"I thought you would see it my way," the queen said lightly and strolled past. "Three days, starting now, little whore. I will be displeased if you fail."

The queen exited the room and as she slunk away, the music struck up again. The vampires around us grabbed their limp human partners and began twirling around us once more.

Zane staggered to his feet and I tried to help him up, only to be pushed out of the way as Ethan shoved him off of me. "Jackie Brighton," Ethan declared. "Stay away from this vampire."

"Ethan, stop it," I said, trying to move around him.

Ethan responded by pulling me away and starting to drag me across the dance floor. "We are leaving, Jackie Brighton."

I twisted in his grip, trying to break free. I was sure that he meant well, but I wasn't going to leave with Zane still weak and barely staggering on his feet. "Ethan, wait a minute. Zane—"

The Enforcer turned back to face me, eyes narrow. "We do not seek the help of vampires, especially not if they wish to destroy your friend. I am ashamed that you even think of doing so, Succubus."

"Wait just a minute here!" I twisted my hand, but he wouldn't free it, and we headed to the marble stairs that led up into the house. In a panic, I sent a surge of my succubus powers through to Ethan. His eyes rolled back in his head and he dropped like a rock.

I glared down at him as I rubbed my wrist for a moment, then leaned over and touched him again to wake him up.

He opened his eyes and stared up at me, confused. I leaned over and offered him a hand. "Sorry to do that, but you weren't listening, and I'm not going to be dragged around like a doll. I'm a person and I can make up my own mind, remember?"

"I am sorry, Jackie Brighton," Ethan choked out.

He closed his eyes and put a hand over them. "I will remember."

I didn't like the way he kept his eyes closed. "You okay?"

"You should stop leaning over," he said in a strangled voice, sitting up.

I glanced down and saw that my breasts were clearly visible. Whoops. I straightened up and put my hands on my hips, surveying the room as Ethan got to his feet. Zane had disappeared in the swirl of dancers, and my heart began to beat rapidly again. Had he left because he didn't want anything to do with helping me? Surely not. Surely he wanted to see me, to spend time together? Right?

Then I saw a figure in a long black trench coat cutting through the dancers. Zane. With the coat on over his wings, he looked like a regular guy cutting through the crowd, lifting a cigarette to his lips. The rope that had kept him tied to the queen was gone. I glanced back at Ethan with a warning look. "Zane is going to help us, so don't attack him anymore, all right?"

"I want what is best for you, Jackie Brighton. I am your protector."

How sweet, if misguided.

"And I appreciate that, Ethan, but I don't want protecting from him." My gaze followed Zane as he headed toward me where I waited on the stairs, almost shivering with excitement.

The grim, world-weary look on his face lightened at the sight of me and his red eyes softened.

"Princess," he said, regreeting me. I reached for his hand, but he moved protectively in front of me, separating me from Ethan with a glare.

"It's okay, Zane. Ethan's my bodyguard."

"He was dancing with you earlier," he growled, his sharp teeth flashing. The back of his coat gave a reflexive jerk, and I wondered if the wings were trying to free themselves. "Touching your bare skin."

Ethan pressed his hands into fists, as if preparing to go after Zane.

I stepped between the two of them, a bit surprised at the fighting . . . over me. "Zane, he was only dancing with me because I made him." When the vampire wouldn't calm down, I added, "I don't know that he's even interested in girls."

This time Ethan gave me an offended look. "I do not like succubi. Your gender does not matter."

Well, there you had it. I gave Zane a bright smile. "See? Ethan is not into immortal chicks." I slid my hands to his leather collar and gave him a playful tug when he continued to loom over me. "We can go now, right?"

Zane's gaze refocused on me, and he grimaced. "Not quite yet. We're waiting for someone."

"Oh?" I tried not to worry, though my mind automatically went to the queen. Then I remembered. "Your bodyguard, right?"

"Caleb. And I have to warn you about him—"

A man approached and looped an arm around Zane's shoulders. He was compact and attractive, with spiky, short blond hair and a facial tattoo that curved around his eye. His nose was pierced, and his bright red eyes gleamed as he assessed me. "No need to warn anyone," said the man, punching Zane in the gut playfully. "I'm just along for the ride."

Zane didn't seem pleased. His eyes met mine, and he gave me a meaningful look, his posture stiff. "Shall we go, then?"

"Sure," I said, though I didn't feel extremely confident. There was something off about the dynamic between Zane and Caleb. Even though Caleb was all smiles, it was clear that Zane did not like him being here. I headed up the stairs, the men trailing behind me.

Outside I frowned at the mess of cars, trying to locate our limo driver in the sea of waiting black stretch limos. Not an easy task.

"We can take my car." Caleb produced a set of keys from his pocket. "It's over in the garage."

"That seems like our best option," I said guardedly, though I wasn't thrilled about the thought of letting Caleb be the one to drive us back to the city. He seemed nice enough, but he had fangs and red eyes, which told me he was no good guy. "Which way is the garage?"

Caleb pointed with the keys, and he and Ethan began to walk in that direction. As I began to follow, something snagged my flimsy sandal. The ground rushed up and I planted, face-first, into the sidewalk. My strappy shoe snapped and my ankle flashed with pain as it twisted.

Zane was immediately at my side, helping to pick me up. "Are you all right?"

I dusted off my scraped elbows and tried to place my weight on my foot. Pain immediately shot up my leg, and I clutched at Zane's forearms, hoping he'd pick me up again. "I don't think I can walk. My stupid shoe—"

He told Caleb, "Why don't you get the car? I'll wait here with Jackie to make sure she isn't attacked."

Caleb's eyes narrowed, though the friendly grin remained on his face. He gestured at Ethan. "Come on, then. We'll get the car and pick you two up in a minute," he said, casting a meaningful look in my direction.

Without waiting for my response, they turned and walked to the back of the house, Ethan walking behind Caleb as if he were trailing a cobra and waiting for it to strike.

I leaned heavily on Zane, who seemed distant. With his free hand, he lit a cigarette and began to smoke as I tried to fix my shoe. Puzzled and a little hurt by his cold demeanor, I plucked my shoe off to see if the broken straps were fixable.

There was a boot print on the back of my heel. Someone had stepped on it to trip me.

But the only person behind me had been Zane. I stared at the print a moment longer, then turned to Zane, shoe in hand. "What the hell is this?"

He dropped the cigarette as soon as Ethan and Caleb rounded the corner of the building, watching to see if they would reappear. Then he turned to me, pulled me close, and began to kiss me with hungry, aching need. His mouth swallowed my gasp of surprise and his tongue stroked into my mouth boldly, demanding entrance.

Emotion swelled through me and I was only too happy to comply. I had my Zane back.

The shoe fell to the ground and I wrapped my arms around his neck, leaning in as he devoured my mouth like a starving man. His tongue flicked against mine repeatedly, tasting me, teasing me. My tongue met his, my fingers curling in his hair, and I moaned with delight. He pulled away after a moment, dazed, his eyes focused on my mouth. Then he began to kiss me again, sucking lightly at my bottom lip, stroking into my mouth with his tongue, then sucking on my lip once more.

It was as if he were starving for my touch, and I was definitely craving his.

Zane finally broke the kiss. His fingers caressed my cheeks; his eyes frantically searched mine. "I can't believe you're here. That I'm touching you again." His mouth hardened in a twist. "I keep thinking this is another one of her tortures—her worst one yet. To bring you to me, only to pull you away again."

My heart gave a euphoric little flip. "I'm not going anywhere, Zane."

He pressed his forehead to mine, as if he needed to touch me again to believe that. "I've missed you. It hasn't been the same without you." He swallowed roughly, and I could hear his throat working. "I thought I could go back to the way I was before, but . . ."

I held my breath, waiting.

He pulled away slightly, giving me a rakish smile. "There's so much I want to talk to you about."

I moved forward, sliding my arms around his waist under the jacket and feeling the tickle of feathers against my skin. "We'll have time to catch up. Don't worry."

"No, that's just it," he said, and pulled me off of him. "We don't."

"We don't?" My arms fell to my sides, and I gave him a hurt look. "What do you mean?"

He glanced around quickly, then moved forward and pressed another fervent kiss on my mouth.

My body instantly ignited with lust again, and when he pulled away, I tried to keep him there with my lips, my head following his as he took a step back. "We don't have time."

"What do you mean, 'We don't have time'?"

He lit another cigarette, his hands twitching as he devoured me with his eyes, sucking heavily on the cigarette as if that could replace my mouth on his. "It's Caleb," he explained, his voice short and terse. "The queen sent him as a spy, not because she expects me to need help. This is yet another test for me, the misbehaving protégé. She's putting you in my reach and has forbidden me to touch you. And Caleb will report back to her."

"Oh." Words failed in my throat, and disappointment crashed through me. "So we can't . . . be together?"

He shook his head, silent. The only sound was the sizzle of the cigarette paper. A long moment passed between us. "I thought it would be enough just to be in your presence again, but . . ." He gave me a rueful look from under a floppy lock of hair, and my heart melted all over again. "You're very hard to resist."

That made my legs weak with desire. "But you just kissed me."

His eyes grew hot as he stared at me. "Oh, I plan on kissing you and touching you every time he turns his back. You have my word on that."

Liquid heat poured through my body at the thought. "I see. And feeding?" I hadn't missed the redness in his eyes—he had yet to feed this night. "Not just yours, but mine, too? I'm due tomorrow and Noah is still in Mexico."

"What about that big warrior guy?" Zane flicked his cigarette away.

I reeled as if slapped. "You'd be okay with me sleeping with him? Really?"

His eyes met mine and I sucked in a breath at the anguish I saw in them. "No, I wouldn't be okay with it," he said hoarsely. "But we're low on options, and I'd rather see you fucking another guy than dying in my arms."

"I don't want to touch him," I said, moving forward to touch his chest. "I want to touch you. Be with you." Tears pricked behind my eyelids, but I blinked them away. "This is cruel."

"That's what she likes to do best," he said, his hand resting over mine for a moment before he moved away again. "I won't be able to stand being near you and not being able to touch you. We'll just have to figure out ways to distract Caleb and sneak a moment here and there."

Sneaking a quick feel in the corner in order to continue my Afterlife? My, how the mighty had fallen. Still, a quick feel from Zane trumped amazing sex with a stranger. "I'll take it," I said. "Feel free to touch me anytime, anywhere. This is going to be as difficult on me as it is on you."

"It'll be a nightmare for both of us," Zane said, gazing at me with hunger. "Christ, that dress—it's a torture. Didn't look like that in the catalogue."

No, I imagined it hadn't. Thanks to succubi genes, my breasts were a very perky double-D, and they made the dress do obscene things. "Next time you're picking out clothes for me, pick out something with a back. Oh, and a front," I said sarcastically.

His wry, bladelike smile returned, and for a moment it felt like old times. "Now where's the fun in that, Princess?"

Fun, indeed. *His* nipples weren't about to snap off from the cold. "There's the car," I said, turning away. "Looks like it's time to put on our game faces."

"I'm going to need more smokes," Zane muttered.

CHAPTER ELEVEN

Since Remy's house was trashed and my apartment had been leased while I was in Mexico, we ended up at a hotel.

Caleb had generously offered for the three of us to shack up at his place, but it was quickly declined. I wasn't keen on taking anyone back to Noah's penthouse, either, because it held way too many memories for me and way too many pictures of Noah and me together for Zane's liking. We settled on the Four Seasons in downtown New City—swanky and expensive. Caleb brought out the credit cards. "You're the queen's employee for the next three days. The least we can do is put it on the corporate account."

Lucky me. Still, considering that my purse only had what I'd taken from Noah's safe in Mexico, a big fat engagement ring, and Remy's necklace, I was willing to let the vampire pay.

Caleb ended up getting us three rooms. One for him, one for Zane, and the last room consisted of a single bed for myself and Ethan.

Zane looked ready to murder Caleb when he distributed the room keys, but I suspected that was part of the vampire's plan. He wanted to remind Zane at every turn that I was officially off limits, and making me room with another tall, handsome man was doing the job admirably.

Perhaps Zane hadn't noticed that Ethan acted like a skittish kitten every time he even caught a glimpse of side-boob, or he wouldn't be jealous.

We stood in the lobby for a few minutes, making plans.

"We'll start tomorrow night," Caleb said. "Night's almost gone already and I haven't had a chance to feed."

I hadn't had a chance to eat, either, and my stomach growled just thinking about it. The hors d'oeuvres at the party had done little to sate my succubus appetite. But feeding my stomach was lower down on my list of to-do items. "I only have three days. Why can't we start tonight? There's still two good hours left before the sun starts to rise."

Caleb's baby-faced smile was disarmingly cute. "Nope. We need to get feeding taken care of before the evening is over, or I'm afraid we'll both be terribly cranky."

Shock hit me like a splash of cold water, and I glanced over at Zane. He needed to feed tonight, which meant he was going to hook up with another woman, since I was off limits. So I'd have to sit by and watch while he seduced another woman . "I see."

"Great, so we'll regroup here at sunset? I'm in room 7401 and Zane is in 7402. You guys are floor two—the honeymoon suite." Caleb winked as if sharing a secret.

Ethan made a strangled sound. Zane's fists curled, and he shoved another cigarette between his lips, only to pull it out again. Couldn't light up in the lobby.

"Spiffy," I said, trying to keep a cheerful face on things. "But no one has mentioned how we're going to find Remy."

"Oh, I have a plan," said Caleb. "She's still here in New City somewhere, looking for another vampire to off, so we'll give her what she wants."

I swallowed hard. "I'm not sure I like the sound of this plan."

"A trap," Zane gritted, and I realized that he already knew about the plan and just hadn't told me about it yet. "We have free use of the club, Midnight. The queen wants us to lure Joachim there and take him down."

I swallowed again, my flesh suddenly covered in goose bumps. "And how are we going to lure Remy there?"

"Bait," said Caleb cheerfully. "She—he—wants your head on a platter. So we're going to give it to him. We'll use you to draw him forth, and when he appears, take him down once and for all."

"Didn't you say he'd taken down seven vampires at once?" I croaked.

"Yes, but you've got us to protect you," Caleb said, with a cocky smile. "You should be just fine."

This didn't sound fine to me. I turned my frightened gaze to Zane. If I was safe—and I wasn't entirely sure I was—would *he* be safe? Or was the queen literally looking to kill two birds with one stone?

At my silence, Caleb smiled and tweaked my nose like I was a child. "Nothing to worry about."

I slapped his hand away.

Zane began to stalk away to the elevator, his long coat fluttering around his legs. I could have sworn that I saw the back of it twitch, his wings probably shivering with forced control.

If that was their idea of a good plan, I was screwed. Zane was screwed. We were *all* screwed.

I turned to Ethan. "I guess we should go see our room, right?"

"Succubus, neither of us sleeps," Ethan said, pointing out the obvious. "I can wait in the lobby for you."

Clearly Ethan wasn't keen on sharing a room with me. I gave his shoulder a friendly smack. "Don't be so worried," I said, trying to keep my voice cheerful. "I won't go on a molesting rampage until tomorrow night at the very earliest. You're safe until then. And sitting down here in the lobby would just make people wonder." A seven-foot-tall warrior with shoulders like a linebacker and long, silky black hair in a half-busted tuxedo didn't exactly blend with the surroundings. "We'll regroup upstairs and figure out what we do from here. I want room service, anyhow. You can watch TV or something."

"Television?" he asked slowly. "I have heard of it but never seen it."

Did they not allow TV in his sanctuary?

"You're in for a treat, then," I said, tucking my arm in

his. "But take it from me. Avoid any channel with 'Spice' in the name."

We ordered room service—steaks, mashed potatoes, a hamburger, some french fries, two chocolate shakes, and a hot fudge sundae for me. Ethan simply got a cup of coffee. There were also Snickers bars and M&Ms in the mini-fridge, so I stashed them in my purse for later. As I ate, Ethan cradled the coffee in his hands and stared at the TV with wide eyes, watching the Lifetime Movie of the Week.

I polished off my food and left him to flip the channels, eager to get out of my skanky dress. Since my bags were still at Remy's house, I made a mental note to head there in the daylight when the vampires were sleeping so I'd have something decent to wear. For now, I grabbed the bathrobe in my room and walked out on the balcony to clear my head. I couldn't stop thinking about the plan to "save" Remy.

A trap. Me as bait. I didn't like this much at all, but what choice did I have?

The air on the wrought-iron balcony was brisk, the wind ruffling my hair. Even only two floors up, we had a great view of the strip in New City. Cars streamed below in scattered fashion—not a lot of people out on the road at four in the morning, but just enough to keep things moving. I stared down at the lit streets, then craned my head up, staring at the balconies that stretched overhead for floor after floor. Which one was Zane's?

The TV flickered in the room, then went black as a commercial began to play. With the lights dimmed, I caught a glimpse of a dark figure several balconies up, and my heart skipped a beat. Someone up there was watching me. Was it Caleb?

The figure above twisted in the black shadows, then leapt down to the next balcony. The iron rungs made no sound as he leapt from balcony to balcony, moving down to where I stood in a white robe, waiting. As the figure approached, I caught sight of a long, shining pair of slick black feathered wings, and Zane's dark, rakish hair. His pale chest was bare in the moonlight, his jacket shed. And as he leapt to the balcony next to mine, he extended a hand outward to me and raised a finger to his lips.

I glanced inside at Ethan, whose gaze was still glued to the screen. The coffee mug hovered halfway to his mouth, undrunk, as he watched *Project Runway* with rapt attention.

He wouldn't miss me for a few minutes. I leaned over the edge of the balcony and placed my hand in Zane's.

He grabbed me and pulled me close, and for a too-long second, I fell into thin air as we both plummeted several feet. Zane spread his wings and began to pump them forcefully, and we flew up the side of the building, my arms locked around his neck in a choke hold.

When we got to the roof, Zane set me down gently. I wiggled my bare toes on the rough concrete as he moved past me, checking all four corners of the roof as if looking for someone. I hugged the robe closer, the wind whipping my hair about my face as I watched his familiar graceful movements. The wings fell loose on his back from his shoulders, a waterfall of beauty that shone even in the weak light of the setting moon. I could watch him for hours, his shoulders shifting as he loped over the roof, his mussed hair falling over his forehead. So very beautiful.

So sexy. And mine. My nipples grew hard, remembering his body moving over my own. The memory made my blood pulse and my skin flush. I needed sex tomorrow, or I'd start the downhill slide into the Itch.

His hand locked around my waist and he jerked me to his side. The hot press of his erection against my belly fueled my own desire. "Zane," I breathed.

"I missed you," he said against my hair, his hands roaming over my back and shoulders as if he needed to touch me everywhere. "God, I missed you. The last six months have been hell."

"I missed you, too," I said, feeling guilty. I'd spent the last six months aching for him, but I'd also had the time of my life on an archaeology dig with Noah. I was a bad, selfish succubus. "What are you doing up here? Shouldn't you feed?" His eyes were still bright red.

He leaned in and began to kiss my jaw, brief, fervent kisses that danced along my chin and neck. "We have to talk first. I can't—I can't drink from another woman with you a few floors away, knowing what I'm doing."

So he wasn't the only one who had been agonizing over that. I held his head close to mine, shivering when

I felt him nip lightly at my neck, then lick at my collarbone. "Where's Caleb?"

"Off with twins. I brought their friend back to my room just in case he checked in, and she's napping, thanks to a 'suggestion' I gave her."

Vampires had a hypnotic charm—I had no doubt that the girl would think she'd had sex with Zane, even if he never touched her. It was a great cover story. "So where does that leave you and me and your feeding?"

I twined my fingers in his hair, pressing his head against my neck harder, as he loosened the front of my robe and began to trail his mouth down the collar.

"God, you're naked under this thing," he groaned, his mouth sliding to my breast.

Liquid heat rolled through my body as his lips found my nipple, and my knees went weak as he scraped my breast with his fangs. My fingers dug in against his skull and all the breath escaped from my lungs. As long as Zane was touching me, I was in paradise. And I was so, so damp with need. "Zane," I protested, my voice weak and thready. "What about feeding?"

He slid down to his knees, pressing his face against my hip, as if he couldn't bear to stop touching me. "Jackie . . . I know it's a lot to ask. I know." He sounded like he hated himself for even asking.

"But you want to drink from me?" I finished for him, my hands sliding to the silky waterfall of black feathers. They all fell in one direction, smooth and evenly marching along the delicate network of bones. I glided my fingers over their backs lightly, loving the sensations.

He groaned and I felt his mouth press against the soft curve of my hip, his face concealed by the fluffy robe. "I shouldn't ask. I know I shouldn't ask. I just can't stand the thought of drinking from someone else with you here."

Even though I knew it was bad, I wanted to do it. Especially with him rubbing his face against my hip and brushing his feathers against my skin.

Torn, I debated the idea. If I let him drink from me, I'd be giving over my control of my body and trusting him implicitly. But . . . I craved the intimacy with him. I'd thought about nothing but his bite and his kiss for the last six months. And right now, I was so turned on that I could feel the heat pulsing loud in my veins, centered near where Zane rested his head. "But . . . Zane, won't you get in trouble? I can't stand the thought of you being in more pain." My fingers left his feathers and slid back to his hair, moving the rakish lock of hair off of his brow.

He looked up at me, hope in his startlingly red eyes. "I can bite you where no one will see it," he said, a hint of a smile curving his mouth up. "A soft, quick bite . . . in a secret place." As if to demonstrate, he leaned in and nipped lightly at my hip.

I squeaked at the feeling of fangs against my skin. More liquid heat surged through my veins, the throbbing centering at my sex. A secret, forbidden bite? "Oh?"

His mouth slid along my hip and his other hand slid around the front of my thigh, his tickling fingers brushing against my sex. His mouth reached the bend where my leg met my pelvis. "There's a large vein here. I'd only need a taste. Just enough to make you sleepy, if you want," he whispered against my skin. "No one tastes better than you."

He ran his tongue along the fold of my hip, starting at the edge of my thigh and working his way inward. By the time he got to the damp curls of my sex, my body was wracked with shivers.

He pressed a light kiss there, then stood. His wings spilled out behind him like a shadowy waterfall gleaming in the moonlight. He cupped my ass and dragged me against his hard erection. "You feel so good in my arms," he said, his mouth pressing kisses along my shoulder, sliding the robe down my arm. "If you don't want me to feed, we don't have to do that. Just let me keep touching you."

I brushed my hand along the front of his pants, outlining the straining cock pushing against the fabric. "Zane, the only person I'm worried about is you. I just don't want Caleb to find out—"

"He won't." Zane pressed a quick kiss on my mouth, smiling again. He sucked on my lower lip gently, eliciting a moan of pleasure from me before tugging on the robe that pooled around my elbows. "Let's lay this on the concrete."

As soon as I took it off, the temperature on the roof

seemed to drop a zillion degrees. Goose bumps covered my flesh and I rubbed my arms briskly.

Zane pulled me down on the robe. "I can keep you warm, Princess," he said in a husky voice. "When my body covers yours, you won't be cold."

Just the thought of that made me tingle, and I laid down, reaching for him. His hot skin pressed against mine, and his wings swept outward, creating a windbreak as they tented against the concrete. He grinned at me. "Better?"

"Much," I agreed, brushing the tips of my fingers against his wings in appreciation.

His hands went to his hips and he shifted between my legs as he undressed, then tossed his pants to the side. He moved back over me, all hot, hard muscle and delicious pale skin, and his mouth captured mine once more. My tongue swiped against his own, fangs scraping, and the taste of blood crept into my mouth.

Against my lips, Zane growled with pleasure, and I felt him push my hips apart, sliding in between them. The head of his cock rubbed against the hot, wet seam of my sex. I moaned into his mouth, biting his lip to show my pleasure. My hips arched against his, rubbing the length of him against my folds again.

"So good," he murmured, and his mouth began to trail down my breasts again. "I don't think I can wait much longer." He thrust against me, the hot slide of his flesh parting the lips of my sex and brushing against my clit. The head rubbed up and down the slick channel, teasing a wordless cry from me. My feet slid along his body, toes curled.

His mouth slid to my breasts again and he wrapped his fingers over each one, my nipples peeking through. "So delicious, my sweet, sweet Jackie. Maybe I should bite you here again. Remember that?"

His mouth dipped between his fingers, capturing my nipple with warmth. A moment later, I felt a hot, intense jolt of pleasure and pain. Blood welled to the surface and he licked it away, teasing the hard points of my nipple as his tongue swirled around it. He moved to the other side and repeated it.

I was writhing by the time he rotated his hips against mine, and my hand reached for his cock. I needed him inside me. *Now.* "Zane," I breathed. "If you don't get inside me in the next minute, I'm going to make you regret it."

"Every moment I'm not deep inside your body, Princess, is a moment I regret." He leaned in and gave me a soft, tender kiss . . . then thrust his cock inside me.

A hot whimper escaped my throat, and my body arched with the intensity of the pleasure. "Oh God, yes!" My legs curled around his hips, my fist shoving against his shoulder. I raised my hips, waiting for the next thrust and was not disappointed. He thrust into me so hard that the robe—and my body—skidded a few inches across the concrete. He grunted with pleasure as well, the next thrust equally rough and hard. I wrapped my arms around him to anchor my body for the next wild thrust. This was not the tender meeting of lovers; this was six months, of mutual pent-up, aching need.

I gladly accepted the next ramming thrust, gasping his name. He pushed so hard into my body that it felt stretched to the limits, yet every thrust seemed to seek a little deeper, scraping along the concrete and shredding the robe underneath us. Harder and faster he plunged into me, his hands gripping my hips roughly so he could shove even harder inside me. Each thrust was equal parts pleasure and pain, but I welcomed all of it as I reached for my orgasm. The stark, aching need on his face was burned into my mind. "Look at me, Princess. I want to see you come," he growled as he slammed into me again.

I was close, but I wasn't there yet, and the next thrust was equally delicious and equally toe-curling. I wanted this to go on forever, and because I was early in the Itch, I didn't have the deep need that pushed me over the edge within minutes. Zane didn't have a similar issue, though, so at his next thrust I slid my hand between us, sliding apart my flesh and exposing my clit. I couldn't masturbate as a succubus; all it did was torture me since I needed someone else to bring me off. But I could still help an orgasm along. When he drove home again, his flesh slid hot against my clit. One more rough thrust and I was gasping his name, locked in the shudders of an orgasm. I held back the scream of pleasure in my throat as he began to thrust harder and wilder, until he cursed, growled my name, and then shuddered, heat flooding through me as he came inside me, hard.

I sighed in contentment as he fell over me, my hands clinging to him. Despite the chill in the air, his flesh was moist with sweat against mine. He pressed a kiss to my brow and sighed at the robe, located somewhere around our feet. "I'm sorry we had to do this on the roof of the hotel."

"You do seem to have an aversion to beds," I agreed, teasing. "Pillow phobia?"

"Bed only counts if you're in it with me," he said, then kissed my mouth one more time before sliding lower. His mouth kissed down my belly, and my body—languid and bruised and scraped up but feeling wonderful—began to awaken again.

"Time for the bite?" I said, wiggling a little under him. It was hard not to get excited at the thought. Vampire bites were a treat I normally forbade myself, seeing as how it shut down my mind and made me share head space with a vampire. Since succubi didn't sleep, it felt like I was letting a bit of my self-control go, trading it for feeling even closer to my vampire lover.

Then again, a vampire bite was also the precursor to a shattering orgasm.

Choices, choices.

He was lapping at my skin at the bend of my hip, and I shivered and arched up. "The sun will be up soon, Zane. Hurry up and do it."

I felt his fangs sink into my skin. Pain flared, followed by a roll of pleasure so intense that my calves locked up, and a shuddering orgasm bolted through my body, a stronger, more powerful cousin to the one that I'd just had. And this time when I cried out his name, even Zane's hand over my mouth couldn't silence it.

CHAPTER TWELVE

I drifted in and out, a hazy fog surrounding my senses. A vampire's bite was a narcotic, leaving me half comatose and drifting in and out of his mind. Through the connection, I had the vague sense of Zane wrapping the robe around me as he stifled a yawn. He gathered me in his arms and descended over the side of the building again, wings lightly fluttering until he landed on my balcony.

Ethan was there—I couldn't focus on his face but could guess that he was disapproving. He took me from Zane and tucked me into the bed.

From there, the dreams got weirder. Flashes of pain swept through my mind. The neck rope. Sharp teeth. Torture. Feathers filled my mind—ripped, bloody feathers. I couldn't focus on why I kept dreaming about feathers, until the dream changed slightly, and I stared up at the face of the vampire queen.

Mercy, said the voice in my dream.

Except it wasn't my voice, it was Zane's.

"I betrayed your trust, and for that I am sorry." Not a true apology. He'd never apologize for maneuvering around her—not when it kept Jackie safe.

The queen seemed to sense his reluctance. She reached forward, her fingernails like tearing claws. The ripping pain shuddered through his wings again, and feathers rained down around him. The delicate bones of his wings were half bare now, the web of skin covering them resembling a plucked chicken's.

"You came to me and I gave you wings. I can take them away again," she purred in his mind.

Not the wings. Not again. "I'll do anything you want."

"Show obedience to me and only me. It will not be easy."

A feather fell to the floor, landing on his clenched fingers and leaving a red stain on his pale fist.

What else did he have to live for? He'd lost one love and traded her safety for wings. He could do it again. A collar was nothing, as long as it kept this love, this woman, safe from the queen.

The clawed hand slashed against his wing again, ripping once more. He screamed in pain, nearly collapsing. "I will do it. I am yours to command."

I bolted awake, panting hard. Sweat covered my brow and I blinked rapidly, staring at my surroundings.

Hotel room.

Bland, pastoral scene on the wall.

Ugly lamp next to the bed.

World's biggest virgin at the foot of the bed.

I was back in my own head. Ethan sat cross-legged in front of the TV, a soda from the mini-fridge in his hand as he watched what looked like *The View*. He barely glanced at me as I swung my legs over the edge of the bed, clutching my stomach as nausea shot through me. Zane's dreams . . . was that what had happened to him while I'd been gone, laughing it up in Mexico?

He'd nearly lost his wings again for me?

"I ordered a lasagna for you from room service," said Ethan. "It is in the small fridge. I thought you might be hungry when you woke up."

Normally I would be. Right now I just wanted to vomit. My head was still filled with bloody feathers. "Thanks."

He clicked the TV off when a commercial came on. "I feel we must talk, Jackie Brighton."

"Just call me Jackie," I said. "And can we talk after I shower?"

He nodded.

Twenty minutes later I was feeling a bit refreshed, more awake, and the visions of bloody feathers were receding from my mind. Starving, I wrapped a towel around my head and one around my body, and headed for the mini-fridge.

Ethan gave me a horrified look. "What are you doing?"

I took the plate out of the fridge and picked up a plastic fork. The lasagna looked kind of hideous cold, but I shoved a big forkful into my mouth anyhow. Yep, kind of gross, but I needed carbs. "Eating," I said to Ethan between bites. "You want some?"

"I meant your clothing."

"Oh." Jeez, I sure wasn't used to being around a dude

who was a prude. "Uh, the only thing I have with me is my dress, and it's kind of, you know . . ."

"Slutty?"

I stared at him, fork frozen halfway to my mouth. "Wow. That stings a little."

He shrugged, getting up from the bed. "LC told Heidi the same thing on the television."

I stared at him. He'd been watching *The Hills*. Funny, he didn't strike me as an MTV fan, but there was no accounting for taste. "I guess."

As I stood there, he took off his shirt, then handed it to me. "You can wear this over your dress until we retrieve your clothing."

"That's very thoughtful of you," I said, taking the shirt from him and smiling. "You're all right, you know that?"

His eyes flickered silver, then faded to black again.

Ha! "You totally got off on giving me your shirt, didn't you?"

He gave me a defensive look and turned his back to me. "Do not be inappropriate, Succubus."

He totally *had* gotten off on giving me his shirt. I smirked as I slipped on the silver dress and began to button his shirt over it. It nearly swallowed me whole, so I knotted it at my waist.

"Are we going back to the house?" I asked Ethan, grabbing a bottle of water and taking a swig. "I'd like to see if we can find some hint as to where Remy disappeared to before I become bait. Not to mention that my clothes are there, and we need to return what's left of your tux . . . or at least pay for the damages," I said.

"We should do something," Ethan agreed. "You cannot continue to walk around with your female flesh exposed."

I choked on the water I was sipping. "Please, please, don't *ever* use that phrase again. Please."

He gave me a chiding look. "We have much to do before the vampires awaken, Succubus. Best that we get started."

We returned to Remy's house after returning the tuxedo. I was now $1,500 lighter and had been the recipient of a firm talking-to from the tuxedo rental employee. Not that I could blame them. It looked like the tuxedo had gone through a war.

I was starting to get used to the sight of destroyed things, I thought as I stared at Remy's house with dismay. If Joachim had caused this much destruction to Remy's stuff, how was my poor friend faring?

A sympathetic hand clapped on my shoulder. It was supposed to be a pat on the back, but given the size of Ethan's hands, it nearly knocked me on my face. "You are upset, Succubus. Retrieve your clothing, and I will begin to pick up the mess here."

"Thank you," I said, the guilty knot in my throat not receding even slightly. I kept staring at the shattered bar, the destroyed couches. Everything Remy had worked so hard for—trashed. "I know you're just doing it to get a fix, but still, thank you."

He stiffened and gave me a wounded look. "Not everything I do is for my own needs."

I gave him a distracted smile and patted him on the back. "You're right. Sorry."

As he grabbed a roll of garbage bags from the kitchen, I went up the stairs to my bedroom. I dug through several boxes of my old junk and pulled out some T-shirts and jeans. I was a woman on a mission, not a tramp on the prowl for some tail. Casual clothes were best.

I moved to Remy's room and began to glance through her things. Where was she hiding in New City? Other than some co-workers, the vampires, and myself, did Remy have any human friends? She mostly loved and left a string of men. Could she have temporarily shacked up with an innocent human?

As I sat on the edge of the bed my BlackBerry rang, and I glanced at the caller ID displayed on the screen. The university? I hesitated, then sent the call to voicemail. If they were calling because I'd left the dig, I didn't have time to try to explain it. Nor could I tell them where Noah was at the moment—best to just avoid that sticky situation entirely.

Then I noticed I had seven messages waiting. Frowning, I dialed over to voicemail and listened to the first one.

"Hey Jackie," chirped one of the assistants, her voice trembling. "This is Becky. Where did you get this painting? Call me." She rambled off a number so quickly that I wasn't able to decipher it. Which wasn't a problem, because the next message was from her, too.

"Is this some sort of joke?" she said when she called back. "Are you testing me?"

Five minutes later, she'd left me another message. "This isn't a joke, is it? Oh God, Jackie. Where did you get this? Did you steal it? Oh my *Goddddddd*." A rapturous trill squeezed from her throat, so loud I had to hold the phone away from my ear. "Do you know what this *is*?"

Well, no. That's why I'd turned it over to the lab to have it carbon-dated and to have someone analyze the words written on the back. My instincts were telling me one thing, but I wanted cold, hard science to prove me right.

Sure enough, the next message was from her again. This time, a few hours had passed between calls. "Jackie, it's Becky again. Call me. Please. This is so exciting. I've talked to everyone in the department and we all agree— it looks like a Da Vinci. The signature, the medium—oil on a panel that's consistent with his other paintings. The time frame, the perspective. Oh my God, Jackie. Oh my God! There's a thumbprint on the back and we're going to run it against a few things. If it's not Da Vinci himself, it's got to be someone from his school. There's no mistaking this. How did you come up with it? *Call me*."

Oh *shit*. I had dropped off a Da Vinci at the university? That was . . . not good. So much for keeping things low-key. I needed to get it back, and fast. I dialed the number that Becky had left on my phone.

She picked it up on the first ring. "Ohmigodohmigod-ohmigod—" she squealed into my ear.

"It's a fake," I lied, cutting into her enthusiasm. "I promise, it's a fake. I had it painted for Noah as a joke."

"A joke?" she echoed, crushing disappointment and confusion coloring her voice. "I don't understand. Why would you ask me to carbon-date—"

"It was a lame joke. It's for his birthday," I said, making stuff up as I went along. "A little bet between us. I told him he wouldn't be able to pick out a real Da Vinci from a fake and so I had this fake made." Okay, even my explanation was lame.

Becky wasn't convinced, I could tell. "But . . . but Jackie, I swear, it looks real. Professor Jergens has studied Da Vinci for twenty years and he says—"

"Jergens?" I laughed, mentally cursing myself. God, why had she shown it to Jergens? If anyone could identify a Da Vinci, it was him. I had to think fast. "That old creep will say anything to try and get you to go out with him. He hits on anything with tits. You could draw a stick figure, and Jergens would tell you that it's a Picasso if it gets you in his office for five minutes."

She paused. Paused for a bit longer. I bit my lip. "That creep," she eventually said. "He totally had me convinced."

I exhaled with relief. "Yeah. It's *supposed* to look convincing."

"It really does," she said in a wistful voice. "It really looks like a real Da Vinci."

That was because it probably was. Noah at Da Vinci's school back in Renaissance Florence? Not entirely out of the realm of possibility. "Can you do me a favor and pack it up for me, Becky? I'll swing by later tonight to grab it. I didn't mean to get you in trouble."

"Oh, it's no trouble," she said glumly. "I was just hoping for something cool to happen. It's always so boring around here."

"True enough," I lied, a cheerful note in my voice. "So did you look at the back?"

"Yeah," she said in a mopey voice. "It's just a date and a name, that's all."

"What name?" I forced my voice to be casual.

"Rachael."

"Rachael?" It didn't ring a bell. "Gotcha. Thanks, Becky."

"Sure. I'll have it wrapped up and left for you to pick up," she said sorrowfully, as if I'd ruined her week.

I clicked off the phone and stared at the wall. Rachael. A woman's name. A Hebrew name, unless I had misjudged the clothing. Why had Da Vinci painted a Hebrew woman? Why was Noah carrying it around? And why was she wearing my face? The questions circled in my head as I finished packing my clothing. By the time I'd finished, I still had no answers. Frustrated and distracted, I headed downstairs.

Ethan had been busy; the living room looked almost

liveable again. If one ignored the shredded cushions, that is. But the couch had been placed back in its original spot, the broken glass had been cleaned up, and the trash had been removed. I could see the floor again . . . and the dark, rusty stains that wouldn't come out of the carpet.

Maybe the trash was preferable.

"Thank you, Ethan," I said, dumping my backpack of clothing on the corner of the couch. "I really appreciate it, and I'm sure Remy would too if she were here."

He said nothing, but I caught the gleam of his eyes again. "You are welcome, Succubus."

"Can you please just call me Jackie, for once and for all? Jeezus."

"Calling you by your first name would imply an improper relationship," he said in a stiff voice. "And I have no wish to imply such a thing."

I waved a hand at him, frustrated. "Can you call me by something else? A pet name of some sort?"

He looked at me with a perfectly grave expression. "Like . . . Fluffy?"

I blinked, surprised. "Not a real pet name. I mean—" His expression grew embarrassed, and I said, "Never mind. Keep calling me 'Succubus.'"

"Very well."

"So did you find anything incriminating?"

"I found a severed foot," he said, and began to reach into the garbage bag. "Did you wish to see it?"

"No," I said hastily, putting my hands up to stop him.

"I'll take your word for it." Jeez. That was disturbing. "Did you find the rest of the owner somewhere around here?"

"Just the foot," Ethan told me. "We'd smell an entire dead body."

That was . . . reassuring. I guess. "Was the foot male or female? Could you tell?" He moved to pull it out of the bag to show me, and I backed away. "Don't show me. Just tell me."

He stared down into the bag for a minute, then at his own foot. "Male, I think."

"Then it must belong to one of the vampires that the queen said that Remy—er, Joachim—murdered." Well, that was a relief. Sort of. I paced around the room, trying to think. "No signs of Remy, though?"

He shook his head. "Nothing that would indicate a succubus has been here. She is just gone."

Well, crap. We were going to have to lure her, after all. I sighed heavily. The last thing I wanted to be was bait.

Trying to wipe the thought of "bait" from my mind, I made a pit stop at the university to clean up the mess I'd created. Leaving Ethan waiting at Remy's house, I ran in to the Archaeology building and made a beeline for the desk of Dr. Morgan's assistant, Becky Lewis.

She didn't look thrilled to see me. "Hi, Jackie," she said, barely glancing up from her computer as I approached. "Dr. Morgan isn't in. He's still in Mexico and will be for the next few months." Her gaze implied I should be doing the same.

I gave her a fake, bright smile and lied through my teeth. "I had to leave early. Medical reasons."

"I see." She didn't sound sympathetic in the slightest. "Did you need something else?"

I guessed that she'd had time to analyze our conversation about the painting and was mad at me. "Just wanted to swing by and pick up Noah's painting. Do you still have it?"

"Oh. That." Becky dug through some paperwork, pretending to look for it. After a moment, she lifted her coffee cup and pulled out the envelope underneath. "Here it is."

I snatched it from her, resisting the urge to check and see if any of the wet brown rings on the surface of the envelope had leaked through to the painting inside. If she had even the slightest inkling that it might actually be a real Da Vinci, I'd never be able to give it back to Noah. So I forced myself to tuck it under my arm, real casual-like. "Cool, thanks. See you."

"Later," she said in the same passive-aggressive tone, and turned back to typing.

I hurried out of the building, and when I was safely back at the car, I tore the envelope apart, checking the painting. To my relief, it was still encased in plastic and the wet envelope had just been for show. Whew.

With the painting safely retrieved, I returned to Remy's house and hid it under my bed, between the mattresses. It felt strange (and stupid) to hide a Da Vinci under the mattress, but what else could I do? It was too big to fit in my pocket. I kept Noah's engagement ring with me at all times, tucked into a pocket, simply because it was too expensive to leave lying around. Leaving the painting at Remy's house seemed like a bad idea, but the hotel safe seemed even worse.

With the painting successfully stowed, I patted my pocket to double check the ring, and then ran off to find Ethan again.

We locked up the house and left it, leaving a note taped to the door in case Ethel should return.

From there, I checked a few of Remy's local hangouts. Her dry cleaner hadn't seen her in a week. Her pool boy hadn't seen her in longer. And her job was furious at her because they were waiting on her to shoot a movie and she was nowhere to be found.

By the time we returned to the hotel, the sun was close to setting and my frustration was mounting.

At my request, Ethan went downstairs to grab us a dinner from the lounge, and I went to the elevator to head up to our room. I needed to put away clothing and the stuff I'd grabbed from Remy's house, and think of a Plan B before the vampires got up.

But when I arrived back at the hotel suite, the door was ajar, and Caleb was there waiting for me. He sat in a chair facing the door, and his face lit up as I saw him. "Welcome home, sweet cheeks. So good of you to rejoin us."

All of my nerves tensed, and alarm bells went off in my head. "Hi. Er, where's Zane?" I didn't see my lover anywhere.

"He's been a tad bit delayed." His long, narrow fingers steepled, then flexed. "Is there something I can help you with?"

Best not to show my attachment to Zane or someone would get suspicious. I forced a bright smile to my face. "Nope. Just spent the day working on my tan."

He shrugged. "It's your friend's funeral if you want to fuck around with the time we have. I don't care either way, dollface."

"If you're going to be a dickhead, we don't need you around," I snapped back at him. "If you don't give a shit, then why are you here?"

He smiled—a beautiful but cold smile. "To keep you in line."

That sent a chill skittering through me. "And if I don't stay in line?"

He tilted his head at me, so pretty and blond and evil. "Why, have you already disobeyed, my pet? Do you have something I should report back to the queen?"

"Pfft," I said, though my heart was pounding. Did he know that Zane and I had hooked up last night? "I was just curious. You make it sound so awful."

"Oh, it's not pleasant when one disobeys the queen," he said in that silky voice.

"Then I guess it's a good thing that she's not my boss," I replied forcefully, digging through my purse for my phone to cover the fact that my hands were shaking.

He leaned back in his chair, his hands stroking his throat. My gaze was drawn to it and I frowned. That was a weird piece of jewelry for a guy to wear. The thick band of gold metal had a pronged bar across his collarbone; it was shaped like an O with a line underneath it. "What's with the choker?"

Caleb stroked it again, his eyes crinkling as he gave me a friendly smile. That baby face didn't fool me—nor did his simple explanation. "It is my *shenu*. An Egyptian symbol that carried great magic. It works twofold— for one, we can use it as a conduit to pull the spirit of Joachim from your friend Remy. And for two, it works as a magical shield. With it, I am protected from those that would harm me. The queen thought I should have some additional protection when we approach your little friend tonight."

Oh, man. I thought of the severed foot back in Remy's house. "You might need more than a necklace. She bites. We found a foot, but not the owner."

Caleb winked at me. "I can take care of myself, baby-cakes. Don't worry about me."

Right. As if worrying about him had ever truly entered my mind. "Since you're up, I'll go find Zane," I said, heading toward the door. "He in his room?"

The other vampire inclined his head, and his eyes grew red as I watched. "He is recovering there, yes."

I didn't like watching the bloodlust come over him. A knot formed in my throat. "Did you say . . . recovering? From what?"

He got up from the chair in a swift motion, and before my eyes could adjust, he'd crossed the room and loomed over me. I got the impression of heat and desire as he sniffed my hair, then snapped his teeth at me, displaying long—frighteningly long—fangs. "Punishment, of course. After only one day, you disobey the rules the queen has set for you?"

He grabbed my wrist and slammed it against the wall, pinning me there. The purse flew out of my hands and skidded across the floor.

Pain shot through my arm, and I whimpered when he pressed his body up against mine. He gave me another boyish look, staring down at my neck with interest. "Is it that you cannot resist vampires, girl? Or do you feel the need to grab any cock and ride it? Because you could have asked me." He smiled at me, all teeth and red eyes and that ugly, thick collar. "I'd be more than happy to accommodate your needs."

I twisted away from him. "Get lost, creep."

"All I'm saying," he said in a low, dangerous voice as he leaned in close to my face, "is that if you value your friend's life, do not fuck him as soon as you are out of earshot, understand me? The queen knows what he did. I know what he did. And if I find out that you've fucked him again, he's going to lose his wings. Permanently."

He snapped his teeth at me an inch away from my nose. "I'm off to feed," Caleb said in his musical voice. "I'll be back here in an hour. Tell Zane that I expect the same from him."

I rubbed my wrist as he stalked out of my hotel room, my heart slamming in my chest. How had he known that

Zane and I had hooked up? What did it mean for Zane?

He is recovering there, yes. Dread curled through my stomach.

I barely stopped to grab my room key before racing out for Zane's room. I slammed into the elevator and pressed the button repeatedly as the doors crawled shut. After an interminably long ride, the elevator dinged open on the seventh floor. I flew down the hall, skidding to a halt in front of Zane's door.

I knocked, my heart pounding.

No answer.

I knocked again. Tested the door handle. Locked, and I didn't have the key card to open his door. I glanced down the hall, where a maid was pushing a cart of towels. "I'm sorry," I said, putting a sheepish smile on my face as I approached her. "I locked myself out of my room. Can you let me in?"

The woman gave me a suspicious look. "No, ma'am—"

Time to turn on the Suck powers. I reached out and brushed my hand over hers, sending a wave of my powers through her. She collapsed to the floor, and I rummaged through her pockets, grabbed the key card, then brushed her awake again, hurrying down the hall before she regained her senses to unlock the door

Zane stood at the window, a tall, lone figure silhouetted against the faint streetlight that streamed in. The room was otherwise dark. The end of a cigarette flared red, and I heard the paper sizzle as he stared out the window.

"I said no towels," he said without turning around.

"Good thing I didn't bring any," I said.

He didn't turn to face me. "You shouldn't be here, Jackie."

I shut the door and dropped the key card onto the desk. "Oh, I don't know about that," I said lightly, my pulse pounding with nervousness. "What's wrong, Zane? Caleb said that you weren't feeling well."

"It's nothing, Princess." His voice was short, terse. "I'll be down to your room shortly, and then we'll go."

Really. I took a step forward and watched him shift subtly, his shoulders setting as if squaring himself for something unpleasant.

I flicked on the light. "If it's no big deal, then look at me."

He turned, slowly.

I gasped. Encircling Zane's neck was a thick black collar. The edge of it disappeared below the band of his T-shirt and swept around his neck like a thick choker. It seemed to radiate an almost blue tinge, and as I stepped forward I noticed that Zane's skin underneath it had reddened, as if it hurt him.

I swallowed hard. "What's that?"

Zane's mouth lifted in one corner in his characteristic sardonic smile. "I've been a naughty boy, Princess." The cigarette went back to his mouth, and he turned back toward the window. "And now I'm being punished."

I moved to his side and touched his arm. "Did . . . did someone find out about us?"

Zane grinned down at me, though I could tell it was painful. His hand moved as if he wanted to tug on the collar, then he placed the cigarette between his lips again. "Yeah. The queen found out and she had Caleb collar me like some sort of dog."

His collar looked nothing like Caleb's. Maybe one was the reward and one was the punishment. "I see. And what does this do?" I touched the collar and it burned, ice cold. The pads of my fingers stuck to it like dry ice and I ripped them away, leaving a layer of skin on the surface. I hissed and stuck my burning, painful fingers in my mouth, sucking on them to make the hurt go away. The thing radiated cold and evil.

Zane flicked his cigarette and glanced out the window, not meeting my eyes. "Whenever I do something against her rules, it will burn me. The worse the infraction, the more it hurts. Since Caleb put it on me, only he can remove it."

My breath choked in my throat. I hated it. And for a moment, I hated Zane for looking so casual about it.

"So this is to stop you from touching me," I said bitterly. "Since you're too far away for her to watch, she's put a shock collar on you instead."

He shrugged. "It is what it is."

I shoved him away. "How can you be so calm about this? She's collaring you like an animal! She's trying to prevent you from being with me."

He gave me a long, hard look. "You think a little piece of jewelry is going to stop me if I want to kiss you, Princess?"

He flicked the cigarette out of the window and pulled me against him. His hand wrapped in my hair and his mouth claimed mine. His tongue thrust into my mouth, seeking, branding me. I gasped at the surge of pleasure and returned the kiss, responding to his touch. The Itch stirred within me, sending my pulse through my veins.

A sizzle caught my ears, and a strange smell, and Zane's hands tightened in my hair. I jerked away, gasping as I stared down at the collar encircling his throat. Tiny wisps of smoke escaped from his skin, and it was even redder. "It's burning you!"

He shrugged. "It burns me with cold if I disobey the queen's orders."

I released him, stepping back. I felt numb. "And what are her orders?"

"Not to touch you. Not to drink from you." He pulled out the pack of cigarettes again and tapped the end repeatedly, not looking at me. "I kiss you, it burns me. I make love to you, it'll eat a hole through my throat. That covers the big stuff."

Great. We were finally together again, and he was going to burn alive if he so much as tried to touch me. "So what do we do?"

His eyes flicked red. "We continue doing what we do, Princess. And if I want to kiss you, she's not going to stop me."

I licked my lips, trying to think. "You need blood. Tonight. Caleb said we had to be ready to go in an hour."

He shook his head. "I'm not drinking from another woman with you here. I'm not doing that to you again."

Sweet, but misguided. If he put his lips on another woman, she'd be a quivering, orgasmic mess at his feet before a minute had passed. I didn't like the thought of that much, but what could we do?

I knew that he enjoyed it. He might not want to, but just like me, he couldn't control his urges.

"I don't want to see you drinking from another woman," I said softly. "It hurts me."

He pulled me close and touched his forehead to mine, our eyes locking. "I don't want anyone else but you, Jackie. You know that. I don't care if this thing burns me."

I cared. I fingered his shirt collar, thinking hard as I stared at the offending black band. "I can't stand the thought of you hurting yourself just to touch me, Zane."

He pulled me close, his hands sliding to my waist, then lower. The collar seemed to flare even colder, but he ignored it, giving me a devilish smile. "Jackie, Princess. She knows she can't stop me from touching you. That's why she slapped this collar on me—to remind me that she's the boss. That I'm in trouble for disobeying her rules."

I swallowed the knot in my throat. I wanted to lay my head on his shoulder, but that would put my forehead right against the collar, and I didn't want to go near it. "And what if she does worse than a collar if she finds out that it's not doing any good? What if she does something worse to you?"

He lost his wings once. He can lose them again . . .

His mouth curved up slightly and he reached out and brushed my cheek with his fingers. "Jackie, not being with you is the worst that she can do to me. If we're not together, what does it matter if I live for four days or four thousand years more?" His thumb brushed across my lip, his gaze going there. "There is nothing for me if you're not in my life."

I shook my head at him. The words were beautiful, but they were all wrong. I didn't want to hear him talking of death—it hurt too much. "Zane, don't." I patted his chest. "Let's not think about immortality or things like that." Or wedding rings or Noah stuck in Mexico, sacrificing himself for me. Because then I'd break down into a sobbing mess. "Let's just worry about that collar right now. And how to get you fed."

"I already told you, not from another woman. Not with you so close to me." His red eyes burned into mine.

No, that wouldn't work. We'd need some sort of donor that wouldn't get too attached . . . Wait.

My fingers curled in his jacket and I looked up into Zane's weary red eyes. "What about a guy?"

His brow furrowed for a moment. "I didn't take you for the type to watch a couple of guys get off, Princess—"

"Not like that," I said, my mind buzzing. "If your mouth touches them, you make them come, right? What if you don't touch them?"

He frowned at me. "Blood doesn't come out of a spout."

"No," I said brightly. "But it does come out of a wrist."

His mouth curled in a heartbreaking smile. "You mean to tell me that you're going to find some guy to cut his wrist open to feed me? This age is full of stupid humans, Jackie, but I think you'll be hard-pressed to find a volunteer for that."

"I know just the guy," I said. "And since it's the right thing to do, he'll love it."

CHAPTER THIRTEEN

Ethan didn't love it. He actually looked rather disgusted with the concept, but at my pleading and Zane's silence, he gave a stiff nod and reached for one of the knives from the food service tray and slashed his wrist.

Blood sprayed everywhere. "Holy shit," I said, wiping a few drops off my face. "A little warning next time."

Zane's hand, held tightly in mine, clenched. He leaned down and licked a drop of blood off of the back of my hand in a sensual move that set my pulse pounding.

"We only have a few minutes before my healing closes the wound," Ethan said, and gestured at the nearby chair. "Sit and I will pour."

Zane sat, his head tilted back, and I watched as Ethan held his cut wrist a few inches from Zane's mouth.

It was the weirdest thing I'd ever seen. Even weirder, Ethan's eyes kept flicking that strange color with every minute that passed. Whatever brownie points he got off on, he was definitely racking them up at the moment.

Zane held my hand as he fed, his eyes on me. As the blood poured into his open mouth, the awful red receded from his eyes. Soon the steady flow of blood from Ethan's wrist turned into a trickle, and Zane raised a hand to indicate that he was finished as well. He nodded his thanks to Ethan.

He sat up and lit a cigarette. "Well, that was weird. My lover watching while another man feeds me. Not in my usual repertoire." He gave me another half-curled smile.

"Whatever gets us through the night, right?" I squeezed his hand.

The club was deserted.

I got out of the car and stared at the front of the club, wary. When I'd seen the sleek neon sign and the full parking lot six months ago, I had walked into a mess of problems. I'd met the vampires, pissed off their queen, nearly sacrificed Remy's life, and put my own at risk to boot.

I guess some things never changed.

The club looked the same as it had six months ago, the neon sign with the blue crescent moon and the rippling letters MIDNIGHT was still on. Beer and liquor signs lit up the windows, and the decorative blue and purple lights that wrapped around the edge of the building twinkled in the crisp night. The building was low-key and charming, like a friendly neighborhood dive. Except beneath the scribbled-on-walls, beat-up dance floor, and smoky atmosphere lurked a very different bar in the basement.

A very popular vampire hangout.

"This place looks disreputable," said Ethan, his voice full of disapproval. "Perhaps your succubus friend will not come here."

"Oh, I don't know about that," Zane said, grinning as he slid out of the driver's seat. He tossed his cigarette butt down onto the empty parking lot. "If I were a rampaging evil spirit, the first place I'd head is somewhere I could get a drink."

Caleb just shrugged his coat tighter over his compact shoulders. "Home, sweet home." He'd changed into a long, sweeping gray duster and a collared white shirt that hid the golden torque encircling his neck that was so crucial to our plans.

Zane didn't seem inclined to hide his badge of shame. It stood out starkly against the paleness of his skin.

Vampires were odd creatures. Far be it from me to try and figure them out. "So what's the plan here?"

Caleb shoved his hands in his pockets and eyed the building. "She's familiar with this place, right?"

I circled around the car to be closer to Zane; I felt better standing near him. "Remy Summore is. Joachim is not. So I don't see how we're going to get him to the club."

Caleb turned back and grinned at me, his face boyish except for the stark tattoo encircling his eye. It looked like a demonic monocle. "Bait, of course."

I crossed my arms over my chest. "Yeah, I got that. But I don't see how that's going to work."

He hopped over the railing of the steps leading up to the front door and pulled out a large ring of keys. "Once Joachim knows you're here, he'll come. At least, I hope he will."

I leaned against the side of the car. "Yeah, well, if you think I'm going to let you tie me behind the car and drag me a few miles to leave a scent trail, you're wrong."

Caleb glanced backward at me, his eyes lit up with an excitement that I didn't share. "We don't need to do anything as drastic as that. We just need your blood."

That sounded ominous.

Ethan frowned and stepped in front of me, holding the bo staff before us as if it could hold back the evils of the world. "I do not approve of this."

I wasn't too keen on it, either. I glanced over at Zane. He wouldn't let Caleb dice me up. "Exactly how does this plan work?"

"There are old symbols that, when drawn, act like beacons," Caleb answered. He pulled a paper out of his pocket and began to unfold it. "Symbols of intense power that can be keyed to lure a specific creature in a variety of ways." He finished unfolding the paper and held it out to me.

I took it from him, uncertain as to what I was looking at. Black scrawls of arcane symbols filled the page, written inside a dark double circle. "What exactly am I looking at here?"

Caleb moved to my side, extending his pinky to point at the paper. "The outer circle must be drawn with chalk.

It binds the symbol. The inner circle allows us to set what sort of symbol we want. This particular circle is a beacon, so we're going to use a food item to invite the creature in. Maybe a circle of coffee grounds. Depends on what the club has."

"And the interior symbols? There's a lot of those."

"Those allow us to pull the type of creature we want—specifically, an angel." His pinky glided over the symbols as if tracing them into his memory.

"So why do you need my blood?"

"The host of our particular angel is a succubus, so we need succubus blood as the medium for the symbols." Caleb's mouth quirked in an unapologetic smile. "If it was a human, we could use their blood, but alas."

I turned to Zane, questioning the validity of Caleb's claim. His expression was grim as he shoved another cigarette in his mouth. "He's right. I don't like it either, but I don't see that we have many choices."

Ethan shook his head, long ponytail swinging. "I swore to Noah that I would keep you safe, Jackie Brighton, and this is dangerous. Letting vampires bleed you out is not keeping you safe."

Zane straightened and moved to stand in front of Ethan. He laid a hand on the bo staff, and his jaw clenched. "Are you saying that I'm threatening Jackie's life? Did Noah send you up here to be a watchdog for him? To keep her away from me?" he sneered.

Okay, this was going to get ugly fast. I stepped between the two men. "We don't have much time and I'm a big girl. It's just a little blood. No problem. Really." I turned to Ethan, who had his jaw set in a mulish frown. "Really. It's fine."

He leaned in, the smooth angles of his face appealing in the moonlight. "Succubus, do you say this because *he* thinks you should do it, or because you think you should do it?"

What a crappily accurate thing to say. I shoved Ethan's shoulder. "Ease off. It's just a little blood amongst immortals. It's not going to kill me."

"No," said Ethan. "But this demon-possessed succubus will almost certainly kill all of us. Are you sure it is worth one life for all of ours?"

I stared down at my small sneakers on the pavement, sandwiched between Ethan's large boots and Zane's Doc Martens. And I thought of Remy. My laughing, easygoing friend with the effervescent personality and sunny smile. Remy was four hundred years old, and she'd seen a lifetime's worth—several lifetimes—of bad shit, but nothing as bad as I'd inflicted on her. She'd taken me in and taken me under her wing without a second thought. Succubi had to stick together, she'd said, and we were the only two in New City.

And what had that gotten her? Possessed by a demonic entity and her life in turmoil. Just because she'd tried to help me out, and I was too stupid and new to listen.

"I'm going to help her," I said softly. "She's my friend. Succubi stick together. That's what we do."

"Then that is what we shall do," said Ethan.

I pushed off of the car and began to cut across the parking lot. Zane and Ethan fell in behind me. "Come on," I said. "Let's find a knife before I chicken out on this."

Cutting one's wrist open? Not as easy as Ethan had made it look. After giving my skin a surface graze, I chickened out and had to have Ethan do it for me. I sat on the metal folding chair that we'd pulled out into the parking lot specifically for this task, and waited for Ethan to strike.

"Okay, I'm ready—"

Before I could finish speaking, Ethan grabbed my arm and sliced it open.

I screeched like a banshee. "Oh my God!"

"Quiet, Succubus. Someone will think you are being murdered in the parking lot," Ethan said in a reasonable voice.

"You could have freaking warned me!" A seeming flood of red blood was coursing down my arm. Dear God, that hurt. There was pain and there was *pain,* and this was some serious hardcore *pain.*

All business, Ethan ignored my howls. He tilted my arm downward so the blood flowed steadily into a pitcher he'd retrieved from the club. "You must do unpleasant things quickly, Succubus. Bandages must be ripped off with haste in order to spare further pain."

Further pain? I was going to black out from this alone. I whimpered, blinking rapidly to fight back the tears that threatened to overwhelm me. So much for hanging with the big boys. Ethan hadn't given so much as a sniff when he cut his own wrist. Me, I was ready to bawl like a baby.

Ethan was the only calm one, too. Caleb had disappeared into the club to start preparing the symbol. Zane had opted to stay near me, but it was obvious that this was an entirely new sort of hell. He paced in the parking lot, coat rustling around his rapidly moving legs. Back and forth he paced, back and forth, and his hand tore through his tousled black hair repeatedly. I wasn't sure if it was because he didn't like seeing me in pain or if the smell of blood was getting to him.

Probably both. Either way, he was making me antsy.

"How much blood do we need?" I asked in a little while. I didn't know how much Caleb would need to paint the symbols, but the bottom of the pitcher was red with blood, and I was feeling a little light-headed. "You're going to leave me enough so I don't pass out, I hope."

"This is enough," said Ethan, grabbing my arm and tilting it upward to slow the blood loss. Succubi had rapid healing, but it'd still take me a while to heal a cut that deep.

Zane moved in closer, his arms crossed over his chest as he regarded me. "She okay?"

"You should lick it," Ethan told Zane suddenly.

Heat flared and I felt the Itch come to life, like some sick puppy dog that had heard its name being called. *Down, girl, down.* "Lick me?" I repeated, just because I liked saying it.

Zane's brows furrowed as he moved to my side. "What did you just say?"

Ethan held up my wrist. "You should lick her wound. It will heal her faster. She is in great pain."

"I'm not sure this is such a good idea," I began, my voice husky with desire. It sounded like an amazing idea, but I didn't want Zane to get hurt by the collar.

"I will take the blood to Caleb so he can finish the symbol," Ethan said, eyes flashing with that strange feeding light of his. "And I will leave you two alone so the vampire may . . . lick you." His voice became strangled at the end, as if it had finally occurred to him what he was saying. He gave us both a quick bow. "I shall return shortly."

Before I could protest, his back was to us and Zane held my wrist in his hands, as if torn by his decision.

"You don't have to," I said softly. "It doesn't hurt that much."

He glanced over at me from the corner of his eyes, his mouth curving into a smile. "You're a terrible liar."

"I am," I said with a wobbly smile. "It hurts like a bitch. But I don't want you to get hurt trying to help me out. Exchanging my wound for yours doesn't make it right."

He just licked his lips. And after a long moment in which I did not breathe, he extended his tongue and licked my wrist, from the top of the cut to the bottom. Slow, sensual, and erotic.

My blood pulsed heavy in my veins, my gaze drawn to

his tongue as it moved over my skin. The Itch had flared, making my nerve endings painfully aware. I wanted him badly. His mouth sensually made love to my arm, lapping at the blood that spilled from the cut, teasing me even.

I was so hot and bothered watching him seal the wound. Who would have thought that cut wrists could be so very exciting?

He grimaced after a moment, and I saw a hint of fang. Zane paused, breathing hard, and I caught the ever-so-faint sizzle of the collar again.

I jerked my hand out of his grasp. "It's hurting you, you big idiot. Why didn't you say something?"

Zane looked at me through slitted eyes, and wiped my blood from his bottom lip in a motion that made me want to lick him all over. "Because I enjoyed it far too much, Princess. I could lick you for hours. Days."

"That's . . . nice," I said in a breathy voice. Very, very nice. So nice that I wouldn't be able to think straight for the next few minutes.

"Come on," said Zane, after nuzzling my wrist for a moment longer. "Let's get you inside and make sure that you're safe."

I nodded and let him lead me in to the club.

Despite the cheerful lights in the windows of the bar, the interior was dark. Spookily so. I released Zane's hand and used mine to feel out the interior. "Can we get a few lights on in here?"

A light switch flicked on, and Zane grinned at me. "I thought you liked being in the dark with me."

Even from here, I could hear the collar sizzle. "Simmer down there, Romeo, or you're going to burn a hole through your neck." I peered around the long, curving bar. "I don't see Caleb. Is he downstairs?"

"Probably." Zane lit another cigarette.

Caleb stepped out of the shadows, all smiling young face and tattooed monocle. His hand looped around my shoulder. "Symbol's done, I think. Want to come admire my handiwork? Your big Nephilim friend went to scout the perimeter. He barely glanced at my symbol. I'm wounded."

"I guess so." I glanced over at Zane. My vampire lover looked as if he was about to chew the cigarette between his lips if he ground his teeth any harder.

But Zane said, "I'll find Ethan." He quickly exited out the front door, leaving me with the overly handsy vampire. Not ideal.

Without waiting to see if Caleb was going to follow me, I ducked through the door behind the bar and into the antechamber. I descended into the downstairs room and ignored the booths that lined the walls, moving toward the pool tables instead. The first time I'd walked into this room, it had been full of vampires, and Zane had been playing pool. I'd been so angry at him—he'd felt up my breasts moments before.

What I wouldn't give to have that be my biggest problem at the moment. I ran a hand along the big, heavy furniture. Could I flip one of the tables over and use it as a barricade? I pushed on the edge of the table, testing the weight. Maybe not. The queen might be protective of her interior decorating, and I didn't want to be on her bad side.

Caleb loped down the stairs after me as if he didn't have a care in the world. "Like my symbol? I think I missed my calling as an artist."

"Indeed." I glanced over at the massive design on the center of the floor. Chalk outer circle, a ring of coffee grounds, and my blood painted all over the center. "Lovely work."

"The symbol should bring Remy here to us. The angel inside her should be able to feel it for miles."

"Joachim's not really an angel anymore, is he?"

Caleb's smile was boyishly charming . . . and cold. "No matter what form we wear now, precious, we all started as the same thing. Joachim's essence is a halo, the same as any other angel's."

I ignored his condescending tone and put on Remy's nullify charm, just in case. "And when she gets here? What then?"

He grinned at me and gestured at the gold *shenu* wrapped around his neck. "Like I told you earlier, we use this to pull him from her."

"That's great and all, but you didn't say *how*."

Caleb unhooked the torque and held it out to me. "The halo needs a vessel—it cannot be destroyed. So the *shenu* will transfer Joachim's powers into the collar. It's like an exorcism."

My fingers trailed on the green felt of the pool table and I circled around it, walking away from Caleb and the collar. I didn't like the thought of taking it from him, feeling that warm metal against my flesh when it had just been against his own. That was too . . . intimate. I was openly skeptical that any sort of exorcism would work on Remy, anyhow. "I think he's too powerful for that at this point, Caleb."

He patted the collar. "Not when we get this on her. Trust me. I've performed this sort of thing before."

Yeah, well, a similar plan had gotten about twelve of his colleagues killed. I opened my mouth to protest, when a loud boom came from upstairs. The floor shook and a light fixture crashed to the floor.

"He's here," Caleb whispered, moving to the far side of me. "Fast work. He must have been in the area."

I resisted the urge to crawl under a pool table and hide. "What should we do? And where are the others?"

Where was Zane? The loud crash from upstairs worried me. Was he safe?

Ethan flew through the heavy wooden doors and down the stairs, his large body smashing into a pool table. Caleb and I jumped backward to get out of the way. Shattered to remnants, one of the wooden pieces of the door wobbled, then crashed to the ground after him.

Ethan got to his elbows and shook his head, his long hair flying. "She's here."

My poor Boy Scout. I raced to his side, helping him to his feet. A moment later, a solitary figure moved into the shadowy doorway. The figure was too slim to be Zane, the hair too long and the figure too graceful. I knew the moment the figure turned its head and red eyes focused on me.

"Hello, Remy," I said in a soft voice. "If you're still in there."

The figure that used to be my friend slunk down the stairs, one slow, predatory step at a time. The eyes flared even redder. "She's in here. Somewhere." Remy's voice had taken on a deep, masculine edge.

Her body was a mess. Her nose had shifted to one side as if recently broken, and still-healing cuts lacerated her beautiful brown skin. Her silky black hair was a snarl of knots, and her torn clothing was covered in dark stains. Wet blood coated her mouth and cheeks, as if we'd caught her mid-meal. At some point, she'd lost a shoe and broken the heel off the other one. Joachim obviously didn't care.

"What do you want?" I said, taking a step backward. I immediately cursed myself. The last thing I should do was to show weakness in front of the monster.

A smile curved his mouth. He'd noticed, too. Joachim-Remy stepped forward daintily, menacingly. She gave a scathing glance to the symbol on the floor. "Old tricks. You must have learned that from the demon bitch you follow."

Caleb quickly moved a few feet away. Being near me made him too much of a target, and I didn't blame him.

Zane was nowhere to be seen. That sent fear skittering through me, and I clutched at Ethan. Had she hurt him? *Killed* him?

Joachim-Remy began to slink toward me, and I took a few more careful steps backward. I'd backed up so much that I'd moved past the pool tables and ended up on the far side of the bar. A bar stool smacked into my backside and I grabbed it, bracing it in front of me to put some distance between me and the creature stalking in my direction. "Now, Joachim," I began, my voice calm and reasonable, "let's talk about this. I think you're getting a little carried away with this whole 'revenge' thing."

"What else do I have left?" she hissed, leaping forward a foot or two. "What do I live for, if not for your misery?"

"Happy hour?" I said, then yelped as a long-nailed hand swiped at my arm. I darted around the bar stool, keeping it between us. It was light enough that I could pick it up and hold it in front of me like a lion tamer.

Joachim-Remy snarled at me, foam flecking the corners of her mouth as she crouched to leap again. Where were my protectors? I stole a quick peek around. In the corner of the room I caught a glimpse of Caleb, the *shenu* held out in front of him. He was chanting, his eyes closed, his face grave.

Okay, so he was doing something that would help us trap Remy. I just needed to do my part and keep her occupied.

Piece of cake.

She snarled and leapt for me again, brushing aside the bar stool like cardboard. She pounced on me, knocking me to the floor.

I yelped, taken by surprise. Before I could recover and

get back on my feet, she crawled over me like a spider monkey and straddled me, wild eyes gleaming. Her long, unkempt fingernails scratched at my face. "You didn't put up much of a fight," Joachim said low in his throat, and there was no ignoring the evil smile that curved his face. He stared down at the acorn-sized diamond around my neck. "Resorting to magic to protect yourself?"

"Don't be ridiculous," I said in a light voice, but the words died when Remy's small hand curled into a fist and smashed into my jaw. Pain exploded, and I screamed, trying to buck her off of me.

Joachim-Remy only laughed, raising her fist again.

But I had other tricks up my succubus sleeves. I clamped my hand on hers, noting that her skin was overly warm to the touch. Not as hot as a demon, but close. She was doing the odd little panting thing that I'd seen her do before, a sign that she was getting worked up and having trouble controlling her body. If I could put her to sleep, Caleb could collar her and we could have Remy free of the possession in minutes. With my skin touching hers, I sent a forceful bolt of my succubus powers through to Remy, trying to knock her unconscious.

Nothing happened.

Remy looked down at me, surprised, and began to roar with laughter. "Did you forget that the necklace nullifies your magic, too, fool?"

I had. Whoops. It was worth a try. And now it seemed that all I'd done was piss her off. I tried to shove her off of me, but her grip was firm. She snarled and her mouth pulled into a wide, ugly, bloodstained grin. "I'm going to have fun dismembering you."

A stool crashed over her head.

She paused, her eyes rolling backward as she struggled to remain upright. Ethan hovered over her, the broken half of the bar stool still in his hands. He stared down at the two of us, and when Joachim-Remy didn't go down, he grabbed my fallen bar stool and repeated the same action.

Crash.

Her eyelids fluttered, as if she were having a hard time deciding if she wanted to pass out or not.

To my dismay, her head rolled back, then snapped forward again, and those red eyes focused on me once more. Her mouth curved into a snarl. "Your friend doesn't know when to stop."

She reached up over her and grabbed Ethan by his shirt, then threw him forward over her body. He landed on me, his back smashing into my face.

Shock waves of pain reverberated through my body, and the world went black for a second. My nose felt like it had been pushed into my head, and pain exploded in my mind like a series of firecrackers. I could taste blood in my mouth.

Over me, I felt Ethan struggling to get up, which only made my face hurt more. "Mmmfck phff," I tried to yell around the small, hard things that littered my mouth— my teeth? Who cared, they would grow back. Right now I needed to get him off of me or we were going to lose this fight.

Hot hands curled around my ankles and jerked me out from under Ethan's struggling form. The wood floor scratched my back, a splinter tore through my skin as she dragged me over the surface and away from the men. I screamed with pain.

"Can't get away now," she breathed, laughing cruelly. "I've waited too long for this."

Blood streamed from my nose, and I reached out, desperate to find something to get Remy off of me.

A large shadow charged overhead and Ethan rushed past, bowling Remy over like a linebacker. The possessed succubus flipped backward as if anticipating his move, and when he feinted to the left, she was right there to angle past. He'd found his bo staff again and it whipped out, snapping her across the head. Remy recoiled but only hissed, undaunted. She grabbed the staff and flipped him with it, and I watched Ethan go sailing overhead again.

Remy took the staff and snapped it in half with her bare hands, leaving a nasty jagged edge. She loomed over me, cocking her head, and pushed the jagged edge between my lips. "You realize that you won't die if I force this into your brain?"

Cold fear washed over me. I said nothing, staring up at her, my palms braced against the floor.

She smiled, a low, deadly smile. "I've thought up all kinds of ways to torture you, my sweet succubus. That's one of the best things about playthings being immortal."

"You weren't worried about that when you killed all

those vampires," I said, careful to try and remain as still as possible. The jagged splinters of the stick tore at my lips as I spoke.

"Yes, but I needed them," she purred, leaning over me. "I don't need you. You have no power on your own. You only exist because of your masters. There is no special halo that lights within you."

Ethan charged at Remy again but she neatly side-stepped, the stick shoving deeper into my throat. I gagged and my hands went around it to stop her as she laughed, a rough trill that seemed so strange coming from my friend's small, blood-covered mouth. "You fools are nothing before me. I have been here for thousands of years, waiting to go free. You think *you* shall stop me?" She turned toward Ethan and grabbed him by his long, black ponytail, swinging him around and flinging him into the bar. He crashed into the side of it, the wood cracking apart as he fell to the ground. "How long before you think your friend understands this?"

She turned to look down at me, and as I watched, the gold collar appeared around her throat.

Remy's eyes widened, and her laughter turned into gagging.

Behind her Caleb watched with avid eyes, a hard, confident smile stretching across his face. He held the collar against her throat, locked around her as she thrashed wildly.

"*NOOOOOOO!*" she screamed, the voice erupting from her throat inhuman. "*NOOOOOOOOOOO!*"

I pushed the stick away from my mouth and scrambled to my feet, weaving unsteadily. Caleb pinned her with that simple golden collar, pulling her body against his own. At my side Ethan moved to stand up straight, and I heard several things pop as he righted himself. No doubt he'd broken a few things fighting Remy, who brimmed with endless supernatural strength.

"Can you stop her?" I called out to Caleb. Remy continued to thrash wildly in his arms, so crazily that I was sure she was going to snap her neck—not that it would stop her for long. But I was frightened for the Remy deep inside, the one that needed our help to be free.

Caleb gave me a cocky grin, nearly hidden by the long, rank black hair that flung in his face from Remy's thrashing head. "I have it under control. It takes a few minutes for the collar to drain her fully."

I could already see the unholy red light in Remy's eyes slowly fading, and the collar growing brighter and brighter. It was as if the power was being sucked into the *shenu*. Joachim-Remy howled and frothed, looking like she was in horrible pain.

One of Ethan's mitts clamped on my shoulder. "You should go see if the vampire is well."

Zane! I didn't need to be told twice.

I dashed up the stairs and past the broken door. The upper level of Midnight looked as if a tornado had blown through it. Napkins and shattered glass littered the floor, and the furniture was smashed to bits. I stumbled past the broken, shattered tables, staring around me. Every bottle behind the bar was smashed. Several of the lights in the room were broken as well, and one had a small trail of smoke leaking from it. All around was the scent of alcohol, thick and sweet.

"Zane?" I called. Below, Remy gave an ear-piercing screech and I jumped. The sound seemed overloud in the silence upstairs. "Zane?" I tried again.

"Over here," said a low, tired voice.

I couldn't tell where it was coming from. Frowning, I shoved past the sea of broken furniture, out to the dance floor. "Where are you? We need your help. Caleb's trying to subdue Remy."

"I'm a little occupied, Princess," said the tired voice. I still couldn't pinpoint it.

Frustrated, I kicked aside a broken bottle and took a few more steps forward. "Well, where are you?"

Something wet dripped on my arm, and I wiped it away. It was dark and thick, and I recoiled in horror at the same time as Zane answered.

"Above you," said the faint voice.

I glanced up, and stared in surprise.

Zane was above me, all right. His hands were braced on one of the rafters, his clothing ripped. Blood dripped from a myriad of small cuts over his body. His wings were extended above him, spread wide as if he were about to swoop down on something. His normally pale face seemed strained.

I was missing something important. "Are you . . . coming down?"

His mouth twisted into a painful smile. "I can't. My wings are pinned to the ceiling."

I stared up at him and noted how very still he remained in place. Each of the wings was curved upward, and the largest feathers were pulled flat against the arching slope of the ceiling. I took a step forward and something glittered. Shards of glass? The floor was crunchy with them. Had some sort of explosion occurred up here and his wings had been pinned? Or was this done deliberately?

I stared up at him. "I don't suppose you can just rip your wings out and wait for it to heal?"

He gave me such a tortured look that I winced.

"Never mind," I said. "I'm coming up there. Just hang tight."

"Hurry," he said in a tight voice.

It took me a few minutes to find the supply closet and a ladder tall enough to reach the rafters. I propped it up in the middle of the room and climbed, then slid out onto one of the beams. Ignoring how high up we were, I scooted over a bit more until I was close enough to Zane to feel his body heat. His wing dripped blood on me, splashing my clothing. I stretched an arm up experimentally, and then looked over at Zane. "Can you hold me while I do this?"

Warm arms wrapped around me, and I noticed the deep body tremble that was moving through him. I said nothing about it, though, just got to my feet on wobbling legs and began to pick the spears of glass—not a normal shattering explosion by any means—out of his wings. There were dozens of them, and he gave a full, racking shudder as I pulled each one out.

Wings were sensitive for angels. Especially for the vampires, though I'd never realized Zane was so affected by them. Then I thought of the dreams that we'd shared of blood and feathers and pain, and wondered if this was a more recent occurrence.

As I pulled the glass from his feathers, a warm feeling of affection swept over me. It was puzzling, but it felt like . . . contentment. Which was odd, given that we were in a trashed nightclub, had just fought the bad guys, and my lover was pinned to the ceiling.

But he was whole, and safe, and that made me far happier than it should have. Being with Zane had somehow made everything right in my world again.

That was startling to realize.

I was able to pluck free one wing. It fell limply from the ceiling it had been pinned to, and Zane carefully let it fall to his side. I noticed the other one, still pinned, twitch in reaction. I murmured for him to keep holding me as I moved down the beam and began to work on that wing, too.

As I began to finish my task, Zane spoke slowly.

"Is she . . . all right?" When she came in, she seemed to be struggling with the power inside her. Like it was fighting to escape her body. Her skin was practically crawling off of her bones. Ethan tried to touch her and everything just seemed to explode around us, like he'd set off a bomb."

That would explain the boom we'd heard. I pulled another shard free. "Strange. Do you think he was having trouble handling all that power?"

Zane made a soft noise of assent, his fingers tightening around my waist as I pulled a bigger shard free. "I think so. When everything settled, I was pinned here so I couldn't help out. She seemed weaker after that—weak enough that Ethan could get close enough to slam a fist into her nose. It didn't stop her, though. She just shoved him through the wall and went downstairs. I couldn't follow."

Poor Remy. So that was how her nose had been broken . . . and how we'd been able to fight her down and get the collar on her.

I dropped one of the bloody shards to the floor and smoothed the wing feather I'd removed it from. "I think she's under control," I said, concentrating on my task. "Caleb put the necklace around her neck and seems to be sucking Joachim out of her."

"Your necklace?" His pinned wing fluttered as I pulled the last piece free.

"No, his," I said, turning toward him. "He collared Remy. Now that she has it on, the power is transferring into the collar. She'll be herself again soon." And I couldn't wait for that to happen. A bubbling sense of accomplishment was rising in me, mixed with relief.

Giddy with happiness, my heart felt as if it would burst, and I leaned in to press happy kisses to his face. Remy was going to be all right after all. "We did it, Zane!"

He folded in his wings, giving a great bodily shudder, and leapt down from the rafter down to the floor. I took the ladder and climbed down while he waited for me. As I moved to his side, he shook his head and glanced around the room, as if something wasn't adding up. "I don't understand," he said. "What's he collaring Remy with?"

I frowned at him. "The *shenu*."

Zane paled and grabbed my arm. "What did you just say?"

I tried to pry his fingers off my arm, alarmed. "The gold necklace. The *shenu*."

"That idiot!" He raced for the stairs and I ran after him, fear clenching in my gut. "It's a transfer symbol."

We ran back down just in time to see Remy collapse at Caleb's feet. All the light and energy had seemingly sucked out of her, and she looked like a pale, wretched copy of herself. Ethan cradled her on the floor, a concerned look on his face as he patted her cheek.

The collar in Caleb's hand was shooting off light much like the halo had, once upon a time. Caleb raised it into the air, a savage look on his face.

"No!" Zane called, reaching a hand out, but it was too late. "Caleb!"

It was too late.

Caleb put on the collar, and the light flared and pulsed as it touched his skin.

A wave of energy rolled through the room, knocking us to the ground. My eardrums exploded, and I barely felt Zane pull me under him before the entire building collapsed around us.

CHAPTER FOURTEEN

I awoke gradually. My head was ringing, but I could hear faint, tinny things, so my hearing must have been repairing itself as I slept. Had I been hurt more grievously than I imagined? It took a lot to knock a succubus unconscious.

Someone heavy and warm lay unconscious over me. My fingers trailed over the muscled arm clenched around my torso, up to the broad shoulders and the base of a wing. Zane. Still wrapped around me, trying to protect me. My fingers continued their exploration and I touched his face, feeling his breath on my fingers. "Zane?"

No answer.

I tried again, prodding his shoulder. "Zane? Wake up."

Nothing.

I glanced up, trying to make out where we were and what had happened. A broken piece of the ceiling was inches from my face, close enough to make my breath hitch shallowly. Were we buried alive? I clenched my hand against Zane's shoulder and forced myself to calm, noting my surroundings. There was a sliver of light coming from somewhere, showing me the broken beams and chunks of drywall that surrounded us. We'd been lucky—we'd fallen into some kind of pocket in the basement of Midnight. When Caleb had put on the collar, the surge of power had destroyed the entire building and brought it down around us.

We were screwed. And not in a pleasant way.

If Caleb—a four-thousand-year-old vampire—had the halo inside him, who knew what madness he was capable of? This was one step away from handing it right to the queen in a gift-wrapped package.

We had to do something . . . just as soon as we escaped the wreckage of the club.

I hoped that Remy and Ethan had managed to find a safe pocket, as well. I called their names a few times, but got no response. I tested my limbs gingerly. Nothing seemed to be overly broken. I ached all over, but I was whole. Noah's ring was still tucked safely in my pocket but Remy's necklace was gone. Next to me, Zane's body felt warm and amazing, so I huddled back down next to him, almost in a dreamlike state.

Zane slept peacefully at my side, and I pulled his arm over me, stroking my hands over his warm skin, sighing with pleasure. My pulse ignited, the warmth beginning to spread through my body. We could just wait out the hours here, snuggled in our cave away from the world, and I could rub up against him—

Oh jeez.

The Itch was in full bloom. I wasn't due for another

day, and I frowned as my skin crawled with need. I must have been badly injured. When I'd had a hole blown through my middle (thanks to an angel wielding a gun), I'd needed sex far more often to heal my body. I recognized the same restless ache deep inside me now, the need for sex to refuel.

And it was getting hard to resist the urge to flip Zane onto his back and straddle him.

We must have been unconscious for longer than I'd thought, and I'd been hurt far worse than I thought. Ignoring the skittering Itch that swept over my body, I craned my neck and tried to find the source of the light to judge how long I'd been asleep.

It was impossible to tell, but the light explained why Zane was fast asleep: the vampire day-sleep.

And I was horny, restless, and trapped.

Not a good combination.

My hand skimmed down my side, sending ripples of pleasure and anticipation through my body. My jeans had torn during the explosion, and I slid my hand down the waistband and let my fingers glide over my sex, parting the lips below. My folds were already slick with need, the Itch throbbing through my veins and making my body react. My nipples were hard, tight peaks, and there was a restless urge in me that needed to be satisfied.

Waiting hours for a rescue—or for Zane to awaken—would be torture. His body, so warm and heavy against mine, was making my own body go crazy with need.

I slid my fingers over my clit, once, twice, the sensation pulsing through me with delight. My other hand brushed across my nipples, teasing them. This eased the Itch's restless hunger. I could do this for a while.

I stroked my body, lost in my own thoughts. This was such a bad idea—I kept telling myself that even as I continued to touch myself, sliding my shirt up to expose my breasts and moving my ripped jeans down so they pooled around my hips and then kicked them off. Clothing was bothering me.

And here I was, all alone. Zane wouldn't awaken for hours. Since a succubus couldn't bring herself to orgasm, someone had to give us relief. Didn't matter who, or if they were willing, and even if Zane was willing, he couldn't knowingly touch me or he'd fry from the collar.

Knowingly touch me . . . I glanced over at Zane, who slept on his side, wings folded tight against his back. His body leaned against mine, his hand loose on my hip. I scooted up slightly, taking his hand in mine.

Ohhh, *lovely.* I hadn't remembered his hands being so very big. They'd touched me a day or so ago, but I hadn't had time to really *study* his hands . . . and they were a thing of beauty. His fingers were long and large—not blunt like a craftsman's, or thin like an artist's, but just right. I took his fingers and guided them so they brushed over the top of my thigh.

An utter thrill shot through my body.

This was terribly wrong, but I couldn't help myself. I guided that warm, large hand between my thighs and brushed his fingertips down my sex.

An electric jolt of pleasure coursed through me, and I moaned aloud. That was far nicer than I had imagined. Soft, light, without force behind it. I slid his fingers against my clit and rubbed hard, nearly coming off the floor with pleasure. My breath came in soft gasps, but even so, frustration was ever-present. I was so close, but I needed something *more*. I swore as I bucked against his hand, almost sobbing with need.

God, I was a sick, sick creature—molesting a sleeping man.

I looked down at his hand between my legs, watched as I guided his thumb, resting on my mound, to slide downward and part my sex. I gasped as it brushed against my clitoris. Using my fingers to guide his, I gave it a rough stroke.

My head tilted back and my thighs locked around his hand, encouraging the pressure.

The clamp of my thighs forced his thick middle finger to slide down through my folds, bringing a new set of sensations. Gasping, I arched and rotated my hips against his fingers, forcing his fingertips to stroke and circle my clit again. And again. And again. Harder and faster, I rocked against his hand, breathing his name and arching my hips to create the friction that I needed so badly. The Itch spiraled through me, wild with need.

Finally, I climaxed. Not in the smooth, easy, pleasant way that sex had always been since I turned. This was rough and grating and shameful, and I collapsed with relief when I felt the aching intensity ebbed out of my body. I lay there for a moment, spent. My breathing eventually slowed, and I relaxed in the languor that followed the abatement of the Itch.

I was a horrible person. I'd just rubbed myself off using a sleeping man's hand. There had to be some sort of rule against that.

But at least Zane hadn't burned himself on the collar, and I'd bought myself another two days. To make amends for using Zane, I carefully straightened his clothes, then wiped his fingers clean on my shirt, though I could still smell myself on him. Well, I'd just have to explain that later.

Once everything was restored, I cuddled close to Zane again and watched him sleep for a few moments. That got tiresome, though. For one, he didn't sleep like regular men, and it was more like watching a dead body. That was a little too creepy for my state of mind, so I peered around. Could I climb out? I tested a heavy outcrop of busted drywall and tried to pull my weight up, but all it did was earn me a shower of plaster pieces and the mini-cave shuddering as it came close to collapsing.

I froze. Okay, bad idea. Someone else was going to have to dig us out. No problem, we could wait a few hours. Or days. Or however long before the queen's men came after us again.

Of course . . . that meant that the queen wasn't going to be happy that Caleb had taken Joachim's power and sucked it into himself. I suspected that he wasn't going to go back to the queen with that little treasure. In fact, I'd bet money that he wouldn't.

So now, instead of just a psychotic succubus, I had to worry about a pissed-off queen and a vampire who could potentially be stronger than her. And crazy. Great.

To pass the time, I decided to mentally go through Egyptian dynasties and pharaohs. Most people would probably go to the old standby of ninety-nine bottles of beer on the wall, but that well ran dry after about five minutes. I started with Narmer. It was a challenge, because I hadn't studied my Egyptian history in a while, so I drew myself family trees on the dusty floor while I waited.

I was somewhere in the midst of the Ptolemies when I heard footsteps overhead.

My breath sucked in. Should I say something? What if it was Caleb? I didn't want to point out where we were. I shifted uneasily. The light overhead seemed fainter than before—was the sun going down? If so, Zane would be awakening soon.

What if the queen had decided to come back and check on things? Would calling attention to us mean instant death? What was I supposed to do?

"Are you sure they're here?" said a low voice. My ears strained to make out the rest of the conversation. A female voice jumped in, her response musical and soft.

Who *was* it up there?

More conversation. I sat up on my elbows and craned

my head, desperate to hear. The low thrum of voices was maddening and my guess was that they were walking away, because I could no longer make out the male's voice.

The female said something sharp and shrill, allowing me to catch her voice. "Don't . . . ridiculous . . . Noah . . . dead . . ."

Noah? Was Noah up there? "Hello?" I called, nearly jumping in my excitement. My head brushed against the broken beams as I tried to stand upright. "Can you hear us down here?"

For a long, endless minute there was no response.

Then, a faint voice called. "Jackie? Is that you?"

Noah!

"I'm here!" I called, clutching at the beams as if that would help me climb them. "We're here! We're trapped down here!"

Overhead, a shadow moved and blocked out the last of my dimming light. I sucked in an anxious breath until I heard the sound of wood creaking and groaning. A massive chunk of the collapsed ceiling moved, the rest of the debris shifting slightly. Faint light trickled in and I could see the orange sky overhead. He was going to get us out.

I moved over to Zane and shook his shoulder, but he didn't awaken. Anxious, I turned back to the hole, waiting to see a glimpse of Noah.

I was not disappointed. After a few more minutes of creaking and groaning and shit being moved, the hole widened a bit more and a blond head peered over the top.

"Noah," I cried, raising my arms up with excitement. "You're free!"

He laughed, the sound a mixture of relief and amusement. "And you're the one trapped. Hold tight for a few minutes more, Jackie, and I'll get you dug out."

I waited impatiently as Noah removed enough debris to clear head space. Soon enough, a rope (made of what looked to be Noah's long-sleeved shirt and undershirt) was lowered down and I grasped it, expecting to have to pull myself up.

But no sooner had I grabbed ahold of the makeshift rope, than I shot up like a rocket into the air, only to be snatched from midair as Noah grabbed me. Holy shit, the man was strong! I'd had no idea. I clung to his neck in surprise, inhaling his crisp, clean, musky scent.

God, I'd missed him. I didn't realize how much until I had my hands on his bronzed shoulders. I clung to him for a moment, enjoying the feeling of being wrapped around him.

"Jackie, sweetheart," Noah breathed against my hair, and I felt him press a kiss into my curly hair. "Thank God you're safe."

"Yippee," said an unenthusiastic voice behind him. I glanced over his massive shoulder at the speaker— Delilah.

My fellow succubus wore her long blond hair in two curling pigtails atop her head, and she toyed with a sucker in her mouth. Her jeans were low slung and her baby pink sweater was so tight that I could see the indentation of her belly button. And her erect nipples. Charming as ever, and dressed a lot more provocatively than normal. I suspected that had something to do with Noah. "Hi, Dee."

She wiggled her fingers, looking less than pleased at Noah's reunion with me.

"Noah, you're here. That's amazing," I began. "But how did you escape the Serim? How did you get out of Mexico? How—"

"We'll talk about that later." He touched my cheek, as if needing to assess for himself that I was all right. "What happened here?"

I pulled away from him and stared at the wreckage of the club. There was a giant mess of debris where Midnight had once stood. "We set a trap for Remy—uh, Joachim," I corrected. "We were able to pull him out of Remy, but then Caleb took him. He put on the collar and everything went kablooey."

"A necklace?" Noah frowned. "What sort of necklace?"

I stared at the ruins in a daze. "Some sort of protection *shenu* thing." Where was Remy? Was this all for nothing? I stepped away from Noah, my eyes searching the wreckage.

"A *shenu*?" Noah grabbed my arm. "An ancient Egyptian *shenu*? Those were used to corral power—to boomerang it."

"No," I said, pacing around the wreckage. Where was Remy? "The *shenu* was used for protection Caleb told me so."

"Yeah, because vampires *never* lie," Dee chimed in.

It was a shame I didn't have time to punch her right now. "Caleb told me he got it from the queen."

"Jackie, did you ever stop to think that maybe the queen wanted him possessed? So he could bring the halo back to her?"

Well, no. I hadn't thought about that. A sick feeling swept over me, and I forced myself to refocus. "That's not important right now. We need to find Remy and Zane."

As if on cue, Ethan arose from the far end of the wreckage, all hulking shoulders and messy dark hair. His shirt hung at his waist, torn. Clinging to his leg like a damsel in some sort of Conan movie, was my friend.

"Remy," I yelled, circling around the ruins of the club to run back to her side. "Are you okay?"

She stared at me uncomprehendingly, then stared up at Ethan in a daze. "Big."

I knelt at her side and touched her cheek, turning her face to me. "Oh my God. We were so worried about you!"

She blinked, then looked up at Ethan again, and caressed his muscular leg. "So big."

Uh oh. Now was not the time. I took her arm and dragged her to her feet, though she resisted all the way. "Remy, say something coherent. Please. So I know Joachim didn't fry your brain."

She blinked again and looked over at me, then threw her arms around me in a bear hug. "Jackie!" she squealed. "You are the best friend ever!" Her mouth landed near my ear and she whispered in close, "And I see you brought me a present."

Ethan? She was welcome to him . . . if he was into that sort of thing. Judging by the dazed look on my Boy Scout's face, he had no clue what hit him.

Remy finished hugging me and moved on to Noah, launching herself into his arms so he could swing her around. "Noah! My boo! How are you, sweet thing?"

He laughed and put her back down again, only to have Remy squeal and move over to Dee, giving her air kisses. "This is so awesome! The gang's all here and my body is all mine again!" She touched her nose. "I think he broke my face, though. And dude, smell my hair—it's seriously rank."

I held up a hand. "Pass, thanks." At least she wasn't holding a grudge. I smiled at Remy's happiness, a bone-wearying sense of relief pushing through me. My friend was okay. Now we just needed to take care of a few other small problems.

Noah gave Remy a pat on the back and then moved back toward me, all purpose and movement. I watched him, my stomach churning in a mixture of happiness and a curious dread. Dee watched him approach me as well, her eyes narrow slits.

"Jackie," Noah said, pulling my hand into his again. He looked at my empty ring finger, and hurt crossed his face. "My safe was ransacked in Mexico. I was hoping you'd taken the things inside it, but I guess not."

"Yes, I have the ring and the painting," I said, squeezing his hand.

"You just chose not to wear the ring?" An expression of pain crossed his face, only to be hidden away by a stoic look. "Let's not talk about it now. This is not the time."

It wasn't, but at the same time, I didn't want it lingering like a big crappy stone around my neck. I grabbed it out of my pocket and shoved the ring box in his hand. "Here," I said. "Noah, I can't take it right now. I just can't."

Behind us in the wreckage, something stirred. I tried to turn to look, but Noah stepped in front of me and pushed the ring box back in my hands. "Jackie, I want you to have it. I want you to know that we can be together, forever."

"Noah," Dee began in an annoyed voice.

"I—Noah," I said, hesitating as he opened the box and revealed the gigantic diamond inside again.

At my side, Remy squealed and clapped her hands. "Jackie! You guys are engaged? You didn't tell me that!"

That was because we weren't. I looked at Noah with uncertain eyes. "We need to talk."

"Jackie, we belong together." Noah wrapped my fingers around the ring.

An animalistic snarl erupted from behind us, and Ethan shoved Remy behind him protectively. Dee instinctively stepped behind Noah.

The hole I had emerged from exploded with debris, and black wings flung themselves into the air, Zane hovering over the wreckage. His face was unholy to look at, his eyes brilliant red, his lips set in a hard snarl. His gaze was squarely on Noah.

"Again?" Zane growled, the sound nearly inhuman in its pain. "*Again* you will take her from me?"

"Uh oh," said Remy.

I stared at Zane, aghast. Did he think I was accepting Noah's proposal? I stared at the ring with horror and looked at Noah. His face was set in grim, angry lines as well.

"She's not yours," Noah said in a warning voice.

"*You can't have her!*" roared Zane in a blood-vessel-bursting voice. He dove at Noah, and our small party scattered as the two of them went flying backward, a sonic boom following them. "*Not again!*"

With an insane amount of force, Zane shoved Noah backward. They both skidded along the pavement, the concrete buckling as the two of them slammed backward, leaving a smoking trench behind them.

What the hell was going on? I shoved the hated ring back into my pocket once more.

"Zane! Noah!" I screamed, following as they plowed through the parking lot. "Stop it! Both of you! We need to come up with a plan to stop Caleb!"

"*Not again,*" Zane roared, plowing a fist into Noah's face.

Again? What were they talking about?

Noah's face, normally so smiling and friendly, was contorted with anger. He flipped the vampire over onto his back and plowed his fist into Zane's mouth. "You're a murdering bastard," Noah seethed. "You don't deserve to touch her."

Zane flung Noah backward and scrambled to his feet, arms flexing as if ready to go another round. Noah moved to his feet, too, circling around.

"What the hell are you two doing?" I called, moving forward.

Dee grabbed my arm, stopping me from moving forward. "Bad idea. This has been building for a few thousand years."

"What do you mean?"

She shook her head. "One of them is going to have to tell you. Until then, let them fight it off."

"It's kind of sexy and hot, don't you think?" Remy said in a fascinated voice. "Two sweaty men, fighting over the love of a woman."

"A succubus," corrected Ethan succinctly. "It is not the same thing as a woman."

"Really?" purred Remy. "'Cause I got the same body parts as a woman. Wanna see?" She plumped her breasts in his direction, her eyes brilliant blue with need.

Ethan froze in place and gave her a deer-in-headlights look.

Noah feinted to the left and grabbed Zane by the shoulders, throwing him forward into a telephone pole. It cracked and fell toward us and we scattered like a flock of birds. I ran for the two men. If I didn't stop them soon, they were going to tear apart the entire parking lot.

Zane launched himself in the air, grabbing the broken end of the heavy telephone pole and swinging it around as if it were a baseball bat. Noah ducked, and the pole went flying. Dee screamed and hit the pavement, and I was tempted to do the same.

Instead, I clenched my hands and screamed as loud as I could. *"ZANE!"*

He paused in the skies, an angry fury of black feathers, then dove in my direction. Noah shouted for me, but he didn't reach me before Zane did. My vampire moved forward and landed before me. He touched my face, his frantic red eyes searching my bleached silver ones.

"I *turned* you," he said, his voice panting and frantic. "You're *mine*. My creation. I made you. I turned you so we could be together. I won't lose you again."

The frantic, unhinged quality in his voice was starting to frighten me. I glanced over at Noah, who was watching close nearby, his eyes narrow slits. I'd never seen him so angry.

What did he mean, lose me again? The six months we'd been apart?

"He can't take you from me again," Zane said, stroking my cheek with hurried, possessive motions. "I made you what you are so we could be together forever. Again."

"Zane, what are you saying?" I shook my head, breaking free of his anxious grasp. Why would he choose to turn me . . . like that?

Maybe he saw the potential inside you and thought you deserved more than wasting away in a bland mortal life. He'd told me that the first time we'd made love.

But maybe it wasn't me he'd been thinking of . . . A cold feeling swept over me.

Remy coughed, really loudly.

"You guys suck," Dee said, coming to my side. "I can't believe it's been, how many months? And no one's told Jackie what the deal is?"

"No," I said, my gaze searching Zane's face, then Noah's. "What's going on?"

Noah turned away from Zane and focused on Delilah, his jaw cold and angry. "Stay out of this, Dee. I'm trying to protect her."

Protect me? Hold the hell up. "What exactly does that mean?"

Noah reached for my arm. Zane snarled and pulled me close, pressing me against his chest. At the sight of me cuddled against Zane, Noah's face darkened and his hands flexed.

I thought for a minute they were going to go at it again, except I was going to be sandwiched between them. I pushed away from Zane. "Tell me what you mean when you say 'again.'"

Zane was mutinously silent.

What was so bad that no one would speak of it? My heart aching, I turned to Noah for the answer. "Again?"

Noah crossed his arms over his chest. "Jackie—"

"*What do you mean, 'again,'*" I gritted. What were they hiding from me? "What happened in the past that made you two hate each other so much?"

You could have heard a pin drop. No one was answering.

Remy raised a fist to her mouth and began to fake-cough. "CoughRachaelcough."

"Rachael?" I gasped. "The shepherdess in the painting?"

The pieces slid into place. The painting of a Hebrew shepherdess. Zane's intense hatred for Noah. Noah's icy dislike of Zane. A woman in a painting with my face.

My world crashed around my ears.

"You guys are fighting over her . . . as me?" My hand began to tremble, and it felt like all the oxygen had been sucked out of my body. "You changed me because of . . . her?"

Not because of *me*? There hadn't been a spark of something special in a lonely nerd who'd stumbled out of a club? I just happened to have the same face as some other chick four-thousand-years dead?

Pain began to throb in my chest. I'd gone from two men fighting over me to . . . no one.

"Jackie," Zane began.

I raised a hand. The world was spinning around me, and I felt like throwing up. "I don't want to hear it right now. I really don't." I'd heard enough for the moment.

"Let me explain," Noah said in a gentle voice.

"No," I said, and took a step backward.

A warm, brown arm wrapped around my waist. Remy.

I felt like crying. Here she'd gone through hell, and she was offering me comfort. I wasn't worthy of her friendship. I leaned heavily against her. "I don't want to talk to either of you." The heavy weight in my pocket felt like a stone, and I grabbed the ring box out of it and flung it at Noah's feet. "Here. Take your fucking ring."

Noah flinched as if I'd slapped him.

As Zane stepped forward, I saw the triumph flash across his face. I pointed at him before he could move another step. "I don't want to hear from you, either."

I ignored the raw pain on his face and turned away from the two men—the two anchors in my Afterlife. The two big, fat liars who'd betrayed me. Zane, for never telling me the truth about why he'd turned me, and Noah for hiding the secret because his feelings weren't entirely for me.

Nothing was really for me. It was all for some other woman.

I wanted to cry.

Remy patted my shoulder. "Come on, Jackie. Let's go home."

I nodded and linked my arm with hers, walking away. To my surprise, Dee fell in line with us, her hand lightly touching my shoulder in support.

We got in the car, and I climbed into the backseat as shocked tears began to pour down my face. Ethan passed me a tissue and I crumpled it in my hand, swiping at my runny nose. I was as wrecked as the club was.

As we pulled out of the parking lot, I heard Zane cry my name in anguish.

CHAPTER FIFTEEN

As my spoon scraped the bottom of my container of tin roof ice cream, I gave a watery sniff. "I'm out again."

Delilah took her spoon out of her Soy Dream pint and generously offered it my way. "You can finish mine."

"No one wants that soy shit, Dee! Gross!" Remy slapped at Dee's hand with her spoon, leaving a wet streak. "What's wrong with you? She's in mourning! Here, you can eat mine." Remy shoved her favorite Ben & Jerry's into my hands. I took the carton with another sad sniff and began to shovel up the ice cream.

Delilah gave Remy a cross look and daintily swirled her spoon over the top of her Soy Dream. "It's an interesting flavor."

"You're a succubus. You don't have to eat health food, you know."

Dee just smiled. "When you're seven hundred years old, you learn to appreciate different textures and nuances of food. I'm currently enjoying the soy movement, thank you."

"Freak," Remy muttered, and grabbed the bottle of

coconut rum. "She's still crying. Time for another round of shots."

"Drowning her sorrows in alcohol and sugar isn't going to solve her problems." Dee glanced over at me, clearly disapproving as I continued to cram ice cream into my mouth. She leaned close and patted my knee. "Jackie, honey. You do know that ice cream will still exist tomorrow, even if you don't get to eat it all tonight?"

"Shut up," I said between mouthfuls, "I still hate you."

Remy held out a shot to me. "Come on. You know you want one." I reached for it, and she gave me an approving "Goooood girl."

"I'm not a dog, Remy," I said but downed the shot anyhow. It burned down my throat, too sweet and overpowering without a mixer, but I didn't care. It was my fourth bottle of rum and who-knows-how-many shots over the course of several hours. "My life is shit."

"Well, my life is back to awesome!" Remy said, falling backward in the pillows on the floor and wiggling like a wild animal. "My body is *mine* again! Yay! Suck it, Joachim!"

"How pleasant," Dee said in a disapproving voice. She gave Remy a light kick to her pajama-clad leg. "You're quite the lady."

"I was a lady for the first four hundred years," Remy said irrepressibly. "It's no fun. That's why I decided to be a slut for the next four hundred." She rolled onto her side and arched an eyebrow at us. "So far, it's much more fun."

Dee gave another disapproving sniff. "Well, I'm glad to see that you're feeling more like yourself, at least."

Remy cupped her own breasts and squirmed happily. "It all feels like myself."

I couldn't help but muster a faint smile at that. Crossing my legs, I leaned back on the mountain of pillows and blankets we'd spread on Remy's living room floor for our makeshift slumber party. "At least you're back to normal. One good thing came out of all this mess."

"Oh yes," Delilah said in a disagreeable voice. "If you ignore the fact that we have a super-powered, crazed vampire on the loose that could bring about the destruction of any immortal in a hundred-mile radius, and the fact that your two lovers are having emo fits as you cram ice cream into your face, then yes." She gave an innocent smile. "I'd say this was an unequivocal success."

Just for that, I shoveled up another mouthful. "You're not helping, Dee. I know we messed up, and that everyone is in danger if we don't get that stupid halo out of Caleb. You don't have to remind me of it every five minutes. Don't you have some dolls you should be sticking pins into?"

"I left yours at home, sorry."

I made a face at her.

Remy flipped over, undaunted by our sniping, and reached for the remote. "Want to watch another movie?"

Both Delilah and I groaned. "*No.*"

"I've seen enough of your pornos, Remy." Dee crossed her legs and sat up straighter. "Besides, my Itch is due tomorrow and I left my usuals at home. So I'll need to find someone." She gave me a sidelong look. "Mind if I borrow one of yours?"

Only if she didn't mind me pushing my spoon up her nostril.

I forced myself to give a casual shrug. "Do what you want, Dee. I don't control either of those men. They're the ones calling all the shots, remember? I'm just the blow-up doll they decided they can't share any longer."

Remy patted my knee. "Don't be so sad, Jackie. You're much better than a blow-up doll. No one has to rinse your holes out afterward."

A choking sound emerged from the kitchen. All three of us turned to see Ethan standing in the doorway, his face flushed dark. He wore a ruffled apron and carried a dustpan. "I'm sorry to interrupt," he said in his awkward, stiff voice. "But I am out of garbage bags."

"No problem!" Remy said, jumping up and bouncing to the kitchen. "Come on, Precious. I'll show you where *everything* goes." The way she purred it made it sound like far more than garbage bags.

I watched them leave and shook my head. "It feels wrong to put him to work like this."

"Oh pooh," said Dee, waving a hand. "He's getting a fix from it, and it keeps him distracted while we're all here. Poor thing isn't used to being around one succubus, much less three. Especially one that's pursuing him."

"I can't believe Remy's not more traumatized," I confessed to Dee. "I'm drinking away my sorrows at hearing that my masters are assholes. She's been possessed for the past six months and yet you'd think nothing happened to her."

"She's compartmentalizing," Dee said. "When you live for hundreds of years, you learn not to dwell on the bad or unpleasant for very long or you're just going to beat yourself down. Remy's lived through some horrible things in her past, and she prefers to enjoy the moment." Dee leaned over and patted my hand. "You know, compartmentalizing is a good skill for you to learn, too. It'll help you through the low moments. And when you're immortal and tied to two selfish pricks? There's quite a few low moments."

"So immortality is nothing but heartbreak, and I need to learn to live in the moment?"

She shrugged. "It's working for Remy, right? She's happy, she's carefree, and she's currently trying to sink her hooks into the hottest man nearby."

Poor Ethan. Remy's single-minded pursuit was going to be a major learning experience. Then again, it might be good for him. He was a little too wide eyed and innocent. But who was I to think that was a bad thing? I'd been all wide eyed myself once upon a time—before two assholes came into my life and ruined it.

I reached for the bottle of rum again and took a swig. "I *hate* men."

"That's a phase we all go through," Dee said, holding her hand out for her turn with the rum. "Comes with being a succubus, I think. I can't believe neither of them told you about the Rachael thing, though. It's very unlike Noah to be so withholding of information."

"Maybe he knew it'd piss me off," I retorted. "I still don't know anything about her, other than we shared the same fat face and it apparently gives immortals boners." Prying the rum out of her hand, I took another large swig and choked on the burning sensation as it poured down my throat. "Have you seen the painting? She's boring looking. Round face. Same horrible hair I used to have. Same dumpy figure. I don't get it."

"Haven't you realized that it's not always appearance that drives a man—or two—mad with love?"

I paused mid-swig and blinked at her. "You know the story? And you haven't said anything yet?"

She gave a dainty shrug and tucked her feet beneath her as she resettled on the pillows. "It's not my story to tell."

"Well, neither of those jerks seems to be interested in telling me the story, so why don't you share it?"

"Very well," said Dee. "Though you won't like it much. Back in the day, both Noah and Zane were a class of angel called a Watcher. The Watchers were charged to mingle with the humans and watch over them from the same plane. Kind of like guardian angels, but they posed as human. They ate at the dinner tables of human men, mingled with humans, and became friends with them. And of course fell in love with human women, since there are no female angels in Heaven.

"Noah and Zane were assigned the same area, Jericho in old Canaan. They knew each other and were fairly friendly, teasing and ribbing each other like brothers. Or so I've been told by Noah." She shook her head. "I can't see it, myself. I've never seen anything but loathing between those two."

Friendly and like brothers? Noah and Zane? They hated each other.

"Noah told me that he fell in love with a Retenu shepherdess named Rachael. Her family was very poor and her brother was a troublemaker, so one of the angels was constantly stopping by to assist the family." She gave a small shrug. "To hear it from Noah, there has never been another woman as kind and sweet and gentle as Rachael. Her laugh was musical, her smile was always welcoming, and she always thought of others before herself."

My stomach churned uncomfortably. Rachael sounded perfect. I laughed like a donkey and scowled more than I smiled. And I sure wasn't musical. "She sounds like a paragon."

"All that, and attractive and wholesome to boot. Noah fell for her, hard. It turns out that Zane had fallen for her, too. But neither of them knew about the other being in love with the same girl: Rachael was a quiet sort, so she never let on that both of them were courting her.

"One of the archangels found out about the Watchers mingling with humans when a Nephilim like your friend Ethan was born." When I paled, she quickly said, "Not Rachael's child, someone else's. Anyhow, the Powers

That Be in Heaven were totally pissed off that the angels were down here making babies with mortal women. It was forbidden, and the Watchers had a choice. They could give up their human women and continue to be angels. If they did so, they'd be reassigned to a job in Heaven that had no interaction with humans. Or they could choose to fall and be with their girlfriends."

"Both Noah and Zane chose to fall," I said softly. "And didn't realize they were falling for the same girl."

"You see the problem," Dee said, a sad note in her voice. "When they found out about each other, it was ugly. They fought and nearly destroyed Jericho with their anger—the city had to be rebuilt almost from scratch. Rachael was very upset, and even more upset when they demanded that she choose between them."

That sick twist in my stomach got even worse. I thought of the two men's reactions, and guessed. "She picked Noah?"

"She did," agreed Delilah. "And it devastated Zane. Back then he was still one of the Serim. Now, wingless, godless, and womanless, he had nothing left. I'm not surprised he turned to the vampire side, once Joachim did. I imagine the lure of wings was too strong to resist— even if it came with a terrible price tag."

The price tag of being the evil lackey of an insane vampiric bitch. Yeah, a definite downside. "Poor Zane," I murmured.

"Poor Noah," she corrected. "You know what Zane did next? He threw a fit, blew out the side of a cliff with his fists, and caused a rock slide. Unfortunately, he picked the hill that Rachael happened to be tending her flock under that day. She died rather horribly."

"He wouldn't do that!"

"You mean Zane wouldn't destroy a woman because she picked his greatest rival over him?" she said in a sour voice. "Just like he wouldn't change a woman into a sex-driven immortal simply because she looks like his favorite piece of ass from ancient history?"

I flinched and stumbled to my feet. I needed to get away.

Delilah reached for my hand to stop me. "Look, Jackie, I'm trying to help you. I have yet to meet a succubus who was turned because someone wanted to help her out. You have to face the facts: we're enslaved to the whims of a bunch of selfish immortals. Forget about your vampire master. He's bad news—untrustworthy, weak, and bitter. If you can, stay away from him." She gave me a little smile and squeezed my fingers. "I'd tell you that Noah's the best of the lot, but he's just as self-righteous as any other. And besides—I want him for myself."

I shook off her hand and stepped away. My head pounded, the horrible story circling round and round in my mind.

Zane hated Noah because Noah stole Rachael from him.

Noah hated Zane because Zane had been instrumental in Rachael's death.

I'd been turned because the frumpy old me was a

stand-in for a girl who had been dead for four thousand years. And there was an element of revenge to my existence. Noah wanted to possess me to keep me from Zane. Zane wanted to possess me because Noah wanted me.

What about . . . *me*? Didn't anyone want Jackie? My stomach heaved.

"Are you okay?" Dee asked, behind me.

"I think I'm going to puke."

"Not on the living room carpet," called Remy from the kitchen. "Ethan just steamed it."

Luckily, I made it to an upstairs bathroom before losing my cookies. I found a bottle of water in my old mini-fridge and hung out on the balcony, watching the sun rise and trying to clear my mind of the horrible thoughts that wouldn't go away.

I kept seeing Zane's face, in anguish at the sight of the ring Noah gave me.

Had he killed Rachael just because he couldn't have her? What would he do if I went with Noah?

And despite knowing the horrible secrets of his past, why did I still want to be with Zane?

CHAPTER SIXTEEN

I sighed, staring out over the rolling, landscaped lawn in the early morning light. So beautiful. So peaceful. And we were all so screwed if we didn't get that halo out of Caleb. We needed a plan to stop him, and I didn't have one.

The pool boy was in the distance, standing by Remy's swimming pool. I watched him for a minute, envious. How simple it must be to be a pool boy, with no bigger worries than skimming leaves out of the crazy rich woman's swimming pool.

I watched him stand by the pool for a few moments longer, then leaned forward and frowned. He looked normal, dressed in grass-stained jeans, a white T-shirt, and a backward baseball cap. Young, kind of a thick body, with square shoulders and a deep tan. Normal. Except . . . he wasn't working. He was just standing by the pool.

As if sensing me watching him, he turned and gazed up at the balcony. Then he began to walk purposefully across the manicured lawn toward me.

A creepy feeling began to stir inside me, and I stood up as he came beneath the balcony.

"Jacqueline Brighton," he said in the hollow voice of the possessed.

The hair on the back of my neck stood up. I had no idea if this was friend or foe—was he possessed by an angel or a demon? I took a step backward. "Who are you? What do you want?"

"The Angel Gabriel sends you a message," said the man.

I should have felt better that it was an angel in the body of the pool boy, but I didn't. Angels were just as quick to mislead you with their version of the truth, and way more self-righteous than any demon that I'd met. Combine that with the fact that the message was important enough to seek me out at Remy's house? I was very concerned.

I raced out of the house and strode across the lawn toward him, the angelic script burning on my wrist. "Who are you? What is the message?"

"The Archangel Gabriel wishes to remind you that the power of the archangels needs to be removed from this plane and neutralized, or else all of the world is in peril."

"I didn't forget. We had a bit of an . . . unexpected snag."

"You need to remove the archangel's power and bring it to Gabriel to ensure the safety of the world."

"I know." I pinched the bridge of my nose, feeling a headache coming on. "It's not like I willfully decided someone else could just have it. Like I said, we'll get it back, and then I'll give it to your boss—if he proves he can be trustworthy."

The pool boy pointed at me. "The Archangel Gabriel gave you his word. You should not doubt him."

The tattoo on my wrist burned again. "I'm not doubting. And don't worry, I'm certainly not going to give the halo back to the vampires. Is there anything else?"

His unblinking eyes stared up at me. "Just that if you do as he commands, you will be granted a boon."

I already knew that. Didn't need a recap. "Any boon?" I asked sarcastically. "Anything at all?"

"Anything," intoned the possessed man.

"Can I go back in time?"

"If you wish."

"What if I want a pony?"

"If you wish," he repeated.

Yeah, that was a joke. "What if I want to bring someone back from the dead?"

"If you wish," he said again.

That made me pause. I could ask for . . . *anything*? Good Lord. "That must be one important halo, if I have carte blanche like that."

"It is."

Well, then.

"Where is Joachim's halo currently?" said the possessed man.

Oh. Er. "It's safe," I told him with a big lying smile. I suspected that he wouldn't care to hear that it was currently attached to one of the fanged persuasion.

"Where is it safe, currently?"

Man. I could see where Noah got his annoying stubbornness from. It seemed to be an angelic trait. "Safe," I edged.

The possessed man continued to stare at me.

"Safe inside someone." When his expression changed, I quickly added, "Don't worry. I'm going to get it back tonight."

That was the deadline the queen had given us to get the halo back, or she'd destroy Remy. Even though Remy was free of the halo now, I wasn't sure if all the rules continued to apply.

And what would she do to Zane once she found out that the halo had gotten away again? I swallowed. "Tonight," I repeated.

"What is your plan?"

I confessed, "I don't have a plan at the moment."

The angel-possessed pool boy stared at me, unmoving. "Have you met James Quinton Cooper?"

"Doesn't ring a bell, no."

"Visit him. He will be able to help you with a plan."

Somehow, knowing that James Quinton Cooper had been vetted by the angels made me want to actively avoid him. "I'll keep that in mind. Thanks for the advice."

"You do not want to fail in this endeavor," he reminded me in a stern, hollow voice. "All of humanity is counting on you."

Gee, no pressure.

"Good luck in your efforts." His eyes rolled back, and I sensed he was about to exit, stage left.

"Wait," I yelped, and grabbed his arms. "I have more questions!"

Too late—his entire body shivered, then he collapsed to the ground, taking me with him. I climbed over his body. "Hello? Are you okay?" I patted the guy's cheek. "Speak to me, angel flunky."

No answer.

His face was red and flushed, so I grabbed his shirt collar and pulled him up, trying to elevate his head. Did possession involve a blood rush? Remy's pulse had moved super fast, so maybe that explained the flush. I gave him a little jiggle, trying to awaken him. "Earth to angel, earth to angel, come in, please. You forgot to tell me how I can find James Quinton Cooper."

His eyelids fluttered, and the pool boy awakened. He slowly focused on me, and an adoring smile lit his face. "Hey there, gorgeous."

His voice was normal.

I let go of his shirt, and he fell backward onto the grass. "Sorry," I said, getting to my feet. "Mistook you for someone else."

I headed back inside the house, pondering the advice I'd just received.

Remy was in the kitchen, sitting up on the counter. Her dusky foot was in Ethan's lap and he was carefully painting her toenails, a look of intense concentration on his face.

"Paint a white flower on the big toe," Remy said imperiously. "And a green one on the next toe. Vary it up."

I skidded to a halt at the bizarre sight. "Am I interrupting something?"

Remy looked up and gave me a cheerful smile, waving me over. "Not at all! I am having Ethan do my toes." She wiggled her brows at me. "Later on, if he's good, he can do me, too."

Ethan's hand jerked, splashing white nail polish across Remy's toes.

"Clean that up," she demanded. "I don't like dirty toes."

"Of course," Ethan murmured, unruffled. As he stood and moved across the room to get a towel, I noticed his eyes flashing like mad.

I moved to Remy's side as she scowled down at the splashes on her feet. "You should be nicer to him."

"I am," she said, admiring her foot. "Ethan's used to orders since he was raised in sanctuary. Giving him orders is the kindest thing I can do for him." She looked over at me and winked. "Well, second kindest."

"I'm pretty sure he's a virgin, Remy."

She pursed her lips, as if thinking about that for a moment. Her nose wrinkled, and then she shrugged, eyes brilliant blue. "I'll be gentle with him."

I shook my head. "Ethan has been a great help to me. Don't mess him up with sex. Not now, when we need his help getting the halo back out of Caleb."

"Let's make sure we find something else to store it in

other than the harem girl, 'kay?" She gave me a chipper look. "Speaking of, any ideas?"

Boy, she really *could* compartmentalize. I shrugged and moved to the fridge, peering inside it. We hadn't had a chance to go shopping, and everything left inside was old and moldy. "I don't know," I said, turning a jar of pickles to see the expiration date on it. Last month. Well, they might be a bit tart but still edible. I pulled it out and looked for a fork. "I ran into an angel, though. He was in your pool boy."

"Oh? Did he have anything interesting to say?"

"No deals," I admitted. I still found that strange. Maybe because I was too used to everyone having their own agenda. Or maybe because my agenda and Gabriel's were the same at the moment. I unscrewed the jar and speared a pickle, then held it out to Remy. She took it and I speared a second pickle for myself. "He did tell me to go find some guy named James Quinton Cooper and get his help."

Remy began to cough, spraying my face with pickle.

"Too bitter?" I eyed my pickle with dismay. I was so hungry.

"James Cooper?" she gasped. "That old pervert?"

I looked at her with surprise. "You know him?"

She gave me a look of horror. "He's Dee's old boyfriend. 'Old' being the key word."

"Old boyfriend, huh?" I said as Remy, Ethan, and I pulled up to a large, two-story house in an older subdivision named Rolling Acres. Every house on the street was cookie cutter—a cute covered porch, neutral colors, immaculate lawns, and a minivan parked out front. All except the house on the end, which had to be James Quinton Cooper's house. Here, the charming wood shingling was in desperate need of a paint job and the yard looked like it hadn't been mowed in six months. Maybe longer.

Remy nodded, propping her sunglasses on top of her head as she stared at the house. "Yeah, that's why she didn't want to come with us. Bad memories."

Bad memories for a voodoo priestess? Now *that* was something. "Do tell," I said, eyeing the house. A zillion wind chimes filled the porch, yet they couldn't hide the fact that the windows were boarded up with wood—on the inside. "We sure someone lives here?"

"It looks uninhabited," offered Ethan. "Should I go in first and make sure the place is safe?"

I snorted. Nothing was safe since I'd turned into a succubus.

"Unless he's moved his wacky mad scientist lab in the last six months, he's still here," Remy said, and pulled something out of the back of the car. "Here, you'll want this."

I caught the piece of clothing she threw at me and eyed it skeptically. "A turtleneck? Really?"

She was busy pulling a green one over her T-shirt. "You'll thank me later. Trust me."

Ethan held his hand out for a shirt.

"You don't get one." Remy ignored his hand. "You don't have boobs."

He flushed. "I see."

"You will," she said cheerfully. "Now hurry up and dress, Jackie. It's hotter than a demon's tit with all these layers on."

Dutifully, I pulled it over my Spinal Tap T-shirt. Pink wasn't my color, but I wasn't here to be fashionable. I got out of the car and headed for the front door, Remy and Ethan on my heels. I lifted the door knocker and smacked it a few times against the peeling wood door.

"This is like the house that time forgot," Remy snarked. "Old James isn't much of a decorator."

"Oh, I don't know," I said, reaching toward one of the wind chimes. "He looks like he's fairly creative." The metal wind chimes came in various shapes and forms. One was made of gears dangling from fishing wire, but the rest seemed to be made of symbols I couldn't put my finger on. I pulled at one shaped like a Y that dangled from a dark piece of chewed rawhide. At the touch of it, a tingle swept over my body.

"Wouldn't touch those," said Remy. "Who knows what kind of juju ol' James has this place spelled with?"

I dropped it immediately. "These are for protection?"

"Probably," she said, moving forward and pounding on the door with her fist. "*Hey, old man,*" she yelled. "*It's Remiza—Noah's friend. Open up.*"

"Remiza?" Ethan gave Remy a slight bow. "It is a beautiful name for a beautiful woman."

She gave him a saucy wink and a flirty push to the shoulder. He never called her "succubus" or by her full name. He followed her around like a lost puppy. He painted her freaking toenails.

Someone had a major crush.

And someone was bound to get his heart broken, I thought as I watched her smile up at him. Remy wasn't the monogamous type, and Ethan was the virginiest virgin that had ever lived. No good could come of this.

My thoughts were distracted as someone came to the door. We heard creaking footsteps long before the chains on the door began to clank as they were undone, then the front door opened.

A tiny old man with sloped shoulders stood on the other side. He held a blowtorch in his free hand and wore a welding mask atop his head. "Where's the angel boy?"

"He's not around." Remy gestured at the torch. "You wanna put that away? We need a favor."

"Oh, oh, of course," said the man, and just like that, shut down the torch. "Won't you ladies come in?"

Ethan stepped inside the house first, brandishing his bo staff at his side. James didn't look too thrilled to see him enter, but his expression perked up when Remy and I followed. The house was something out of a pack rat's wet dreams—wall-to-wall clutter lined the rooms. Every piece of furniture was stacked high with old newspapers, magazines, boxes of miscellaneous parts, old computers, and God only knew what else.

"So nice to see you, ladies," he said to my boobs, and wiped a bit of drool from his mouth.

Greaaat. Just what we needed. I leaned over to whisper to Remy, "I'm starting to see why Delilah wouldn't come with us."

She nodded. "Plus, it'd violate the restraining order if she came within one hundred feet of him."

Oh boy. This just got better and better. "How do they know each other?"

"Delilah was his girlfriend about sixty years ago. She dumped him and he refused to let her go no matter what sort of voodoo she cast on him. Noah kind of watches over him to make sure he doesn't head back to New Orleans and harass her again, but mostly we just try to avoid the old perv."

The elderly man moved to my side, stroking his wrinkly hand down my arm. "You're a pretty, pretty one, aren't you?"

"That's me," I said in a flat voice. "Nice and pretty. And I need your help."

It left a sour taste in my mouth to say that, especially when his eyes lit up.

"You need my help?"

"That's right," I said, forcing myself to be cheerful. "An angel sent me."

"I'll say he did," said the old man, brushing his hand over the front of his pants.

Ew. I resisted the urge to cross my arms over my breasts. "I mean a *real* angel. Like, Gabriel. He told me that you could help me stop a vampire that's been possessed by a crazy archangel."

He smiled. "Well then, young lady, you've come to the right place."

Relief passed through me. "I have?"

"Yes. Come down into my laboratory with me." He took my hand in his.

I glanced backward at Remy, who made a shooing motion with her hands. "We're right behind you."

Yippee. I allowed the old man to drag me through the cluttered house. The place reeked of loser bachelor pad and crazy old inventor. Opened bags of ramen noodle littered the kitchen countertop, and the walls were bare of everything except for magazine centerfolds and some Dallas Cowboys cheerleaders posters. He led me to the basement, going down a long flight of rickety steps into inventor wonderland.

The basement was huge and littered with junk, garbage, and antiques. James continued to lead me back to a desk where several full bookshelves lined the walls, and the desk itself was covered in all kinds of schematics and drawings.

"Nice place," I said, prying my hand free as he sat in the single chair in the room. A calico cat appeared and began to rub against my legs, purring. I reached down to pet it. "You've got a great mad scientist vibe here."

"Not a mad scientist in the slightest," he said, shooing the cat away from my legs. He placed his cane against the desk, then patted his knee. "Now come and sit and tell me what you need."

I didn't like that gleam in his eyes. I grabbed Remy and pulled her forward. "Remy'll sit with you."

"Succubus," Ethan began in a warning tone but was silenced when James raised his hand.

"I've seen her titties on tape," he said. "Ain't got nothing new under that shirt. It's you I want to see." He wiggled his eyebrows at me.

Ethan's breath choked out of his throat, and Remy gave me a smirk.

"I don't want to sit on your lap, Mr. Cooper," I explained patiently. "If I need to sit, I can sit on the floor."

He screwed up his face and scowled at me. "Did you want my help or not?"

"I do."

"Well?"

I waited.

He waited.

With a loud sigh, I moved forward and sat on his bony knee. "If you touch my boobs, I am out of here."

"Understood," he said, his eyes level with my rack. A smile creased his wrinkled face. "Now, tell me what my sweet red firecracker needs from her Poppy." His hand slid to my ass.

"For starters, you can call me Jackie. And for double starters, don't ever call yourself Poppy again." I pushed his hand off my ass.

Remy sat on the floor at my feet, followed by Ethan.

She petted the friendly cat, her expression serious as she stared up at James. "It's so good of you to help us, Poppy."

I narrowed my eyes at Remy. She was so dead when we got home. So. Very. Dead.

"There's this evil archangel who is possessing people," I began. "He was possessing Remy for a long time. When we moved him out of her, he got transferred into a vampire who used an enchanted collar that was supposed to trap the power but transferred to him instead. And now the archangel's super-powerful and is probably going to kill everyone, so we need something to get him out of the vampire."

James rubbed his chin thoughtfully. "Can't kill him or destroy him, I suppose."

"Right." I clasped my hands in my lap. "We need some sort of vessel to contain him. He can't be destroyed, just transferred."

"Well, the obvious solution would be to move him back to a different object, or a less dangerous person."

Gosh, why didn't I think of that? I thought sarcastically.

"Now get up, because you're killing the circulation on my knee."

I gladly got up and watched as he began to sort through some of the papers on his desk. "How did you say he was transferred out of Remiza?" he asked.

"A collar," she offered.

"A *shenu*," I corrected. "Everything I've read says it was a protective amulet, but the vampire used it to boomerang the power into himself." Evil bastard.

"He is a vampire," the old man said, his voice dry and raspy with age. "Were you expecting puppies and kittens?"

"I kind of like you, James," Remy said.

"Ancient Egyptian magic?" The old man shuffled to a nearby shelf covered with old, dusty books. "I think I know just the thing to solve your problem." He pulled down a book, flipping through the pages. "*Djed . . . djed . . . djed*," he muttered to himself. "It's in here somewhere."

"What's a *djed*?" Archaeology was one of my passions, but I didn't recall every single symbol in ancient Egypt's long, symbol-filled history. "An ankh? The crook and flail? A sistrum?"

The old man crowed, his finger stabbing at one of the pages. "Here it is! I remembered it because it has to do with semen."

I stared at him. "Beg your pardon?"

James ran his fingernail under a paragraph of text in the book. "The *djed* was a fertility totem and a symbol of intense power. It represented the base of the spine. The ancient Egyptians believed that semen sprang forth from there." He flipped a page, reading further. "The *djed* ensured that the carrier would bring stability with him wherever he went."

"So we need that?" I said, leaning in to look at the book. Stability sounded like just the thing.

He nodded. "It's like a power magnet. Whoever carries it pulls *in* power from his or her surroundings. It calls power to the bearer and stabilizes it. I think it should be able to give you the edge over this vampire that stole your halo."

My hands clasped in relief. "So we can use this *djed* thing on Caleb and get the archangel's spirit out of him?"

"If we have a spine," he agreed in a mild voice. "A spine from a sacrificial animal is required. That, and some magic spells." He flipped the page. "A few incantations, make the staff magic, and you're good to go. You just need the spine."

"Where are we going to get a spine to smack a vampire with, old man?" Remy asked.

"I have one." He peered at the shelves full of clutter. "Somewhere around here."

I took a step backward, eyeing him. "You just happen to have a spine laying around?"

He shrugged his rounded shoulders. "You never know when an emergency is going to call for ancient magic. I was trying to make one for myself because I loaned my last *djed* out to a very nice warlock. Handy things, those *djed*."

"So you'll give it to us?"

"For a price. It'll take a few hours for me to do the proper incantations, but I think I can squeeze it in this afternoon."

Here it comes. I crossed my arms over my chest. "And what sort of price are we talking?"

He stared at my breasts again. "I want to touch those."

"Ew! No."

"Fine," he said angrily, throwing his hands up. "No *djed* for you!" He began to stomp away.

Ethan and Remy sprang to their feet. Remy pinched my arm hard, and Ethan looked as if he wanted to attack James for even suggesting such a thing.

"What's the big deal, Jackie?" Remy hissed at me. "It's not like you haven't shown them to anyone else. Hell, you've shown them to Luc and to Noah and to Zane—and I bet even Ethan has seen them."

A flush of shame crossed my face. Ethan *had* seen them. I kept my arms crossed over my chest protectively. "So what? That doesn't make it any less gross."

"You will not touch her breasts," Ethan said in a low, angry voice, looming over James's much smaller form. "The succubus said no, and that is the final answer."

Remy rolled her eyes and stepped forward. "Look, I'm sure we can figure things out if we're all reasonable," she said in a soothing voice. "What about a quick grab? Over the clothing, no nipple. I think that's perfectly acceptable, don't you, Jackie?"

I gave her a horrified look. "No!"

"I want under the clothing," James bargained. "No nipple." He gestured with his hand. "Unless she wants to throw a little something special my way."

"I sat in your lap, but that is it," I ground out.

"Fine," he said, turning away from us again. "Let the vampire keep the halo. See if I care. I'll be down here in my basement with my *djed* and my books."

Remy gave an irritated sigh, then moved back to James's side, putting her arm around his shoulders. "James, dear. Let's compromise. We need that staff, which means we need your *djed*. Jackie doesn't have time to go out and sacrifice an animal on her own." She gave me a warning look.

"That's right," I echoed. "No time. Very busy."

"How about," she said in a low coo, "you make us that nice *djed* thing with whatever you have laying around, and I let you touch my breasts instead."

"Remiza!" Ethan sounded scandalized.

I kicked him. "Let her show them if she wants to!"

James still looked unconvinced. "I like the redhead. I've seen your boobs on the television before—"

"I'll throw in a motorboat," she coaxed.

Frowning, Ethan leaned down to me. "What is a motorboat, Jackie Brighton?"

"It's where he sticks his face between her boobs and rubs it all around," I replied. That was not going to go over well with the Boy Scout. "Ethan, maybe you should leave—"

"A motorboat for a *djed*," James declared triumphantly. He rubbed his arthritic, wrinkled hands together. "You have yourself a deal!"

"Super!" Remy reached for the hem of her shirt and began to tug it upward.

"I'm leaving," said Ethan in a disgusted voice.

CHAPTER SEVENTEEN

By the time we hit the highway on the way back to Remy's house, my eyes were a brilliant blue. Judging by the looks Remy was giving Ethan, she had a plan to fix her Itch.

I, on the other hand, did not have any plans for my Itch, and it would be returning all too soon. After all, I'd been used and abused by both of my boyfriends and was now flying solo.

Maybe I'd starve for a few days. Punish myself as well as my body. Served me right for being gullible enough to fall for their stupid lies.

The car hit a speed bump, causing a surge of pleasure to course through my lower body. Damn. I must have been thinking about the Itch too much—thinking about it made it show up. I clamped my legs tightly together and bit my lip, determined to ignore the sensation. Maybe it was back so fast because I was still healing.

"Oooh, that felt good," Remy said, glancing over at me with a grin. "Want me to turn around and go over it again?"

"No," I gritted. "Let's just go home."

"You're in a cranky mood."

"I'm still pissed at Noah and Zane. So get used to the cranky, because it's probably going to be around for a few days."

She said, "You need to do what I do, my friend. Hakuna matata."

"I can't believe you're spouting advice from *The Lion King*." Actually, I could. That was even worse.

"What I'm saying is, don't let the bad crap bother you. Put it in storage to think about some other time. Like, three weeks from never."

"I can't just shut it off, Remy," I said in a tired voice. "And I can't stop thinking about the Itch, either."

She glanced in the rearview mirror at Ethan. "I hear you," she said in a purring voice. "Neither can I."

"Remy," I warned in a whisper, "he's innocent. Don't mess with him. That wouldn't be fair."

"Oh pooh," she said, swerving around a car at a stop sign. "He's a good guy, and he's big and handsome. Best of all, he can't command you like the last two men you were with. So his drawbacks? Very small in comparison to the very, very large parts of him, if you know what I mean."

I flushed. "Don't be sick."

"I'm just saying." She cut around another car and nearly hit a parked one with her swerve. "You know why I love humans? Because they can't control me. And you know why I love the average human man? Because when he gets an amazing roll in the sack, he is grateful for it. He adores me for it. An immortal thinks he has rights to my body, or that he owns me. And I'm a little tired of being owned by people. That's why I like human dick instead of immortal dick."

I could see her point. "But we're not talking about my love life, Remy. We're talking about you and Ethan."

"I know. And he's a perfect blend of both worlds—he's hot, young, fierce, and has no power over either one of us, so he's safe." She pulled into the driveway with a screech. "I'm just saying . . . if we asked, I'd bet he'd be happy to be the meat in a succubus sandwich."

Oh God, that sounded really hot. "Passing on all sandwiches!"

Ethan leaned forward. "Do you require a sandwich? Would you like for me to prepare one for you?"

"No!" I blurted. "Not hungry!"

Remy gave him a sly smile. "I think she likes being the meat, not the bun."

He shook his head. "I do not understand you."

"Trust me, you don't want to know, Ethan," I retorted.

"Maybe he does," Remy purred.

I jerked my seat belt off, escaping out the door. I didn't really want to hear any more innuendo from Remy—it was making my blood pound in my veins. And poor Ethan—he was free to do what he wanted, but I wondered if Remy would come on a bit too strong for him. I supposed he had to learn about women at some point. And it'd be a favor to her, which he'd get off on, as well.

Win-win situation for them. Too bad I wasn't as casual about jumping into bed with another man. I wanted

Zane. And Noah. Preferably together. But that was just the Itch talking; I was still mad at both of them.

And I was even more hurt than mad.

I sighed as I walked up the driveway to Remy's house. Still jittery with the Itch and distracted by thoughts of Zane and Noah, it was difficult to compose my thoughts. Focus. Focus. Remy's giggles floated through the air, and I winced, picturing her seducing Ethan over the hood of the car. Didn't want to think about that. Ugh. Pushing the door open, I stepped over the threshold and stripped off my extra turtleneck.

Noah was waiting inside the house.

He stood up from the couch at the sight of me. He wore a suit like he normally did on weekdays, with the collar open and loose, displaying a tanned chest, and his golden blond hair brushed against his collar. His beautiful forehead was creased with worry lines that smoothed as his gaze roamed over me, making sure that I was well.

I stopped at the sight of him. Blood coursed through me, hot and thick with need. I licked my suddenly dry lips. "How did you get in?"

He gestured at the door. "Remy's wards are broken. Feels like they have been for some time. I let myself in. The door was unlocked." He looked at me with eyes the pale silver of a satisfied immortal.

That irritated me—he didn't need sex for another three and a half weeks. I needed it in the next day or so. I hated him for that, too. "I don't want to see you. I'm still mad at you."

"Jackie," he began, moving toward me.

I put a hand up to block him. "No. I told you I don't want to see you. Why can't you respect that?"

"Because you're not giving me a chance," he said, anger edging his voice. "I didn't choose to turn you. Zane did. Why are you blaming me?"

A good point—not that it mattered. Rage and hurt blasted through me, and I slapped the turtleneck sweater against his broad chest. "Because you *lied* to me. You never told me the truth about Rachael." I hit him with the sweater again for good measure. "That makes you just as wrong as him."

He grabbed the sweater, using it to tug me forward. He pulled me into his arms. "Jackie—"

I batted his hands away, still furious, but they kept coming back to stroke my arms. The Itch spiraled through me, and I moaned with need. "Noah, don't," I whispered. "Please."

His hands dropped and instead of stroking my skin, he pulled me against him in a tight bear hug. Nice, and at least it wasn't inflaming my senses like before. I settled into his embrace, pressing my cheek against his lapel. Under the clothing, he was warm and smelled wonderful, and a bolt of sheer longing washed over me. I didn't want Noah and Zane to be bad for me.

I wanted to go back to being ignorant.

Noah stroked my back. "I'm sorry that you're mad, Jackie. I was just trying to protect you."

Great, he had to go and ruin it by talking.

I pushed away from him with irritation. "I don't need protection. I'm not twelve, Noah. I'm an adult. Just like you."

"You're only twenty-seven years old," he said in a gentle voice. "I'm four thousand years old. Trust me that if I think something strange is going on, I probably know what I'm talking about."

"Funny that you bring up age, because I seem to recall you offering me a ring a few days ago, and you didn't have a problem with me being twenty-seven then."

His jaw clenched. "That was different, Jackie, and you know it. I want to marry you because I love you and I can keep you safe."

The whole "keep me safe" thing was the part I kept sticking on. Keep me safe from everything? From anything in the outside world that would hurt my feelings, like the truth? Would I wake up in fifty or a hundred years to find myself living in a bubble, cut off from everything and anything that might possibly wound my tender sensibilities?

A bitter smile touched my face. Would he even know that he was hurting me? The protective instinct was so strong in Noah. I loved him for that, even as it drove me insane. He couldn't change the way he was.

Just like I couldn't change how I felt. "Noah, I don't want to be protected. I can't be." I pushed away from him, my hands still resting on his chest. "You're not doing me any favors by trying to shelter me from everything. Protecting me from the truth only means it hurts more when it comes out. And you know it always will."

Noah's jaw set in a stubborn clench that told me that what I was saying wasn't sinking in. "Jackie, listen to me for a moment."

Well, hell. I had no choice after that command. I gave him an exasperated look, silent and obedient.

He ignored the annoyance on my face, and shoved up the long sleeve of his jacket, exposing the tattoo on his wrist. The delicate wording crawled across his skin in a language I couldn't read—angelic. I wore a similar tattoo on my own wrist now, thanks to Gabriel. "Four thousand years ago, I gave my word to a woman I loved." His voice caught in his throat, but he continued on, his voice harsh. "I promised that I would always keep her safe. And I wasn't able to fulfill that promise."

My eyes filled with tears.

"I promised Rachael that I'd watch her and take care of her. I never imagined that Zane might destroy her. When I found her body, it was too late. She was dead." Anguish racked his voice, and he shook his wrist at me, emphasizing the tattoo. "This is why I still wear the mark to this day. Because I could not keep my word."

I stared at the swirling script written on his skin, Gabriel's word burning into my own. Poor Noah. I was so torn. Part of me wanted to hate Rachael. I was just the poor imitation of her, the replacement model. But I couldn't hate her, any more than I could hate Noah or Zane for trying to hold on to her memory with me . . . even if it was grossly unfair to me.

My anger diminished a little, mixed with sadness. I was so confused about the whole thing; I didn't know what I wanted anymore.

He pulled me close to him again. "Jackie, say something to me. I can't bear to see you look at me with such sad eyes." His hand caressed my cheek with longing. "This pain is exactly what I wanted to protect you from, until you were ready to learn the truth."

"Trust me, this wouldn't have been easier to learn fifty years from now," I said in a soft voice. Being second choice never got any easier. "Let's not fight about this right now, all right?"

"Your eyes are blue," he said, leaning in to lightly brush his lips against mine. "Your need is coming. I can help you with that."

"I don't want your charity, Noah. I can't *believe* that you would stoop to offer that."

"Not charity," he said in a husky voice, pulling me close despite my reluctance. "Never charity."

I felt the hunger spiral through me, felt my fingers flex against his chest. "I don't know that I can trust you—or Zane—anymore. I don't want to be a replacement body for someone else."

He lifted my hand to his lips, kissed my palm. Hot fire scorched through my body. "You're not. My feelings for you are for *you*."

I wasn't sure I trusted that, but the blood was singing

in my veins and I couldn't think past his lips skimming over my palm. I moved forward, letting the tips of my breasts brush against his jacket, and sucked in a breath at the sensation that flowed through me.

"Don't hurt yourself just to be a martyr, Jackie," Noah said, releasing my hand and cupping my face. He lightly kissed my eyebrow, then kissed the tip of my nose. My breath fluttered out of my throat as he continued to press small, light kisses along my cheekbones, then my jaw. My fingers curled on his lapels and my mouth sought his in desperate longing. His tongue swept into my mouth and I met its welcome stroke. Heat flared through my body, and I felt the Itch pulse harder than ever.

Even though my feelings were mixed, there was no denying the Itch. As his hand slid down to my breast my hand was sliding to his cock, stroking it through his pants. His tongue flicked into my mouth, darting and suggestive, and I didn't need much convincing after that. When his hands slid to my ass and hiked me against him, I wrapped my legs around his waist. Unfazed by my weight, he began to carry me toward the stairs. I kissed Noah passionately as he held me against him up to my room, then tossed me down on the bed.

His warm body was laying against mine a second later. "We need to satisfy your Itch, Jackie. There's time to think about other problems later." And his mouth swept over mine again.

"Yes," I said against his lips, though it came out more like "Yeth" because his tongue was sweeping into my mouth again. "But what kind of girl am I if I use you when I'm mad at you?" My fingers wouldn't stop roaming over his clothing, desperate to touch the golden skin underneath.

"A human one," he said, giving my jaw a small nip, and I was lost at that. If Noah wasn't going to hold it against me, I wasn't going to, either. I didn't protest as he sucked on my lower lip. My tongue met his, flicking against it with desire and need. Noah always tasted so good.

His mouth began to press small kisses up and down my throat and cheeks, slow and soft, tasting me with every brush of his lips against my skin. I shivered with pleasure. His fingers stroked over my bare arms until my body was a mass of quivering nerves, and my hips began to rise with every touch. He ignored it, taking his sweet time as he pressed his mouth to every inch of exposed skin. Then he slid a hand under my shirt and began to hike it up, exposing my stomach. I wriggled as he kissed down my throat and then moved to my belly, continuing to hike my shirt as he kissed and licked my flat stomach. His tongue dipped into my navel, and when I shivered, he kissed the prickles away. Slow. Methodical. Seductive.

So, so good.

He glanced up at me, and his silver eyes had changed to a deep, liquid blue. "Clothing off."

I didn't need to be told twice. As he shucked his gray sports coat and button-down shirt, I kicked my shoes off and shimmied out of my T-shirt, jeans, and my bra and panties. He didn't chuckle at my eagerness like he usually did, just moving back to my side when he was equally unclothed, his hand brushing out to touch my cheek again in a soft, tender move.

"So serious," I breathed, trying to lighten the atmosphere a little.

His mouth dipped to my shoulder, sending ripples of pleasure through me. He didn't reply to my comment, only continued to kiss my body as he pressed me down onto the bed again. There was nothing but affection and desire in each small, tender kiss. As he lavished attention on my belly and hips, I ran my hands over his broad shoulders, careful to avoid the scars on his shoulderblades. My hands grazed his chest, his biceps, and the tattoo that burned when I skimmed my fingertips across it.

Noah's vow. Tears clogged my throat and my fingertips moved away from the tattooed script. She'd always be first in his heart.

As if sensing my emotions, Noah moved back up and his hands brushed the tears spilling over my cheeks. I felt his breath whisper over my mouth, felt him press another soft kiss to my upper lip. "Don't be sad, Jackie. I can't stand to see you sad."

"Then close your eyes," I said tightly, though the tears were already drying. It had been a command, if a subtle one.

He moved down to my breasts and began to press the same light, teasing kisses on them that he had the rest of my body. I arched against his mouth and let the sensation take over my body, the Itch throbbing its demand. His mouth coaxed my nipples into points, first one, and then the other. Just when I thought he was going to drive me into madness, he closed his lips around one nipple and gently bit, sending shock waves through my body and a gasp escaping my mouth.

He sat up and pulled me toward him until we were both in a kneeling position. He caught my hand and interlinked his fingers with mine. "Will you touch me?" he said in a low, husky voice.

Just the sound of it sent a thrill through my body, and I didn't miss the fact that it wasn't a command, but a request. My one hand linked to his, my other skimmed along his body, eager to comply. First, his shoulders, then down the wall of muscles that made up his stomach. Remembering where his kisses had pressed along my body, I dipped a teasing finger against his navel, and skimmed the smooth, tanned flesh just above his cock. His body clenched slightly in anticipation, and my fingers teased a bit longer, moving to the thick cords of bronzed thigh before stroking their way back up again. His linked hand squeezed tight and he leaned in to press a light kiss on my shoulder. Our bodies were so close that the head of his cock butted against my belly, and my nipples grazed his flesh as he leaned in.

Such a tease.

My fingers slid around the thick shaft of his cock—Noah's equipment could put most men to shame. I wrapped my fingers around the thick length, enjoying his hiss of pleasure. A bead of slick moisture had formed on the crown, and I played with it with my thumb, spreading it over the head of his cock.

Noah groaned with pleasure, and his hand clasping mine grew tight. I liked that our hands were linked—it formed a delightful shivering bond between us. Instead of just seeing how Noah reacted to my touch, I could feel it in the way his hand moved. When his fingers clenched involuntarily, I knew he liked something. And he definitely liked my fingers on his cock.

Which was good, because I liked that too. I played with the wetness on its head a moment longer, then lifted my hand to my mouth, expecting his gaze to follow.

It did.

I raised my wet thumb to my mouth and let the tip of my tongue lick it clean.

He groaned and leaned forward, biting my naked shoulder. I gasped as the sensation sent a thrilling mixture of pleasure and pain through me. My free hand slid back down to his cock and I gave it a swift stroke. He leaned back slightly and groaned, eyes closing with pleasure, and I suddenly wanted to kiss him. My hand pumped his cock again and I leaned in to capture his mouth with mine.

He wouldn't let me move too close—my lips barely grazed his own before he pulled back, his tongue flicking against my mouth in a maddeningly sensual move.

"Not fair," I said lightly, moving up against him. With his cock still in my hand, I aimed it at my own sex, hot and wet with need, and slid the head against my body. My hips flexed involuntarily, needing him inside me, and his blue eyes burned into my own.

"Are we going to play like that, then?" he said in a low voice. His hand—still interlocked with mine—bore me down, and I released his cock and let him push me backward on the bed. His hand disentangled from mine and our palms were no longer linked.

Noah grasped my thigh and slid his hand down it, and I opened willingly for him. That was more like it.

He ran the length of his cock along my damp seam. I nearly came off the bed, gasping with pleasure. He did it a second time, this time letting the thick head of his cock part the lips of my sex just enough to let the head brush against my clit, eliciting a moan from me.

Torturer.

I hooked one leg around his waist, trying to encourage him to enter me. His cock rubbed against my wet, slick sex again and slid to the opening of my core, the head brushing against the spot where I needed him most. I arched my hips, my body clenching with need, and was rewarded with the sensation of the head pushing in, slowly, teasingly.

And then he stopped.

I gasped, needing more. My foot dug into his buttocks, trying to ram him forward to give me the relief I desperately needed. My other leg followed until I had both wrapped around his waist. He ignored my writhing and leaned over me, his eyes so very blue.

"I need you," I blurted, reaching up to link my arms around his neck. "Please, Noah."

His hands locked under my hips and waist, and he rocked backward in a swift, powerful motion, resting on his knees. The sudden motion pulled me upright, my body against his, seating me heavily on his cock and leaving me breathless.

He held me against him as I grew used to the sensation of being filled by his cock, my body pressed against his, breasts to breastbone. His mouth nipped mine lightly, and he flexed his hips, causing shock waves of pleasure to undulate through my body. I wrapped my arms tighter around his neck and returned the kiss, my tongue flicking against his as he gave a small thrust and rolled his hips again. Due to the position, neither of us were able to move much, but it didn't stop the sensations from sweeping over our bodies. My breath caught with every small thrust and every roll of his hips, and his tongue would make an accompanying thrust. Speared on top of him, tongues mating, his next motion sent a small orgasm coursing through my body. I clenched against him, rolling my hips to try and make it last longer. My legs tensed around him, and I moaned his name against the next thrust of his tongue.

In the next moment, we rolled forward again, and I was pinned under Noah once more on my back. Gone were the small, controlled thrusts that he'd given while

I was on his lap. He pulled almost all the way out, and then slid back to the hilt, sending another spiral of sensation through me. He did it again and again, each thrust becoming harder and faster until I was raising my hips to meet him and crying out his name.

The orgasm that had already begun continually spiraled through my body, growing more intense with every thrust until I climaxed again—this time so hard that my vision blurred and a sob tore from my throat. He came with a shout a moment later. With another thrust or two he collapsed on top of me, all damp golden skin and heavily breathing male.

I panted for breath as well, wrapping my arms around him and rubbing my feet against his thighs. God, that was amazing. I always felt energized after sex, and right now, I felt like I could take on the world.

Noah propped up on his arms and studied my face, his eyes bleached back to silver again. He leaned down and kissed me softly.

Who said succubi couldn't be led by their hormones? Not me. I was feeling very good.

To my disappointment, he got up off of me and began to dress. I watched him pull his briefs on and step into his slacks.

"So where does this put us?" I asked, propping my head up on my hand and watching him.

He said nothing as he continued to get dressed, and I sighed and sat up, scooting over to the edge of the bed to do the same. The intense look had returned to Noah's face, meaning that the gears were turning upstairs and I'd find out the answer as soon as he'd figured it out.

He tucked in his shirt and then leaned over to kiss the top of my head. "Good-bye, Jackie."

His hand lingered on my hair for a moment, and then he moved toward the door.

"Wait," I yelped. "What do you mean, good-bye?"

He turned, the banked emotion back in his eyes. "I mean that I'm leaving you, Jackie."

I bolted up from the bed, wrapping the sheet around my body in an awkward toga. "What do you mean, you're leaving me?" Fury rushed through me. "You can't leave me! I'm the one you guys are fighting over. I get to pick who leaves who." I stabbed my finger in his chest. "Those are the rules."

The corners of his mouth lifted in a sad smile. "I thought you already decided who you were choosing, sweetheart. I offered you a ring and you turned it down."

"But . . ." I gave him a beseeching look, blinking rapidly. My hand reached for his, found it, and squeezed. "Noah, that's not fair. You're asking me to commit to four thousand years.

"I am," he said in a soft voice.

The tears I'd been holding back were replaced with anger and I glared. "This again? You've got to be kidding me. I *can't* choose, Noah. Right now, I'm so mixed up over you that I can't decide whether to kiss you or slap you."

"I know you can't choose, sweetheart." His serious

eyes met mine. "That's why I'm opting out. There's too much tangled up between us right now. I know it's wrong for me to force you to choose, but I can't sit here and watch you go to him every night. I hate the bastard, and I can't stand the thought of him touching you, feeling like he owns an equal part of your heart. I won't share someone with him again. It eats me up, Jackie," he ground out. " I can't function like this.

"I'm not good for you this way. You said yourself that I protect you from too much, and it's true. That's part of my nature, to guard you and protect you. You're an adult, and immortal—you're free to make your own choices, not have them crammed down your throat by my actions."

My throat locked, any protest I might make dying in my throat.

"I wasn't lying when I said we needed time away from each other," he said, his voice firm. "We do. There is business that I've neglected, and it's time I took care of it once and for all. Zane can help you with your needs."

"Oh yeah?" I bristled, irritated that he was deciding everything for me once more. "What about *your* needs?"

His mouth twisted, becoming a little hard and bitter. "There's always Delilah."

I recoiled as if slapped. "So that's what this is? You're throwing me over for that jailbait because you think *that's* what's best for me ? Is this all to get back at me because I won't wear your ring?"

I moved back in the bed, reached between the mattresses and pulled out his hated Da Vinci, and held it out to him. "Don't forget your precious picture of Rachael, Noah. Wouldn't want you to lose that," I said angrily. "Heaven forbid someone forget what she looked like."

He took the painting from me with gentle fingers, his eyes caressing it with the expression of someone that held far, far too much affection. For her. Everything was always for her.

It hurt. "Once again, it all boils down to that woman, doesn't it?"

The expression on Noah's face grew shuttered. "*You* won't make a decision, and I can't stand to see you in his arms, so the only other choice I have is to pull myself out of the equation entirely. If you won't commit to me, it isn't fair for me to remain here and try to bend you to my will." He gave me one last kiss on the forehead, then said softly against my skin, "You've already chosen, Jackie. We both know this."

I did know it. I knew it in my heart, even though I wanted to protest. I was frozen in place, unable to move lest he remove his mouth and disappear out of my life forever.

"Say it, Jackie."

The world seemed to move in slow motion as I spoke, hating myself as I did. "Zane can't live without me. You can."

Noah's mouth thinned into a hard line, his eyes going flat. "The fact that you believe that tells me everything I need to know. Good-bye, Jackie." He touched my cheek. "Don't follow me."

He left the room, tucking the painting under his arm.

"Fine, then," I shouted after him. "Leave me! I don't care. I don't need you!"

Silence. The world swam in front of my eyes, spun queasily as I tried to process what had just happened.

Noah had left me.

My rock, my angel, my protector—he'd given up on me.

Zane can't live without me. You can.

Why had I said something so stupid? I must have wanted to hurt him like he was hurting me.

The fact that you believe that tells me everything I need to know. Good-bye, Jackie.

Damn it. And damn him for making me feel guilty. Hitching the sheet up, I opened the bedroom door and headed down the hall, and stairs. If this was a guilt trip, I wasn't going to fall for it.

But Noah's things were gone. The living room was empty. The driveway was empty of his car.

He'd left. And I couldn't follow him because he'd commanded me not to.

I screamed in rage, my hands fisting in the sheet. "You *bastard!*"

He'd really, really left.

Remy and Ethan raced into the room, staring at the sight of me. "Jackie? What is it?" Remy asked.

"Noah left me," I snarled, my hands wrapped in my

toga so tightly the fabric began to rip. "He said it was for my own good. Do you believe that asshole?"

"He left?" Delilah popped in from around the corner, car keys in hand. She was trying very hard to keep her face straight but was having a difficult time keeping her smile tamped down. I stared at her as she gave me an apologetic little smile and wave. "My, look at the time. I really should be going. I'm just going to . . ." She gestured at the front door, then ran for it.

Dee and Noah. I shrieked in rage again.

"Oh dear," said Remy.

"I'll get the ice cream," said Ethan.

CHAPTER EIGHTEEN

"You sure you're up for this?" Remy asked as we drove toward James's subdivision. "I can just pop in and get it if you want to."

"That's okay," I said, putting on a brave face. "I made my decision, right? This day was bound to come someday."

"Noah Gideon is a good man," Ethan said from the backseat. "I am disappointed that you sent him away, Jackie Brighton."

Yeah, well, at the moment I wasn't feeling too keen about it, either.

As we pulled up to a stop sign, she frowned over at me. "I wanted to ask you about that." I winced in anticipation. "You picked Zane over Noah? Are you on drugs? Untrustworthy vampire over rich Serim? Am I the only one who sees the problem with this scenario?"

"I see the problem with this scenario," Ethan chimed in helpfully.

I turned to glare at Ethan. "Stop it. I'm not crazy, Remy . . . I just . . . it's hard to explain."

"Hard to explain?" She cocked her head and gave

me an exasperated look. "To a porn star succubus who recently had a tiny possession issue? I'd say I'm game."

I looked down at my hands in my lap and shrugged. "I told Noah he didn't need me, and Zane did."

Her screech was loud enough to make the car windows in the car vibrate. "You did *what?*"

"I might have not thought it through," I confessed.

She stared at me with curious eyes. "Jackie, hon. Are you in love with Noah? Or Zane?"

That was the million-dollar question. I looked down at my lap and gave a heavy, deflated sigh. "I should be in love with Noah, right? He's a good man, good to me, rich, handsome, kind, caring, considerate, thoughtful—"

"But?"

I swallowed hard, allowing myself to admit the truth. "I love Noah, but I'm not *in love* with him. I think I'm in love with Zane." Even though he was totally wrong for me and had used me to get his way, I still wanted him. And I still wanted to be with him, more than anything.

It was stupid and wrong.

Ethan sighed.

Remy sighed as well. "You are?"

"I am," I said, a wondering sense of emotion filling me like it had yesterday when I'd freed his wings. "Only I didn't realize it until just now. I'm mad at him and furious that he's used me to replace someone else—that hurts me more than I can think about. I don't know where that leaves us, but I know that if he walks out of my life again, I won't be able to stand it."

"And Noah?" she asked. "He just walked out of your life. How does that make you feel?"

"Like the world's worst person ever," I admitted, wringing my hands in my lap. "I love Noah, but it's not the same desperate sort of need that I feel when I'm around Zane. Noah's like a warm, fuzzy blanket. Zane makes my pulse race and my heart pound." I glanced over at her. "You think I'm a bad person for choosing between them, don't you?"

"I do not approve," began Ethan, but he stopped at a glare from Remy.

"Don't be ridiculous," she said. "It's their own fault—they didn't want to share you. They have to be happy with whatever you decide. It's your life. No man is allowed to control it." She gave Ethan a pointed look. "You belong to *you*."

It was a little weird that she felt the need to make that point to him. What had gone on with them?

Ethan spoke up. "Perhaps the man only had her best interests at heart. Perhaps the succubus should not be so selfish with her favors."

Oookay. Clearly they weren't talking about me anymore.

"I was happy with both of them, but Noah wants more than I can give him," I interrupted. "He wants to protect me from the world, and I think it's time that I start to take my own lumps, for better or for worse."

Remy nodded. "I hear you. Noah's a big boy—he'll recover." She cast a glance to the backseat. "People should be free to do whatever they want."

"Remiza," Ethan began.

She put a hand up. "Don't want to hear it."

I finally asked, "Did something happen that I should know about?"

Remy gave me a meaningful, I'll-tell-you-later look. "Nope. Besides, we're talking about you and Noah. You're fine, kid. I promise. Let him sulk for a while and get it out of his system." She turned into James's neighborhood.

That was good to hear, because right now I felt as if I had lost my best friend. "I'm fine. Really. Promise."

"Awesome," she said. "Then let's go get our *djed*-thing from the old pervert."

I nodded, glancing around us. "Odd that there's no traffic," I said, keeping my voice light.

"Maybe there's a soccer mom meeting or something. Who knows," she said.

As soon as we turned down James's street, I could tell something was seriously wrong. Cars were everywhere. Not just lining the curb and in driveways, but scattered on lawns and stalled in the middle of the street. Doors were left hanging open, as if the passengers had been in a desperate hurry.

Remy parked behind a Jeep Cherokee that was blocking the middle of the road.

"Something's wrong," I said, getting out of the car to stare at the abandoned neighborhood. At a nearby house, smoke poured out of a window, and I smelled burning bacon. The front door was wide open. "Where did everyone go?"

"I do not know," Ethan said, striding ahead. His stance had changed from the easygoing, loping behemoth I usually saw to the tightly coiled muscles of a predator. "Stay behind me."

Remy moved to the trunk of her car and grabbed the tire iron. Weapon. Good idea. I popped open the glove compartment, searching for anything that might be able to protect me, but all I found was an ice scraper. I took it anyhow, feeling better with something in my hand.

We crept down the deserted street after Ethan, sticking close together. Evening had fallen. I immediately thought of Noah. Had he gotten someplace safe before the dark fell? Delilah would have taken care of him, I was sure. The thought left a sour taste in my mouth, and I forced myself to think of other things. I had made my choice, and I had chosen the vampire. He should be awakening now.

Vampires. Awakening.

I stared at the empty neighborhood. "Oh, shit."

Remy grabbed my arm, jerking closer to me. "What? What is it?"

"Caleb," I said. "The sun's down. I bet he's the one responsible for all of this."

She shivered.

"Be careful," I said to Ethan. "Let's stay close together, just in case."

We saw no one else as we went down the empty street, arriving at James's house just as the streetlights came on. Remy and I paused at the end of the driveway, clutching our makeshift weapons. Nothing seemed out of place but then, James's house had looked derelict earlier this morning.

"Should we enter?" I asked, uncertain.

"I will go in and investigate, Jackie Brighton." Ethan gave Remy a quick glance, his eyes flashing in a feeding frenzy of good deeds. "Succubi, you stay here and watch yourselves."

"And what if something bad happens to you?" Remy said, irritated. "How long are we supposed to stay out here?"

"If I do not come out in a half hour, leave without me," he said, his face grave.

"Why? What's the point in that?" I asked. "We need the *djed* to bring Caleb down. If we don't, we're going to have to confront him again tomorrow, or the next day. And in the meantime, he'll just keep killing more people. He's already killed a dozen vampires."

Ethan frowned at us. "You will stay out here because I command it."

I shook my head. "You're not the master of either of us. I like you, Boy Scout, but there's some things that you shouldn't take on alone."

Remy hefted the tire iron. "We might as well go in with him."

She had a point. A scary, scary point. I swallowed hard. "I'm thinking we should go in together, yes."

Ethan shook his head, his big shoulders bracing to disagree. "If there is something wicked in that house—"

"Other than that old pervert," Remy added.

"—then I will need all my senses about me." Ethan gave us his best stern warrior look. "If you are out here, I do not have to worry about your safety while I fight."

"But you can't take down Joachim," I said. The archangel's rampaging spirit had the power of twelve vampires and God knew how many mortals, if they even counted. Ethan was big and strong, but he didn't stand a chance against the Big Bad inside Caleb.

"If I die, I will die protecting you," he said in a cool voice, but his eyes flashed repeatedly.

"Martyrdom is not sexy," snapped Remy. "So don't think you have either of us fooled."

"It is not martyrdom." He touched Remy's cheek. "I have enjoyed getting to know you, Remiza." And before she could respond, he turned and moved stealthily toward James's house.

I leaned over to Remy, both of us watching Ethan as he snuck up on the house. "So what exactly happened between you two? You guys are being totally weird."

"Nothing," she said in a sullen voice.

"Okay, goo—"

"Maybe a little sex. Just a little."

"Just a *little*?"

"On the hood of the rental car."

I resisted the urge to hit her with the ice scraper. "I told you to leave him alone! He's innocent, Remy!"

She waved a hand at me, dismissing my concerns. "Please. Your boy wonder wanted it just as much as I did. And besides, have you seen the size of that man's equipment—"

I moaned and put a hand up, cutting her off. "I do not want to know!"

But now I was picturing it. And getting turned on. I hated my friends sometimes.

"Anyhow, long story short, we do it, and he's kind of quick and to the point, but the equipment makes up for it," Remy said. "So I thought, that's that, right? Little did I know that he was going to get all possessive and stuff. I shouldn't dress like this. I shouldn't speak like this. I shouldn't do this. I shouldn't do that. I should let him walk in front of me to protect me, blah blah blah blah." She rolled her eyes, clearly exasperated. "I've had four hundred years of men telling me what to do, and I'm not going to let some sexy dweeb with a ten-inch dick—"

I groaned.

"—tell me what to do with myself! Can you imagine! He's only twenty-eight! Scarcely a baby."

"And a virgin," I added helpfully. "You totally deflowered him."

She snorted, hand on hip. "That explains his staying power. He's lucky that I can get off with a good power stroke—"

"What is this, TMI day? Jeezus, Remy!"

Crash! The entire house shook.

I clutched Remy's shoulder. "That didn't sound good."

Remy pulled the tire iron close to her chest. "Do you think Ethan is okay in there?"

Crash! One of the house numbers swung on its nail and fell to the porch.

"I'm going to guess that's a no," I said. "Come on. He might need our help." I gripped my ice scraper and headed toward the house.

After all, succubi couldn't die, I told myself. We could just hurt . . . a lot . . .

Remy and I crept onto the porch. The front door was ajar slightly, and the lights were off inside. There was a faint coppery scent in the air that I didn't like, but some things were better off not discussed.

My fellow succubus didn't seem in a rush to enter the house, so I took point, moving forward. I gave the door a nudge and watched it swing open. The interior was pitch dark, and I could hear nothing. Fear pounding in my throat, I reached inside for the light switch.

It flicked on.

Remy began to gag.

The entire living room was covered with wall-to-wall bodies. They were heaped on top of the furniture and covered every inch of the floor. I swallowed hard, repeatedly. Dear God. They'd all been murdered. "Now we know where the neighbors went to."

"I think we need to find you a better weapon," Remy whispered, then gagged. "Gross, I think I just saw someone's pet."

Still swallowing, I edged inside, going toward the kitchen. "James's cat?"

"No," she said, putting the back of a hand to her mouth. "A dog. Don't ask me to show you."

"Don't worry." I tiptoed into the kitchen and found it still cluttered with dishes and gadgets. I picked through a pile of crap as quietly as possible, looking for a knife, then pulled out a few drawers. Nothing. I frowned, thinking hard. His basement had been full of artifacts and gadgetry. I'd find something to use as a weapon there.

Of course, if I were a psychotic, possessed vampire intent on world domination, that's also where I'd be waiting for more victims. So that was out.

A shout filled the house, and Ethan shot past us, his body punching a hole through the wall and disappearing out into the front lawn. Remy crawled under the dining room table, which was covered in stacks of old newspapers and dust. That seemed like a good idea, so I crawled under after her, waiting to see what was coming.

A thump, and then another. Remy clutched my hand and we huddled together as footsteps approached, neither of us daring to move.

Blood-spattered boots stopped not three feet away, and I clutched my scraper tighter. A body dropped heavily to the floor in front of us. Remy and I jumped, her squeak of distress hastily smothered by my hand clamping over her mouth, and we stared at James's dead, broken form.

Then Caleb crouched down to look under the table, grinning at us. His eyes were bright red and the look on his face was wild. "Heard you girls were looking for a magic staff. I thought I'd help you along with matters."

I stared at James's body.

"Are you going to kill Ethan?" Remy squeaked.

He tilted his head, staring at us. "Can't kill an immortal, love. Or at least . . . not quickly. As you girls are about to find out."

CHAPTER NINETEEN

Caleb/Joachim didn't kill us right away. To my surprise, he didn't kill us at all. Instead, he grabbed Remy by the wrist and dragged her to the basement, leaving me no choice but to follow him below. There, he'd picked up a chain—the only one in the basement—and shackled her to the window, then turned to me with an evil look. "Going to run away, little succubus?"

I trembled, but held my ground. "Not without Remy."

The answer seemed to amuse him. Before he could respond, he shuddered, his eyes rolling back in his head. His wings gave a great shiver, and I felt the evil inside him pulse heavily. The room shook in response, dust fluttering from the ceiling. Remy cast a wide-eyed glance at me and twisted her wrist in the cuff, anxious.

Caleb regained himself a moment later, then stalked to the far side of the room. I snuck over to where Remy was chained and crept behind a crate next to her. It was stupid to hide—he knew I was there—but I felt better. "What's wrong with him?"

"I think it's a power overload," she whispered, her

eyes on Caleb/Joachim. "Maybe he can't handle everything."

I peeked around the large, heavy crate marked "Antiquities" and stared at the vampire pacing at the other end of the cluttered room. Caleb did not seem to be handling Joachim well: his eyes were hollow and shadowed, his cheeks shrunken. The tattoo stood out starkly on his pale skin, and as he paced, I watched black feathers flutter to the ground. He was shedding his wings under his torn, disheveled clothing. He twitched repeatedly.

"What's he waiting for?" Remy whispered at my side, her hand drawn over her head in the ornate cuff. Apparently old James had a fetish for bondage equipment.

"Maybe he's waiting for some sort of wacky ritual?" I whispered from behind the box.

I'd expected him to torture us. Demons knew a lot about torture, and whatever Joachim was now was worse than a demon. Worse than a dozen of them.

But to my surprise, after he'd bound Remy against the wall he had then left us alone. Which made me suspect that he was saving us for other, more nefarious things.

As succubi, Remy and I could only be killed by sexual starvation or the deaths of our masters. It pretty much made us invulnerable. It also made us the perfect "spares," in case Joachim ran his current vehicle—Caleb—into the ground.

That thought made me quake with fear.

I continued to watch him pace across the floor. Slowly. Methodically. Even steps. What was Caleb/Joachim waiting for?

Remy's handcuff shook slightly as she shifted against the wall. "Do you think Ethan is all right?" Her liquid eyes were a deep, emotional silver. "He hasn't come back to check on us."

"I don't know," I said softly. "I would have thought he'd come back for us if he was alive, so . . . Maybe . . . maybe he's invulnerable, like us. I don't know enough about Nephilim to say."

At my words, Caleb's blazing red eyes turned to focus on me.

I cringed behind the crate.

Caleb/Joachim paused, then very slowly moved to the box. He brushed it aside as if it weighed nothing, and I blinked up at him, frozen in place. Confidence, my brain screamed at me. Be cocky and confident, like every other immortal.

"'Sup," I croaked. "You need something?"

He smiled, exposing teeth that had grown disturbingly long and razorlike in the past twenty-four hours. "I need to feed," he said in the cracked, broken Joachim voice. "The blood hunger is strong in this body."

I slid backward on the floor a little. "I'm AB negative," I blurted. "Very bitter taste. You wouldn't like me."

His gaze turned sharply, focused on Remy. "This one, then."

She flinched, jerking at the chain. Trapped against the

wall, she was helpless to move as the possessed vampire approached.

"Wait," I yelped. "Don't touch her! I've, er, been taking vitamins," I offered, clambering to my feet and shoving my wrist under his nose. "Lots of Flintstones chewables. Very tasty."

He grabbed my wrist with both hands in a jerky motion. His hands were hot, like a demon's, and I flinched. He sniffed my skin like an animal, then ran his tongue along the inside of my wrist, where the angel's word still burned in my skin.

It sizzled against his tongue, and he hissed. He flipped over my hand and sunk his daggerlike teeth into the back of my wrist.

Agony lashed through my arm as a thousand icy-cold needles sank into my skin, digging deep, and I nearly collapsed. Then he began to make loud sucking noises, drinking my blood.

A vampire bite was normally a precursor to a quick, sweet orgasm. This was . . . not. This was something else entirely. I could feel the corruption and hatred lingering inside Caleb, the spirit of Joachim warping the vampire powers to something even more awful. As he drank from me, my skin crawled and I resisted the urge to retch, the sickness and corruption inside him feeling as if it were seeping under my skin.

I think I would have preferred the orgasm. This just made me feel cold and dirty and afraid.

As his mouth moved against my skin, the power in the

room shuddered once more, and it rolled over me, blowing my hair backward like a strong gust of wind.

"Are you okay?" Remy said in a wobbling voice.

I gave her a weak thumbs-up.

God, I was going to pass out from the pain. My other hand fisted tight, knuckles pressed to my mouth to keep from screaming. I was immortal, I reminded myself. It would heal. It would heal.

But he continued to feed long past the point that I knew any sane vampire would stop. I began to feel light-headed and weak, and I pushed at him, whimpering my distress.

His only response was to dig his teeth deeper, bringing another hiss of pain to my lips.

I had to do something, or he was going to eff me up badly. I planted my free hand on his cheek and pushed harder. Nothing. He refused to be turned away from my wrist. I took a step backward. The room swam before my eyes, and it took a moment for me to realize that he'd followed me. I took another step backward and sure enough, he followed, his mouth still locked on my wrist.

"The staff," Remy said, pointing with her unchained hand behind me. "Get the staff!"

I reached for the desk, feeling around. A thick brass rod lay on the far end and I dragged it forward until I could wrap my hand around it. The rod was strung through the holes of the vertebrae, but only looked half done. There was a partially-drawn symbol at the top that looked like the creator had been interrupted. I grabbed it and whapped it against the side of Caleb's head.

No reaction. No wailing. No "I'm melting."

He just grinned, releasing my wrist after giving the flesh one long, last lick that made me shudder. "Your *djed* is not finished, stupid girl."

He grabbed me by the throat, then shoved me across the cluttered desk and against the wall. My mangled wrist hit against the brick, and my head smacked it hard. I nearly lost my grip on the *djed*.

"The nice thing about a succubus," Caleb told me with a hiss, "is that you are an endless blood supply. That is the only reason you continue to live."

"You can't kill me," I bluffed, fear coursing through me.

His smile was slow and cruel, his tattoo crinkling around one red eye as he watched me with a predatory gaze. "You'll never know what you can achieve unless you try."

Okay, I was officially scared. Even more so when he stretched my mangled arm higher along the wall, leaning in to sniff me.

I averted my face and scrunched my neck down, trying to hide the vulnerable parts. He leaned in, and my face was so close to his neck that I detected the faint gleam of gold under his shirt collar.

The *shenu*? Was he still wearing it?

If so, what did that mean for the possession?

I had to be sure he was wearing it. Half against my better judgment, I used the *djed* to smack him on the neck, deliberately brushing against the collar of his long trench coat and the buttoned shirt underneath. More gold revealed, confirming my suspicions.

Then the *djed* was knocked out of my hands and Caleb flung me across the room. I crashed into the opposite wall, next to where Remy was strung up.

Good thing we couldn't die, because the number of bones that felt shattered right now was enough to nearly destroy me. My lungs felt completely deflated and I lay unmoving as I struggled to regain breath, waiting for the world to come back to me.

"Jackie?" Remy whispered quietly. "You okay?"

I mustered the world's weakest thumbs-up to let her know I was alive.

"That was fucking stupid," she whispered back.

"*Shenu*," I wheezed as Caleb returned to his methodical pacing. When she shook her head at me, uncomprehending, I used my slightly less broken hand to circle my neck. "He's still wearing the gold collar."

Her eyes widened. "Do you think the transfer wasn't complete?"

I nodded. "I think Joachim's bound more to the collar than to Caleb. Look at how awful he looks." Indeed, the vampire looked as if he were on the verge of collapse at any moment. "That's why he's keeping us here. We're the blood supply and the backup plan."

"I don't think I like being a backup plan," she said faintly.

Me, either. I didn't move from the ground, keeping very still. "What's he doing now?"

"Just pacing," she whispered, her gaze glued to the vampire. "What's he waiting for?"

As my lungs slowly began to fill with air again, I pondered the same question. Joachim was acquiring power, so why was he staying here? It could only be a trap. Zane was the most powerful vampire, next to the queen, and killing him would clear a path to Nitocris. After that, it'd be easy for him to destroy Noah. And with that much power . . . who knew who he would take on next?

Suddenly the Archangel Gabriel didn't seem so invincible.

"What does he want with us?" Remy said, nudging me with her toe.

I stared at the endlessly pacing vampire, at the strange calm that had come over him.

"We're not a threat," I whispered back. "We're not even the backup plan. We're bait."

Her eyes widened, then she murmured, "Zane."

My heart was ripping out of my own chest at the thought. "He won't come for us," I said, hoping against hope. "He doesn't know where we are."

Remy pondered this for a moment. Then she said, "Unless Ethan went for him, and that's why he hasn't come back to save us."

Shit. She was right. I pictured Ethan chasing down Zane, his eyes flashing with a whopper of a good deed.

My good hand clenched with frustrated anger. The Boy Scout was going to get my vampire killed.

The house creaked and groaned, and a few flakes of plaster fell on my head. I brushed them off, glancing up at the ceiling. Was the weight of the bodies upstairs too much?

Caleb began to chuckle, the sound low and unearthly. Then his torn jacket ripped apart as his shedding wings burst free.

"Not a good sign," Remy whispered, her chains shivering.

No, it was not. I got to my feet as the house groaned again, more plaster raining down.

"What is that?" said Remy.

I could guess, remembering the torn-up parking lot from yesterday. Sure enough, the house gave another loud groan and part of the ceiling fell in. I scurried out of the way just before a giant wooden beam came crashing down. Dust rained thick, and I pulled my wounded hand close to keep it safe. Wind whipped through the basement, scattering papers everywhere.

"Caleb!" called Zane in a furious voice. "Where do you have her?"

No—not Zane alone. He'd be killed!

"She's safe enough," the possessed vampire laughed. "And she tastes delicious."

The chimney of James's house came sailing down into the basement. Caleb neatly sidestepped it and it left a meteor-sized crater in the floor.

"Come out of that hole and fight," Zane snarled from above.

Caleb's wings beat madly and black feathers rained about the basement. "Come and kill me, if you can," he sneered. "Or do I need to take another bite of your pretty redhead again?"

Zane dive-bombed into the room, tackling Caleb, and the two of them crashed across the floor, slamming into another beam.

"Zane," I screamed as Caleb caught him and easily flung him across the room. My vampire snarled and picked himself up, his gaze skimming the room frantically. Relief flashed across his face as he saw me.

Relief was short-lived, though. Caleb jumped atop a fallen beam and sprang at Zane, tackling him to the concrete floor. It buckled and shattered, and I felt the room tilt wildly.

It was a clash of titans. What was left of the basement shook madly as the two vampires duked it out. Over and over, they pummeled each other.

Zane would slam a powerful fist into Caleb's side, but it would do no good. He ignored Zane's punishing fists and grabbed him by the throat, his strength clearly surprising Zane.

I hardly dared to breathe as Caleb tossed Zane off to the side again, making a wall collapse. The fight seemed to go on endlessly. Zane would recover, pick himself up, and surge back at Caleb again, only to be batted away. He would rise again, bloody and bruised, and the same would happen, over and over again.

Caleb barely had a scratch on him.

Zane kept turning to look at me to make sure I was safe, and every time he did, he lost a little ground with Caleb. If I remained close by, Zane was going to die.

I had to do *something*. I ran over to Remy's side. "We have to get you out of here."

Her eyes widened. "We can't leave Zane behind. Caleb will kill him."

I choked back my tears. "I know—I'll come back to save him, but we can't do anything with you chained down here."

Scrambling, I raced over to James's trashed desk, but found nothing useful. But the shelf next to the desk held a hammer. I grabbed it and dashed across the room just as Zane gave a bloodcurdling scream and I heard the rip of feathers.

Oh God, his wings! Caleb was holding him down, a handful of shiny black feathers in his hand. The *shenu* seemed to pulse under his shirt collar.

Before I could attack Caleb, someone with long black hair jumped from above with a wild yell. He landed on Caleb's back, swinging his staff, only to be flung aside like a pesky ant. Ethan shook himself and went back to the fight, with boundless energy.

Two of them—good! I ran back to Remy's side with the hammer. "Stand still!"

She winced, closing her eyes.

I swung. *CLANG*. Reverberations swept up my arms and I staggered, trying to hold on to the hammer. Nothing.

I swung again. *CLANG*. Still nothing. The wall behind the cuffs chipped, but that was it.

Above us the ceiling cracked and sagged, and Remy shrieked. "It won't hold out for much longer."

Ethan slammed into the wall next to us. One of the gigantic shelves teetered, and as I watched, the ceiling at the far end of the room began to sag.

It wasn't going to last long, and Remy and I would be buried alive. I swung the hammer again, with the same result.

"It's not working," I yelled at her over the din. "It might be too hard to break!"

She yelled back, "I'll try something else!" She leaned up to the cuff and spat on it, once, twice. Then she began to twist her hand, jerking at the cuff. I heard a crack of bone and turned to look at Zane, but he was dropping a crate on Caleb's head. I turned back to Remy.

She shook her now-free reddened hand, wincing. "It's lucky that I've done that before."

I stared at her. "Did you just break your own hand to get out?"

"Hell, yeah," she said, ducking the splintered remains of the crate that flew in our direction. "It's better than the alternative."

"Why didn't you do that earlier?" I shouted.

"Why would I break my own hand for nothing?" she yelled back, cradling it close. "It fucking hurts!"

God. Immortals.

We crept around the back of the room as the two vampires continued to fight. Zane was slowing, even with his supernatural strength. Blood covered his face and one of his wings drooped. Ethan continued to jump in and attack Caleb, but every time, he was batted away.

What he had in brute strength and energy, he lacked in skill. Caleb and Zane had had thousands of years to hone their skills.

As we crept around the room, the cat wound around my legs and I nearly tripped on it. Stupid cat!

I picked it up and put it on the desk, out of the way. Instead of running for its life, it cocked its head and meowed at me. No sense of self-preservation.

The house shuddered as Ethan was thrown through the roof and disappeared. The stairs—the only way out of the room unless you could fly—cracked and leaned heavily to one side. Pretty soon we'd be stuck down here for good, unless we could find a way to stop the possessed vampire.

Caleb grabbed a fallen Zane by the front of his torn shirt, hauling him forward. Zane raised a hand, only to have it easily blocked by Caleb. Zane was at his end, but Caleb seemed endlessly strong. As I watched, Caleb leaned in and sank his fangs into Zane's shoulder.

"No!" I screamed.

Zane gave a full-body shudder, his eyes rolling back in his head and his entire form going limp. Caleb's *shenu* pulsed, glowing so bright that I could see the outline of it through his torn shirt.

The collar! I had to get it off of Caleb, to get him off of Zane.

I grabbed the hammer and hefted it. "Remy, get out of here. Find Ethan and run."

"What are you going to do?"

"I'm going to get that collar," I said, the power surging into the room whipping my hair. Zane was fading before my eyes as Caleb and the collar pulsed and grew stronger.

Remy looked as if she wanted to argue, but she nodded and disappeared up the broken steps.

I raised the hammer and swung. It smacked Caleb on the neck with a loud clang, sending reverberations through my body. A surge of pure evil shot through me, and I shuddered.

I raised the hammer again for another swing, and another, but I might as well have been hitting the wall for all the difference it made. A sob caught in my throat. "You can't have him," I snarled, raising the hammer with tired arms. "No one gets to fuck with that vampire but me."

Zane's eyes opened again and focused on me. His fingers strained, as if reaching for me, and I frantically pointed at my neck. *The collar*, I mouthed, then raised the hammer one more time.

Zane's eyes lit with recognition and his hand shot forward, grabbing on to the glowing collar. Caleb jerked backward, and my blow landed on the side of his head instead of on the collar.

The room exploded with power.

CHAPTER TWENTY

Caleb went flying across the room, the image of Zane holding the flaring collar burned into my retinas. The pulse knocked me off my feet, shoving me backward. I gasped for breath in the miasma of the room, struggling to recover. Evil filled the basement—evil and hatred.

Squinting at the bright light, I stumbled to my feet. As the haze cleared from my eyes, I gasped.

Zane stood in the center of the room, collar still clutched in hand. It pulsed as if lit from within, and Zane's eyes were glued to it as if entranced. At the far side of the room, crumpled and broken, lay Caleb. His chest still rose and fell as normal, though; it would take more than a blow to the head to destroy a vampire.

"Thank God," I said, lowering the hammer with exhaustion. I took a wobbling step forward. "Are you okay?"

Zane ignored me, his hand beginning to shake. The collar glowed and Zane's eyes grew even redder.

Uh oh. I moved forward, keeping the hammer close. "Zane?"

His hand began to shake and throb, his eyes wide. His mouth curled into a snarl, his wrecked body beginning to tremble as he began to slowly inch the collar toward himself.

Put me on, I heard the air whisper.

Oh shit. Shit!

Caleb hadn't meant to put the collar on, after all—it had talked him into it. Just like it was talking to Zane!

I had to do something, and fast. But what? I stretched a hand to the collar, then withdrew it sharply—I didn't want to put it on myself. There would be no way I'd be able to resist its power.

"No," Zane gritted, even as his hand moved toward his neck.

"Zane, stop," I cried out, moving forward. At my feet, the cat meowed and tried to wrap around my leg again. I pitched forward, nearly landing on the collar, and managed to shy away. Good lord, if I'd touched that thing . . .

Wait—it needed any vessel to possess!

I dropped the hammer and picked up the cat. "Good kitty. Nice kitty," I murmured.

"Jackie . . ." Zane whispered, sounding strained.

I thrust the cat under the outstretched collar, forcing its head through the loop. "Drop it, Zane! Drop it!"

The light flared again.

The cat struggled in my arms, all claws and fury, then it gave an unearthly yowl.

The collar hung off the cat, sliding down to fit around her chest. I snapped it shut around her, then jerked my hand backward when she swiped at me with a vicious paw. I dropped her to the floor, and her red eyes narrowed and she hissed at me.

I'd just created a feline Cujo. I warily backed up a step as the cat crouched, preparing to spring at me.

A large crate suddenly slammed down over the cat, hiding it from view. I heard it thump against the wood, but the huge crate didn't move. Zane leaned on it, one wing listing, and gave me a wan smile.

"Good job, Princess."

He looked bone tired, pale, and streaked with blood, some his own, and some not. One eye was nearly swollen shut. He looked vulnerable and exhausted.

I gestured over at Caleb's fallen body. "So do you think Caleb's really evil, or was it just the collar?"

The crate thumped angrily again.

"Oh, he's evil," said Zane in a weary voice, still laced with humor. "But it was definitely the *shenu* driving him. I could feel the hate and the need in it when I touched it. Caleb's been the queen's faithful warrior for millennia. He wouldn't betray her like that."

No, it seemed the queen had everyone well and good under her thumb, my own lover included. My gaze slid to the control collar she'd put around his throat.

"Come here, Jackie," Zane rasped.

Part of me thought I should resist, but he looked as if he were about to collapse—and so was I. I moved a step forward, then another, finally standing close enough to him to smell the metallic tang of the blood covering him, to see the midnight pulse of his collar.

He grabbed me by the waist and lifted me to sit atop the crate. The cat thumped against it once again, as if trying to attack me through the wood. My breath caught in my throat as he leaned in, his eyes raking over me. I swallowed. "What are you doing?"

"Checking you over. Making sure that you're not hurt." He took my trashed arm in gentle hands and pulled off the remnants of his shirt, then began to wrap my arm.

Tears burned in the back of my throat. Here he was, wings torn, weaving from exhaustion, and covered in blood—and he was tenderly wrapping my wound as if I were the only one hurt. His touch was incredibly gentle, careful to avoid the jagged edges of the wound and ensured that I was taken care of. "I should be asking that about *you*. Are you all right?"

He gave a slight shrug, which emphasized how much his wing was listing to one side. "My body will heal. That's one benefit of being immortal." His mouth pulled up on one side in a sardonic half smile. "My heart is not quite so quick to mend."

"Zane . . ." I whispered.

He fell to his knees before me, holding my hand. He pressed it against his forehead and exhaled long, his shoulders shaking. "I never meant to hurt you," he said, and kissed my fingertips. "Never."

I swallowed hard, realizing we were talking about Rachael now.

"But you did hurt me, Zane," I said softly. "All those times you kissed me—it wasn't me. It was her." It still hurt just to think about it.

"Jackie, that's not true—"

"Just don't lie to me anymore, Zane. I'm so tired of the lies."

"Then tell me what you need to know."

I swallowed hard. "Did you kill Rachael? When you found out she chose Noah over you?"

His flinch could be felt, and he sucked in a ragged breath. "I . . . yes." He swallowed hard, his throat working. "I was angry and I took my anger out the only way I knew how. I didn't know she was nearby . . ." Zane's words were filled with self-loathing. "If you're asking if I regret it? Every day for the last four thousand years. One reckless, stupid mistake . . . and I destroyed her."

I swallowed the lump in my throat. I couldn't hate him for that—not when he clearly hated himself. "I see. And that's why you turned me?"

His forehead felt hot against the backs of my fingers. "It *was* the reason I turned you. When you landed at my feet and you were drunk and disheveled and warm . . . you looked just like her. It made me ache just to see you. Back then you were just another girl, so it didn't matter to me if I ruined your life. So after I bit you, I delivered you to Noah, knowing that he'd be unable to resist taking you to bed as well."

I flinched and tried to pull my hand out of his. At least he was honest, even if it hurt.

But he wouldn't let me go.

"When you turned, you didn't look much like her anymore. That's why I didn't recognize you when you first came into the club. And you're nothing like Rachael in personality. I didn't like you much at first, Jackie. And I called you Princess because you were so prissy about being a succubus."

I swallowed hard.

"You crept under my skin, Jackie. With your jokes, and your smile, and the fact that you tried so hard at everything, even if you weren't good at it. That you were so determined to be moral and good, despite the succubus curse. I admired that about you. Before I knew it, I was falling in love with you. *Not* Rachael's double. Not the girl I loved four thousand years ago. *You.* The Jackie who gets excited about old vases and teases me about hieroglyphics. The Jackie who isn't afraid to tell me what she likes, and likes me for what I am." He kissed my fingertips again, ignoring the faint hiss of his black collar as it burned him. "The Jackie who takes my hand and pleasures herself when I'm asleep, because she wants to be with me."

Heat crept up my cheeks. "How did you know about that?"

"I was asleep, not dead," he said, a hint of the old Zane's grin returning to his face. "And my dreams took a decidedly interesting turn once you started touching me."

He said he loved me . . . but did he mean it? Or was he just afraid of losing to Noah again? How could I know for sure? "I . . . still need time to think about this, Zane. I don't know."

Zane simply nodded. "I can wait for you."

I ignored the warm, fuzzy feelings his words brought forward. The cat thumped underneath me again and began to yowl. "Help me find a cat carrier for this little bugger," I said to Zane. "I've got someone to deliver him to."

Zane looked wary. "Who did you have in mind?"

"The Archangel Gabriel."

His scowl showed his anger. It was obvious that he didn't approve. Too bad.

When he opened his mouth to speak, I raised a hand. "Just trust me on this, will you?"

He clamped his mouth shut and nodded once. "I trust you, Jackie," he said huskily. "And I will follow your lead, wherever you want it to take us."

The warm fuzzies coursed through my body again, but I forced myself to tamp them down. "Right now, let's just get this out of here before Caleb wakes up and insists I give the queen our little kitty cat."

"It must be quite a deal that you've made with the archangel," Zane said in a rough voice.

Gabriel's favor to me *would* be worth it—I could ask him for anything. Even to go back through time, to resurrect the dead . . . anything I wanted.

A thought suddenly occurred to me—and my heart gave a heavy, aching thump as I realized what I would ask from Gabriel.

Zane was stranded here on the mortal plane with me, a pale shadow of the woman he'd truly loved. Sure he professed to love me now, but if Rachael was standing next to me, I wasn't sure which of us he would pick. It was easy to choose me when he had no other options. But . . . I could give him those options. As I played with the thought in my mind, I realized that it was brilliant. It was unselfish.

It was going to be so hard to do. I could ask Gabriel for Zane's redemption. Then Zane would be free to return to Heaven and receive his wings again—real wings, not demon-spawned ones.

And best of all, he could be with Rachael. He wouldn't have to settle for her replacement, like he'd been forced to settle for replacement wings. I could give him everything back—his wings, his first love, eternity in Heaven. *Everything.*

It felt like a knife in my breast, and tears spilled down my cheeks as I realized that I loved Zane. With all my heart and soul.

I loved him so much that I'd have to let him go back to the arms of the woman he loved more than Heaven itself.

Chapter Twenty-one

"Here, kitty kitty," Remy said, wiggling her finger in front of the cat carrier that Ethan held.

The cat yowled and swiped at her through the bars of the cage. Hissing, it attacked the front of the carrier as if, by sheer persistence, it could somehow get through the reinforced bars.

Remy jerked her hand backward and grinned at me. "Joachim's still a little ticked off at being a cat, I think."

"Let him stay ticked off," I said, watching the two vampires having a conversation on the sidewalk—probably about Joachim. "He's a cat. He can't do anything but piss on the carpets."

She giggled.

I wished I was as happy as she was. We had the halo and were set to deliver it. Soon we'd be free of Joachim's evil forever, and I'd have a boon from an archangel—no mean feat.

But it felt like my life was about to be over. I was going to lose Zane forever.

I rubbed at my breastbone to stop the ache. Remy and I sat in a rental car, parked at the curb of a church downtown. The streets were dark and empty with the onset of dawn except for the two vampires clad in full-length trench coats, smoking cigarettes under a street-light.

After forcing our demon cat into a reinforced cat carrier, we had escaped the destroyed house. Zane had torched it and all the bodies within, and we drove away before the authorities could arrive at the massive fire. I thought of all the families who would wonder endlessly what had happened to their loved ones, and sadness nearly overwhelmed me. All those innocent people dead, because of one evil halo. It had to be destroyed before Joachim could cause more damage.

We'd returned to Remy's house to find Dee's stuff gone and a note stuck to the front door. She and Noah were going to take a little time away from New City. If we needed her, we could call her cell phone. I tossed away the note. Hell would freeze over before I'd call and check and see how she was doing with my boyfriend.

Make that ex-boyfriend, who'd given me up to Zane.

Zane. Who, if my plan came to fruition, would soon be happily in Heaven, reunited with both his wings and his first love. It would leave me terribly vulnerable—with only Noah left as my master (and him not speaking to me). I'd be in a tricky situation, but it wouldn't be enough to stop me from carrying forward. Zane's happiness was more important than anything else.

Zane, who didn't know that he was about to get the biggest gift ever. I blinked away sudden tears, gripping the steering wheel. I had to be strong. If I blubbered like a baby, everyone would guess what I was about to do. But the love I kept trying to fight kept surging forward.

How was I stupid enough to love a man who had used me as a cheap replacement for the true woman he loved? And after knowing that, how was I stupid enough to continue to have feelings for him?

And how was I ever going to let him go?

Outside, I watched the vampires argue. Both were nearing hibernation and their eyes were reddening with the need for blood. Both were smoking heavily to try and take the edge off, since feeding wouldn't happen until after they had finished day-sleep.

Caleb began to pace.

My gaze focused on my lover, my heart doing a little flip at the sight of him, his hair in its familiar tousle that fell over his forehead. Underneath his coat, his wing had been bound and bandaged—I'd done the bandaging. The rest of his body was scarred and bruised, but he was healing quickly. Another day and he'd be fine.

Caleb had not fared as well. He still had that hollow-eyed, worn look. His wings had nearly lost all their feathers while he'd been possessed—I guessed that was part of the curse, since Joachim had been condemned to never have wings again. Still, Caleb should have been thankful that we'd saved him and that he remained relatively whole.

He didn't look thankful at the moment. A cigarette hung from his mouth and he continued to pace, arguing with Zane. They kept glancing back toward the car where we waited, Remy and Ethan watching over the cat in the backseat.

When Caleb shook his head for the third time, I couldn't stand it any longer. "Be right back," I told Remy and Ethan, and got out of the car. I stalked toward Caleb and Zane, hugging my long-sleeved sweater close to my body. The wind was picking up as the new day eased onto the horizon.

"Hi there," I said, approaching the two of them and trying not to wince when two reddening pairs of eyes focused on me. I probably smelled like a succu-buffet.

Zane threw down his cigarette and ground it under one boot. "Everything okay, Princess?"

I gave him a thumbs-up and glanced warily over at Caleb. "Something wrong that you two want to share with the rest of the class?"

Caleb's expression darkened. "You really think giving the halo to Gabriel is a good idea? He could take the halo from you and then destroy us all."

I raised my wrist, displaying the archangel's mark. "I have his word that he won't. See?"

Both vampires stared at my wrist for a moment, and then Caleb shrugged. "I still vote we should turn it over to the queen."

"Yeah, well, it's not yours," I retorted, shoving my sleeve down over my wrist. "And you know how well you controlled yourself when Joachim possessed you. You murdered an entire subdivision without even thinking about it. Now imagine that power given to the queen."

"She's my queen. What do I care what she does?" Caleb sneered.

"You'll care when she murders everyone on Earth," I retorted. "Then who do you plan on drinking from? Each other? Won't *that* be a clusterfuck."

Neither one said anything, and I didn't blame them. I'd have nightmares thinking about the situation myself.

Caleb shrugged again. "The three days is up, anyhow. I have to return to Queen Nitocris and tell her that it's been disposed of. She won't be pleased that I had it in my grasp and lost it."

"When is she ever pleased?" Zane said.

"And when are you going to tell her your news, Zane?"

Zane grew very still. "I'm not sure."

"Tell her what?" I said in a sharp voice. Zane wouldn't look me in the eye. Why did he look so guilty? "Tell the queen *what*?" I repeated.

Zane glanced over at me, his mouth lifting on one side in a heart-melting smile. "Tell her that I'm not returning to the fold."

My heart hammered with a mix of hope and fear. "But . . . I thought . . ." He'd given himself up to her six months ago to save me from her wrath. What would happen to him—and to me—if he elected to go for his freedom?

And did this mean we could be together? Hope began

to spiral through me, only to be crushed by the realization of what I was about to do.

I wouldn't get to keep Zane. I was going to give him up because it was the right thing to do.

God, I *hated* the right thing to do.

"A shame, isn't it?" Caleb flicked the ashes from his cigarette, grinning. "That you died trying to get the halo away from me. Another vampire, sacrificed to the noble cause."

I held my breath.

"It *is* a shame, isn't it?" Zane's gaze remained on Caleb's smiling face. "And all that was left of me was the slave collar."

Was that a dare for Caleb to take the collar off of Zane? Better yet, would it work?

Caleb's expression didn't change as Zane continued to stare at him, eyes locked. I held my breath, waiting to see whose will would win out.

"A real shame," Caleb finally agreed. "Nothing left but the slave collar—and my memories are too fractured for the queen to pull anything from them." He gestured for Zane to lean in, and with a spoken word, the collar unhooked and fell to the ground. Caleb scooped it up. "She's not going to take it well, you know," he told Zane. "You always were her favorite. The crown prince." His mouth twisted into a sneer.

"Favorites change over time," Zane drawled. He looked over at me and I flushed. Was that a reference to me and Rachael? "She'll focus her attention on someone new. A far more obedient prince—like yourself, maybe."

"Maybe," said Caleb. His shrewd gaze slid over to Zane. "Now we're even. If I see you again, I'll have no choice but to destroy you, lest I be proved a liar."

"We're even," Zane agreed. "Nothing more."

Caleb grinned. "As long as we both understand that." Caleb turned and walked down the street.

"I should have destroyed him," Zane said casually, then he gave me a small, heartbreaking smile. "You've made me soft, Jackie."

Warmth coursed through me at his words, and I moved a little closer to him, inhaling his scent. Cigarettes, leather, and cologne. I loved that scent. I was going to miss it so terribly much.

I forced myself to change topics. "Why is Caleb going to lie for you?"

"Because it helps him in the long run," Zane explained, his gaze caressing me, desire in his eyes. "There'll be room at the top for another favorite of the queen, and Caleb's had his eyes on that for a long time. It's the best situation for him."

I longed to move into his arms, to cuddle against his warm chest, but there was no sense in torturing myself. "So you're free of the queen?"

His smile tugged up on one side. "I don't know if I'll ever be free. If *any* of us are ever free of the demands we place on ourselves. But for now, yes. I'm free to be with you. Free to touch you." He moved to pull me close to him. "If you want me to."

Though I hated myself for doing so, I pulled away. I couldn't let him touch me. Not when I was resolved to do what I had to do. I swallowed the knot in my throat and ignored the flash of pain that crossed his face. "Come on," I said hoarsely. "Let's go deliver that halo and get on with our lives."

"Whatever you want, Jackie," he said, his eyes shining with love and pleading for me to forgive him.

I turned away, heading back for the car.

Remy hopped out of the backseat and handed me the case, which immediately began to rock back and forth. "Man, he hates you," she said with a grin. "I'm guessing Joachim doesn't like being a kitty."

"He won't be one for much longer," I said, and slapped the side of the case to give him a jolt. "We're about to deliver him home." Case in hand, I slowly approached the church. I glanced over at Remy. "Think this will be safe?"

She shrugged. "Nothing we do is safe anymore, girl-friend. But this is the best option we've got."

She had a point. As I moved to the double doors, I glanced at Zane. He'd lit up another cigarette and hung back from our small group. "Ready to do this?"

He gestured at the door. "I can't go in, remember? Consecrated ground. You'll have to go without me."

I handed the cat carrier to Ethan. "Go inside and I'll be with you in a moment. I want to talk to Zane first."

After watching them enter the large double doors, I turned back to Zane and put my hand on his chest. "Will you stay while we get this all figured out?"

His mouth twisted a little. "I can't go in and protect you from whatever is in there, Jackie. Why should I stay?"

I wanted him to be there when I received my boon from the Archangel Gabriel. He'd then be free to be with his true love instead of her sorry clone.

Tears blurred my eyes as I regarded him. "Will you just trust me and follow my lead on this?"

His expression was grave. "I'd follow you to the ends of the earth, remember?"

I pulled his mouth down to mine, my heart breaking. The taste of him was so overwhelming that the tears I'd been fighting slipped down my cheeks, and I slid my fingers down to his neck, feeling the smooth skin where the collar had been. He was free.

And I was about to lose him of my own will.

"Why are you crying, love?" he said in a husky voice.

I pressed small, urgent kisses to his mouth, tasting his lips and tracing them with my tongue. "No reason," I whispered between kisses. "Just stay. Please. For me."

"Always," he whispered, nearly undoing me.

But I could do this. I could keep Zane safe. I could make him happy again. That was what I wanted.

I pulled away from him and gave him a tremulous smile. Straightening my shoulders, I moved to the church and pulled the door open. Glancing backward, I saw Zane watching me with intense eyes. He gave me an encouraging wave and I moved forward into the church, letting the door shut behind me.

Remy and Ethan still stood just inside the doorway, and Remy had her hands up in the air. I couldn't see over Ethan's massive shoulders. "What's going on?"

The two parted.

The entire Serim council waited in the church.

"Welcome, Jacqueline Brighton," said Ariel, striding forward with a smile. "I see you've brought us a gift."

The row of Serim stood in line, their shoulders straight and their faces impassive, unforgiving. At the center of the welcoming party stood an imperious figure in white robes and a beautiful pair of white wings: the Archangel Gabriel.

Crap—an ambush.

"Looks like we're late to the party," I said cheerily, hiding my dismay. "How did you know we were coming here?"

Ariel reached for my arm, pulling me forward to escort me to the archangel. "We knew you would be in New City. It was just a matter of locating you. Luckily, we are able to track wherever the Nephilim go."

So they'd known where Ethan was at all times? *Gee, thanks for helping us out of all the messes we'd been in.* "You tracked us?"

"I did. Bonjour, ma belle," said a familiar voice. A man stood at the far end of the room, rising from a pew, and I groaned at the sight of my nemesis, Luc.

"Not *you* again," I said. "You're working for them now?"

His gaze flicked to Ariel and he gave me a cynical look. "I do whatever my master commands. I am not at liberty to disobey. Remember?"

Ugh. Ariel was Luc's master? I suddenly felt sorry for the incubus. A few things slid into place. Luc's unhappiness, Ariel's vendetta against me—it all made sense. No wonder I was in such shit with the Serim council. I'd messed with their favorite plaything.

No time for that, though. I gestured at the cat carrier. "I'm here to uphold my part of the bargain."

Ariel's eyes narrowed at me. "You wish for me to impregnate you?"

"Hell no," I blurted, stepping away from him. "I brought the halo."

The Serim's mouth curled into a sneer. "I am supposed to believe that you were able to recapture the halo?"

"It's in the cat carrier," I said.

As if on cue, the cat yowled loudly.

"It's in . . . the cat?" Ariel gave me a disbelieving look. "What were you thinking?"

"Once called, the halo must have a vessel," intoned Gabriel, moving past Ariel toward Ethan and the cat carrier. "You have brought it back."

"Yes, and it's mine," I pointed out, stepping in front of the cage. "Before I give anyone the halo, I have a few conditions."

"No conditions," shouted Ariel.

"Then I'll take it and leave," I retorted.

"We will take it from you," Ariel roared, striding forward.

"Really?" I said in a light voice. "Because the last time I checked, stealing was a sin. Remember?"

Silence fell.

"Madness," muttered someone in the Serim council. But I could have sworn I saw Luc's mouth twist into a half smile.

Yeah, I was getting the same giddy rush at outmaneuvering Ariel that he was. Of course, that giddy feeling disappeared when the archangel focused his clear-eyed gaze on me, disapproval stamped on his face.

I swallowed hard. "My conditions are simple," I said quietly. "Do you want to hear them?"

"State them," ordered the archangel.

"Very well," I said, rubbing the word burned onto my wrist. It stung like the dickens, probably because I was mere inches away from Gabriel. "For starters, I want to be cleared of all charges set on me by the Serim council. Noah, too."

"Noahiel has already received his punishment," Gabriel said in an emotionless voice.

My knees went weak. "What? Is he . . . all right?"

"He is alive and well, and wholly outside of your concern," Gabriel said. "He resides under my protection. Are those the only demands you have?"

Blinking at the abrupt change in topics, I struggled to clear my head. "No, I have more," I said slowly. "I want Ethan to be free of whatever obligation he has to serve the Serim council. He should be free to go where he likes."

"He has no master to obey, Succubus," said the archangel. "He has always been free to go where he chooses."

"Just making sure," I said, then gestured at my wrist. "I want the cat to be safe, too. It's just a harmless animal."

"Done," intoned the archangel.

"And you gave your word that I can ask anything I wish for in return for the halo." I raised my wrist and pointed at the marking there.

His gaze became flinty. "I have not forgotten."

"Then it's yours." I took the cat carrier from Ethan. A low murmur started from the Serim council, but I ignored it, crouching low to set the carrier on the ground. I glanced up at the archangel looming over me. "Are you ready?"

His eyes were emotionless. "I am. Release the beast."

I opened the carrier door.

An orange and black streak flashed out of the cage, yowling. It dove under the pews, scrambling to get away.

Gabriel raised a hand into the air, his eyes lighting with power. The room grew thick with power and the scent of vanilla grew strong. Gabriel seemed to glow from within, and my internal tuning fork went wild in response. As I watched, the cat lifted into the air. The golden *shenu* around its neck flared brightly and began to pulse. The cat twirled and scrambled midair, trying to escape, and I could feel the power inside the cat struggling against the overwhelming feeling of warmth and purity that seemed to be radiating from the archangel. With a flick of Gabriel's wrist, it floated over the pews toward him.

He reached for it with both hands, and the moment he touched it the world pulsed, with a shift of power so strong, it knocked me to the ground.

I struggled back onto my feet. My eyes took a moment to refocus, then I saw Gabriel cradling the now-calm cat against his chest. He stroked it with a gentle hand, radiance surrounding his head in a halo of light.

The golden *shenu* was nowhere to be seen.

"Joachim is at peace now," Gabriel said calmly. "And safe from harming himself and others. You have done a wise thing, Jackie Brighton."

"Thanks." I watched him pet the cat for a moment longer. "Is the cat okay?"

In response, Gabriel handed her back to me. She was purring, and warm in my arms. I cradled her, stroking her soft head. If there was an evil rampaging archangel in her anymore, I didn't feel it.

Gabriel asked, "Is there anything else you require before I leave?"

I swallowed hard and bent down to put the cat back in the carrier. "Yes. We need to go out on the street."

"I cannot leave consecrated ground," Gabriel said. "You know the rules."

"You can if you're inhabiting someone." I turned toward the Nephilim who stood with Remy. "Ethan, would you be his vessel? Just for a few minutes?"

Gabriel stretched out a hand, expressionless. Ethan glanced over at me, and then reached out to take it. There was a flash of brilliant light, and I blinked rapidly to adjust my eyes, then I saw Ethan with a halo of light surrounding him, his eyes completely white.

Well. That was . . . interesting. I forced myself to smile. "We ready, then?"

The smooth white eyes turned to me and Ethan's shoulders straightened, his posture more erect than I thought humanly possible. "Lead me to where you wish to go."

CHAPTER TWENTY-TWO

S ucking in a deep breath, I steeled myself. I could do this. I could. I could. My hands trembled as I pushed the church's doors open and I stepped into the cool dawn air, half hoping that I wouldn't see Zane when I emerged.

He was there leaning against the side of the car, trying to look casual. Only the drum of his fingers gave away any anxiety. He stood at the sight of me, coming alert with a wary look at Ethan behind me.

"Zane," I breathed, stretching my hands out to take his. "You're here. Good."

"You told me to wait," he said in an even voice, his gaze locked on Ethan's towering form. "And Ethan looks like a white blur . . . so tell me why there's an archangel following you."

I'd forgotten—a vampire couldn't look upon the face of a pure angel.

"It's Gabriel," I said, giving his hands a squeeze. "I agreed to turn the halo over to him in exchange for a favor." The knot in my throat choked me for a moment.

Zane remained silent, watching me. His thumb grazed the soft flesh of my hand, encouraging me to go on.

I drew a deep breath and lifted my head, tears swimming in my eyes. "I'm using my favor for you."

He shook his head. "I'm not following you."

"I'm granted anything I ask for, Zane. You can ascend back to Heaven. You can have wings again. Real wings with no strings attached."

In shock, he stared at me, then back at Ethan, then back at me again. "I don't understand."

I swallowed hard, then confessed the next part—the most important part. "You can be with Rachael again." My voice wobbled at the end.

He stared at me, eyes wide with disbelief.

I couldn't seem to stop crying. "See, I made a deal that if I got the halo back, I could have anything I wanted. I couldn't think of anything that I wanted for myself that was important enough." I began to smooth his jacket, his sleeves, something to keep my mind focused. This might be the last time I saw him. Smooth, smooth, stroke, stroke. My fingers moved along his collar. "And all I could think about was you, and how losing Rachael broke your heart, and how you're separated from her forever, and cast out here on Earth, and I know that's not what you wanted." I swallowed hard. "An eternity in exile without her."

"Jackie—"

"And I know that the queen won't forgive you if you leave her again," I interrupted. I didn't want to hear his happiness. Even though this was the right thing to do, it was tearing me apart. "Not for good. And I want you to be safe, always. I can't bear the thought of something happening to you, and in Heaven you'll be safe forever. And happy. And in love. And—"

"No."

"And—I'm sorry?" I said, swiping at my nose. "What did you say?"

His smile was gentle, and his fingertips brushed away my tears. "I said no."

"I . . . I don't understand."

"Jackie," he said, his hands sliding to my waist. "I loved Rachael a very, very long time ago. My memories of her are four thousand years faint. Long before I met you. Before I chose to wear dark wings. I'm not the same person I was back then.

"I fell in love with you the first time you hit me with your purse—or the first time you scowled at me in the nightclub. Or the first time you looked at me with something other than hate in your eyes." His voice grew very soft. "Ascending would be a dream come true for any of the fallen *except* for me."

"But why? Why, when it can keep you safe from the queen?"

"Because *you* won't be there." He ran a thumb along my lower lip, his eyes soft with emotion. "Because I'd have to wake up without you at my side. I've known that hell for the past six months, and I don't intend to ever let it happen again."

"But the queen! She'll kill you."

He shook his head. His normally playful smile was gone, replaced by an intensely passionate look. "I would rather spend one more day in your arms than an eternity without you, Jackie Brighton. I love you." He pulled my hand to his chest and placed it against his heart. "This beats for you, and only for you. Not Rachael. Not the queen. For *you*. I love you, and I hope that someday you'll forgive me for turning you."

I burst into tears, pulling my hand from his grasp to fling my arms around his neck. "Oh Zane," I sobbed.

He laughed, the sound warm against my neck. "Glad to see I've made you so happy."

Zane loved me for *me*. He'd picked me over Rachael. He'd picked me over redemption. "Oh Zane, I love you so much."

He stroked my back as I sobbed. "You do?"

I pulled away, nodding and wiping tears from my face. "I love you and I want us to be together." I pulled a deep, shuddering breath. "Noah and I are over for now." I wasn't sure if the ache in my heart would go away anytime soon, but he'd made his choice and I made mine. I leaned in and began to press kisses on Zane's jawline with frantic adoration. "I love you and I want us to be together, and I'll let you take my blood every night—"

"Whoa, slow down there, Jackie," he began with a chuckle.

"You can call me Princess all you want. As long as it's not her name."

"It's always been yours." He played with a lock of my curling hair. "She chased sheep for a living. I called you Princess because I couldn't think of anyone better for a vampire prince."

I pressed my face against his neck, breathing in his

scent. "You sure you don't want Heaven over me?" I said in a soft voice.

"When I'm with you I *am* in Heaven."

Damn, I was going to start crying again. I looked over at Gabriel/Ethan, suddenly embarrassed.

So maybe . . . maybe I could use the archangel's favor for Noah. He could ascend and reunite with Rachael, and I could stop feeling so guilty. "Gabriel," I said, pulling away from Zane slightly (though I kept my hand firmly in his). "I have another friend I want to use the favor on instead."

The sightless eyes focused on me. "What favor do you speak of?"

I frowned. "You said that if I returned the halo to you, then I could ask anything I wanted."

"I said that if you returned the power of the archangels to me, you could ask anything you wanted," he said in the deep, sonorous voice. "I have not forgotten."

"Well, that's what I just gave you. It wasn't some souvenir," I retorted.

"Jackie," Zane said faintly. "What did you promise to do for him?"

"I promised to return the archangel's power."

Zane shook his head. "There were *seven* archangels, Jackie. The seven seals of Heaven. Almost all of them fell when the rest of us fell." He eyed Ethan/Gabriel. "Except him and Michael."

"*Seven?*" I echoed. Oh, hell. When Gabriel had told me that I had to return the archangel's power, I had assumed it meant one archangel. Had he meant *arch-*

angels'? As in plural, not possessive? As in, I wasn't done with the job yet? Not by a long shot? "No!" I protested. "No way. That's cheating."

"It is not cheating," said the angel, stone-faced.

"You didn't explain that there were five more freaking halos." Could angels ever ask for anything without making it a double-sided deal?

"The deal was always for *all* halos. How you chose to interpret it is not my problem."

I gritted my teeth, my fist raising.

"Jackie, Princess." Zane placed his hand over mine, stopping me before I did something reckless, like punch Ethan/Gabriel.

I forced myself to exhale slowly, trying to calm down. "All halos. Then I get the reward."

"That is correct."

I swear, they must have given out merit badges for sneaky promises up in Heaven, because this was ridiculous.

"The seven seals are the guardians to the gates of Heaven," Zane explained to me. "If all of them fall, then there is nothing to stop Lucifer from taking Heaven for his own."

I pointed at the church. "So that halo in there . . ."

"Is one of the seven seals," intoned Gabriel. "I am another. The Archangel Michael is another. Two were recollected in days long past."

So that meant . . . "There are still two remaining?"

"That is correct," said the archangel.

"Fuck me," I said in disgust.

Zane grinned. "I'll handle that,"

EPILOGUE

"We decided to call the cat Angelbait," Remy told me as I entered the kitchen. She was feeding the cat a can of tuna on the floor. "He doesn't have anyplace to go, so he might as well stay here. We could have a halo addicts support group or something." She grinned at me, dipping her peanut-butter-covered spoon into a jar of jelly and then shoving it into her mouth. "He likes Ethan, too," she said around the spoon.

I smiled at her and moved past, digging in the fridge. Now, where had that gone? I pulled out a container of honey, eyed it, and then put it back in the fridge. Not quite what I was looking for. "I don't suppose you've seen a jar of uh . . . stuff?"

"Body butter?" she asked helpfully.

A blush crept up my cheeks. "That's it."

"Goes great with peanut butter," she said, then giggled.

"Remy!" I turned around and sure enough, she was swirling her spoon in it. I snatched the jar away.

"What?" she asked in a hurt voice. "It's strawberry flavored and we're all out of jam."

Cheeks on fire, I screwed the lid on as quickly as I could. "It's not yours."

"Well, what kind of dipshit puts their sex stuff in the fridge, anyhow?"

Lord, I was never going to stop blushing. "Ethel thought it was a snack. She put it there and I couldn't find it."

"I *see*," she said in a voice that made me want to smack her in the face. "Anything else I'm going to find in the fridge?"

"No! Shut up!"

"Can I borrow it later?"

"Get your own," I retorted. "Besides, you'll scar Ethan for life if you try this on him."

She rolled her eyes and hopped off the counter. "I'm breaking him in easy, I promise." She bent down to pet the cat. Angelbait sniffed the peanut-butter spoon and began to lick it. Yick.

"So how are things going with you and Ethan?" I ventured.

Remy shrugged. "Not bad. Could be better. He still thinks you should go after Noah, by the way."

"Noah made his choice. I made mine. Tell him to quit trying to make me feel guilty about it." Nothing was going to ruin my happiness right now. Especially not the world's largest Boy Scout.

"Yeah, I told him to shut up about it, too, but you know how he gets. He has this possessive thing that I'm trying to break him of. So far it's working. He's promised not to freak out whenever he sees me on TV anymore, and I promised to show him what a Cleveland steamer is."

"Remy!"

"I'm *kidding*, Jackie. Jeez. You're as bad as he is." She gave a gusty sigh. "Ethan and I aren't too bad, now that I got fired from *The Big Sleazy*. Oh well." She sounded glum. "I guess I can always do an autobiography, or something boring like that. Ethan's lucky he's got some big equipment, or he'd be back to that sanctuary."

I headed over to the kitchen table to examine some paperwork there. "Just don't break his heart, or we'll have the Serim council back here with new kinds of torture."

"Pass on that," she said, making a face and following me to the table. "So, any luck with the halo hunt?"

"No," I said in frustration. I flopped down on a chair, staring at the maps spread over the table. With no clue of where to find the two missing archangel halos, we'd started by cross-referencing ancient artifacts and old temples. Visiting everything that seemed to be a likely site would take years, and I had no leads. No more hints from possessed pool boys, and no signs from above.

Clearly, these other two halos weren't as big of a threat, or they'd have offered more help. I was on my own for the next leg of the scavenger hunt, it seemed. "I swear, just when I think I'm getting free of angelic entanglements, I get launched into another. It isn't fair."

"Of course it's not fair," she said, moving over to pat my shoulder. "Cheer up. Something is bound to turn up. It always does."

I glanced out the window—sunset. Time to go. "I'll be back later. Right now I've got a date."

"Don't do anything I wouldn't do," she said, winking.

Yeah, like that left anything. "By the way, Remy. I still have the nullifier necklace I gave you back in New Orleans. Do you want it back?"

She wrinkled her nose in disgust. "No, thanks. That thing just reminds me of Joachim and he's better off as a bad memory."

"Gotcha." That suited me just fine. Zane had originally gifted the necklace to me, and I'd kept it for sentimental value. Too bad I couldn't wear it regularly—the nullifier charm worked on succubi too . . . and I really didn't have any desire to have my libido dampened at the moment. I grinned and sprinted up the stairs to my wing of the house.

Sunset was my favorite time of the day, and I looked forward to it with enthusiasm. As I headed back to my rooms I passed Ethel, the little old maid who kept Remy's house, and smiled at her.

"Hello, Miss Jackie," she said in a disapproving voice. "I cleaned your scarves again." She held it out to me, clearly scandalized. "Don't get them so dirty."

I took the black sashes and shoved them in my pocket. "Thank you."

She merely sniffed and continued down the hall. I raced toward my room, grinning with anticipation, and shut the door behind me. The bedroom was dark, the blinds shut, and the bed occupied.

Zane's black hair was tousled on the pillows, wings neatly tucked underneath him. He was naked, the sheets slung low on his waist. I admired the sight, then set down the jar of body butter. Pulling the scarves from my pocket, I tied one of his wrists to the headboard, then straddled him to tie his other one.

"Well," he said in a sleepy voice against the vee of my legs. "This is what every man dreams of waking up to."

I laughed and swung off of him, bouncing next to him on the bed. "Evening, vampire."

One hand flexed, then the other, and he smiled, displaying white fangs and eyes bright red with interest.

"You ready for another game tonight?" I asked.

Zane chuckled, a low rasp that did incredible things to my insides. "Your wish is my command, love."

At the affectionate term, my heart swelled. I leaned over and kissed him, filled with happiness. "I love you."

He smiled into my kiss.

My tongue played along the points of his fangs, then I slipped away to straddle him again. "Tonight's game is called Bite Me. Very exciting stuff."

"Sounds like my kind of game. What do I get if I win?"

"You get to bite me all over."

"And if I lose?"

"You get to help me study maps again to figure out where the halos are. Tonight's continent," I said, trailing a finger down his washboard chest, "is Australia."

His smile flashed. "Fuck that. So how do I win?"

"We bet on how many bites it takes for you to make

me come." I leaned over him to press a kiss on his chest. "I bet ten."

Zane's breath hitched. "I bet one."

"One?" I scoffed. "I need one bite just to get wet."

"Princess, never dare a vampire when it comes to his bite," he said, teeth flashing. "He might take it as a personal challenge."

I arched an eyebrow at him. "You're on."

It turned out he was right. It *was* a personal challenge.

And it did, in fact, only take one.

Turn the page
and step inside Midnight Liaisons,
a paranormal dating service
open to every vamp, were, and angel

The first book in
a fun, sexy new series
by

Jill Myles

Coming soon from Pocket Books

"Midnight Liaisons," I answered as I cradled the phone to my ear. "This is Bathsheba. How can I help you?"

"Hi," the man breathed nervously into the other end of the phone. "I'm looking for . . . company. Tonight. Maybe a redhead."

I winced. There was no way to misunderstand what he was looking for, as he'd clearly stated "redhead" in a rather obvious (and breathy) fashion. We got at least one of these kinds of calls a day and I'd become an old hand at deflecting the creepiness of the occasional misguided caller. "Midnight Liaisons is a dating service, sir. Not an escort service."

Now please, never call me again.

There was a pause on the other end of the line. "Oh," he said. "Well, that's fine. How can I access your website to look at the dating profiles? It won't give me a password."

"The password is your Alliance ID number." I fought to keep my voice pleasant. "Or I can check your credentials and get you set up with a temporary log-in. If you can tell me who your pack leader is, I'd be more than happy to send through the background check—"

"My what?"

Definitely a civilian on the line. A "natural," as my

boss liked to joke around the office. I decided to play dumb anyhow. "If you don't have a pack leader . . . perhaps your master?" If this guy was familiar with undead society at all, he'd catch the hint.

"Huh?"

"Coven? Fey King?" I couldn't resist. "High Lord?"

"What are you talking about, lady?" The man on the other end of the line was irritated at me. Gone was the smarmy tone, replaced by your typical, run-of-the-mill angry customer. Except he definitely wasn't one of *our* customers.

"I'm sorry," I said in my most sugary voice. "But Midnight Liaisons has an exclusive clientele. Our dating service is open to referrals from current clients only. Have a nice day, sir—"

"Now just a minute," the man began, but I hung up on him anyway. The chances of him ever becoming a client were slim to none, after all.

Across the room, Sara snickered at me as she typed. "You always get the weird ones."

"Of course I do," I said, turning in my chair to glance at her. Sara's eyes were glued to her screen, but she had a smile on her face. "We get weird calls because the company name sounds like an escort service. And I get them because you're not answering the phone."

"I'm busy," she said, but her mouth quirked.

"Part of your job is to answer the phone," I retorted, exasperated. "I'm the office manager! If any one shouldn't have to answer the phone, it should be me."

"But you're so good at it," Sara soothed me, grinning. "I'm not half as patient with them as you are."

"Then maybe I shouldn't have hired you to work here."

Sara had heard my complaint a hundred times before, but it was an empty threat. Seeing as how she was my baby sister, she could get away with—and usually did get away with—just about everything. She flipped through the slender stack of profiles on her desk as if searching for something, ignoring my sputtering with the good-natured humor of someone completely safe in their job. "Midnight Liaisons is a stupid name, I admit. But what else was the boss supposed to call a dating service that caters exclusively to the paranormal?"

"Bangs For Fangs? Flea-collared Submissives?" I quipped, turning back to my screen to get rid of the flashing software pop-up reminding me to log the call into the database. "Fresh Meat for Deadbeats?"

I could hear Sara's snort of laughter across the small office. "You're too hard on them. They're not all jerks just because they have fangs or tails."

"Says the woman that doesn't answer the phone," I replied, but smiled. It was a weird business, but generally I liked my job, weirdos and all. The hours were strange, the clientele were even stranger, but it paid well, I ran the office like it was my own, and I got to watch over my baby sister. Life was good. Strange, but good.

Across the room, Sara sucked in a breath. "Uh oh."

I turned in my chair again to glance back at my sister. "Uh oh? Why 'uh oh'?" While my job was to set up new profiles and match up clients unable to manage on their own (in addition to running the office), Sara had the task of personal follow-up and account maintenance. It was her job to check in with our clients to see that dates were still on, to follow up after the date to ensure everyone enjoyed themselves, and to update profiles with "exclusive" status if necessary. It was the easiest job in our small office. Sara usually finished it within hours and then flipped her computer over to gaming mode, spending the rest of the day playing Halo or something equally obnoxious. "Something wrong?"

"Profile #26742, that's what's wrong," she said with an anxious note in her voice.

Oh boy. I flinched. I didn't even have to access the profile to know who it was. "What's Rosario done now?"

Rosario was what Sara had lovingly referred to as "trouble." She cancelled on dates regularly, was aggressive as hell, and had given more than one guy problems, and not just of the flea-and-tick variety. Some guys were into it—they expected a werewolf chick to be fiery, especially a Latina one.

Everyone in our office hated her.

"What's she done now?" I repeated, anticipating the complaint call certain to come in.

"She's accepted a date with a cat shifter," Sara said, sounding puzzled. "Through the website. Don't worry, I can handle it."

A nervous quiver settled in my stomach. "But Rosie always cancels on the cats." We had a string of complaints in Rosie's file a mile long. If someone canceled on a date, they were charged an inconvenience fee. But our boss Giselle had decided a while back that she liked Rosie, so she waived her fees, and Rosie used and abused her privileges.

I suspected that Rosie and Giselle had some sort of hidden agreement that involved a bit more than what the standard contract said, but I wasn't about to ask. The only reason Rosie was still allowed in the dating service was because the pool of female Alliance members in the database was so small compared to the male membership. Especially one as attractive—and willing to date—as Rosie. We couldn't afford to lose her. She was brisk business, even if I questioned her motives.

"Not just any shifter," Sara amended as I headed over to her desk. Her eyes flicked back and forth as she regarded the screen. "One of the new accounts. The head of the Russell clan."

The Russell clan was powerful, but to my knowledge, they'd never used Giselle's services before. "I don't recall setting up—"

"His account is starred."

A star on someone's account meant someone powerful and dangerous, and not to piss them off, or the boss would do terrible things to us. It also meant Giselle had circumvented the regular account set-up process and had taken care of this one on her own. She had a vested interest in its success.

We'd learned long ago not to mess with the starred accounts. Not if we valued employment.

"Oh boy," I breathed, tucking a limp strand of blonde hair behind my ear. "Have you called Giselle yet?"

Giselle was the hundred-year-old siren who had started Midnight Liaisons. Our boss, and a bit of a hardass. She wouldn't be pleased about Rosie, and she'd be even less pleased when she found out Rosie had screwed up a starred account.

"Hell no, I haven't told her," Sara said, looking at me as if I'd grown another head. "I can handle this. Just give me a minute."

"Sara," I warned, my hand going to my hip in exasperation. "This isn't like one of your games."

"Sure it is," she said, not looking at me as she typed furiously, her gaze fixed on the screen. "I can fake a database failure and wipe out all the records for the past twenty-four hours—"

"Sara! No, jeezus no." I tried to grab her wrists, but my little sister was smaller and quicker than me. "Don't you touch the database. Giselle will freak out if the records dump again."

Considering that my sister had pulled this same stunt twice in the past year, I suspected that Giselle was starting to grow wise to Sara's hacking skills.

"If we lose the account, we're in deep shit, Bath. Much deeper shit than a data-loss."

No kidding. Not only did Giselle have a sensitive relationship with the Russell clan (read: tenuous), but she had little tolerance for humans in general. The only reason she staffed her business with quiet normal girls like Sara and myself, I suspected, was because we could work all hours of the day. Giselle's circle of friends were limited by things like daylight and a full moon.

Sara turned frustrated eyes to me. "We can't tell her, Bath. That's just out of the question."

How could we not? But when Sara sniffed, holding back tears, I caved. My feisty sister, crying? That wasn't like her at all.

"We'll fix this, don't worry." Leaning over her desk, I gestured at Sara's computer monitor, determined to take control of the situation. "Pull up Rosie's profile. See if she logged where she was heading with her hot date tonight." Midnight Liaisons strictly monitored the activities of clients. The date, time, and location of a date was recorded and detailed—for their protection as well as ours. You never knew when an interspecies war was going to break out because someone had dated someone else's bitch. Literally.

Sara's fingers tapped on the keyboard and then she whistled. "She logged it, all right. Dinner at Del Frisco's and a couple of nights at the Worthington afterwards."

I made a strangled sound in my throat. "Dinner and a private party, eh?" Rosie moved in faster circles than most girls, human or otherwise. Still, Del Frisco's was pricey. At least she was getting this guy to treat her right.

The phone on my desk rang again and I started in surprise. It was unusual to have two calls so close together again due to our small client pool, and it almost never happened before dark.

Which meant my freak was probably calling back again.

Time to fix this. I narrowed my eyes and marched back to my desk. "Give me a moment, Sara, and we'll figure this out." The phone rang a third time before I picked it up and answered in my breathiest voice. "Midnight Liaisons," I said, and before he could answer, I continued. "If you keep calling us, you fucking pervert, I'm going to call the cops and tell them you're soliciting our business for sex."

The voice on the other end chuckled. A deep, low laugh rumbled through the receiver—most definitely not my last caller. Warmth flooded through my body at the liquid sound and I could feel my face flushing at the sensation.

"Do you call all your customers perverts," the man asked, "or am I just lucky?"

I bit my lip. "I'm sorry. I thought you were— Oh, never mind. How can I help you, sir?"

He paused for a moment, as if still amused at my response. "I have a bit of a problem," he said in a delicious voice, pleasant and smooth. "I had a very important date tonight and she just cancelled on me."

My heart sank. The bad feeling in my stomach lodged firmly in my throat. "What is your profile number, sir?"

He gave it to me and I typed it in the system, though I already knew what it would show. Rosie's date.

The caller's profile pulled up, the information on it minimal. Leader of the Russell clan—oh *hell*—and very much a VIP with our service. No picture in our database, his log history was brief, his profile number new. He hadn't used our service before setting up the date with Rosie.

My super-seductive caller was named Beau Russell. I'd have bet money he was absolutely gorgeous. Tall, blond, and handsome to match his cougar genes. A sensual face to match the sinful voice. And lots of muscles.

"You got quiet over there, sweetheart." He paused and then said in a low voice, "You see my problem?"

That drew me back to earth. I quit picturing the client's abs and tapped on my mouse, my cheeks hot. "I see Rosario Smith cancelled on your date, correct," I said. "And I'm not your sweetheart."

"Rosario agreed to spend the week with me," he said, his voice tensing. "This is an extremely important time frame for me, and it's vital I have a companion."

In the span of a moment, his sexy voice had changed from delicious to condescending. "Well then, sir, I would suggest next time you examine Rosie's profile a little closer. If you looked at her date history, you would see she has a few bad habits." Like accepting dates from cat shifters and then dumping them at the last minute. "A bit of simple research could have avoided this heartache."

He chuckled low in his throat at my tart lecture. "You'll have to forgive me for not being too familiar with your system, sweetheart." His voice thrummed low in my ear. "I'm not used to searching for women online."

No, I'd bet not. If he was half as sexy as his voice, they'd be falling all over him on a regular basis.

"Regardless," he said. "It's the eleventh hour and I need a new date. So either you fix this or we have a big problem. Is Giselle in?"

I ignored the last part of his statement. Obviously he was on good terms with my boss. Obviously this was bad news for me. "I can't force Rosie to go out with you, sir."

"Call me Beau," he said, the inflection in his voice changing to coaxing. It made my thighs quiver. "And if Rosario won't go out with me, I need you to find me another date."

I brightened. "I can do that." We were a dating service, after all. I put his number into the profile generator and today's date. "Give me just a moment and I'll go through the database. I'm sure we can find you someone on short notice."

"No vampires," he said, "or any sort of undead." Then he paused. "What's your name?"

I typed his search criteria into the system, trying not to frown. The whole "no undead" thing kind of limited my query by a lot. Female shifters were rare, and if I counted out both men and undead, we might have a problem getting someone for tonight—and the next week. "My name is Bathsheba Ward," I said absently, crossing my fingers as I waited for the profile results to pull up.

Just as I gave him my name, the door to the office

rang and a gorgeous man walked in the door, a pair of sunglasses obscuring his eyes.

My jaw dropped. The man was flipping beautiful—tall, dark, tanned. His suit was expensive, and he grinned, flashing a pearly-white set of teeth at me. Even at my desk, I could smell the thick musk of his cologne. A bit heavy, but typical of the confident sort.

He must have come down to the office for a new profile set-up. Giselle always preferred that I handle those in person. I raised a finger to my customer, indicating that I needed a moment, and blushed when he nodded and sat down directly across from my desk, eyeing me with interest.

"Bathsheba?" The man on the phone sounded amused and I had to drag my attention back to the phone call. "That's a bit of a mouthful for a modern girl. Are you a vamp?"

Intensely uncomfortable, I squirmed in my seat and tried to look busy, avoiding the scrutiny of the man across from me. "If I was a vampire," I said lightly, "I'd be a piece of burned toast right now, seeing as how it's midday." Sunlight poured in from the window behind my desk and the entire front of the strip-mall office was nothing but windows. "I'm human. Sorry to disappoint."

"Oh, I'm not disappointed," he said in a low husk that made my toes curl.

Between the phone call and the man across from me that looked altogether a little too interested in my conversation, I was going to die of embarrassment. Sara was shooting me puzzled looks from across the office and that only added to my discomfort.

My search results returned and the computer pinged at me. One lousy, lone profile popped up on my screen and I pulled it up with desperation. "It looks like we've found you a good match, Beau," I said, turning on the sales pitch. "Lorraina Murphy happens to be free tonight, and she's very interested in dating all kinds of shifters, according to her profile."

He made a rumbling sound of assent in his throat. "And what is she?"

"Shifter," I said evasively.

"What kind?" he pressed.

"Avian."

An uncomfortable pause. "You're going to have to be more specific than that."

I held back a sigh, knowing where this was headed. "Harpy."

The man across from me smiled.

There was a pause on the phone as there always was when the harpy's profile came up. Then, very softly, he said, "I'm not going to go out with a harpy, Bathsheba."

Well, I couldn't blame the man. Harpies had a bit of a reputation. Plus, they gave psycho-girlfriend a whole new meaning. They tended to get unhinged over small stuff and then things got really ugly. Shit hit the wall, literally. "We have a doppelganger on file," I said, desperate. "Jean can pose as a man or a woman, depending on your needs."

The phone grew very quiet.

Then, "Bathsheba, are you married?" God, his voice sounded sexier than ever.

Say Yes. Say Yes. Lie and say you are married. "No," I breathed. "I'm not." I didn't dare look up at the man across from me, and busied myself with flipping through a stack of files on my desk. *Look busy, look busy.* Too bad I couldn't hide under my desk.

"Seeing someone?"

". . . No." It was hard to date guys when you couldn't tell them where you worked. Besides, Giselle had us keep weird hours.

"Then it sounds like you're my date, doesn't it?"

"The Alliance of Supernaturals doesn't permit human/ supe dating unless allowed by a special visa."

"I'm a lawyer. You leave the details to me."

"Mr. Russell," I said, desperate, "I don't date clients."

The man across from me sat up and leaned forward, as if his interest had sparked. He murmured, "That's a real shame."

I didn't think my face could possibly get any redder. Not. Humanly. Possible.

"Make an exception . . . or let me talk to Giselle." The man on the phone wasn't going to take no for an answer, and I turned all my concentration back to him. I was starting to get a little irritated at his high-handed demands.

"I think you are making a mistake, Mr. Russell."

"Beau."

"Whatever. Still a mistake."

"Why is that? You have a lovely name, a sexy voice, and you're free tonight," he said, his tone cajoling. "You're at least an auxiliary member of the Alliance if you're working for Giselle, so there won't be anything awkward to explain, like why I grow a tail sometimes. And you already think I'm a pervert, remember? So there won't be any surprises."

Was that a joke? I made a protesting noise in my throat, but it came out as a dry squeak.

"I have to say, I'm looking forward to it," Beau continued. "I'll get the chance to put a face to that sweet tongue of yours," he said in a low, seductive voice.

I blushed again. Dammit.

It took me a moment to recover, and I thought hard. I gave Sara a frantic look. She sat at her desk, hands covering her face, shoulders slumped. Sara needed her job badly—and it was her job to monitor pending dates and warn clients of any disastrous mismatches. If anyone got in trouble, it would be Sara for not catching a situation sure to end in disaster.

I turned away from my desk, phone clutched to my cheek, trying to get a semblance of privacy. "Just dinner," I breathed into the receiver, warring with my own instincts. I couldn't look at the man across the desk from me—I didn't want to look at him as I caved like a deck of cards and gave in to Beau's demand. Everything in me shouted that the date was a big mistake, but I couldn't abandon my sister. Lord only knew what she'd do to the database. "I won't go back to the hotel with you."

"Unless you want to," he added.

I rolled my eyes at his cockiness. "I won't want to. Trust me."

"We'll see," he said, supremely confident. "I'll meet you at the restaurant at seven thirty. See you then, sweet Bathsheba." He hung up before giving me a chance to respond.

Dazed, I set the phone down, trying to regroup.

The man across from me smiled. "Hi," he said, extending his hand over my desk.

"Was that him?" Sara interrupted, drawing my attention away from the new customer. Her voice was muffled from her hands over her face. "Am I totally fired now? How much do you think I could get for unemployment?"

"Not fired yet," I said, my heart hammering in my chest with nervous excitement. I gave the man across from me an apologetic look. "Could you excuse us for a quick moment?"

"Of course," he said, giving me a quick nod.

I raced over to Sara's desk for a more private conversation, trying not to seem too flustered. I had a date with a mysterious stranger tonight. One that was going to try to seduce me, regardless of what I looked like. A man with no standards, except when it came to the undead and harpies. A man with an amazingly sexy, powerful voice. I was thrilled and terrified all at once.

She gave me a guilty look as soon as I came over to her desk and tried to hide her screen.

"Don't kill the database yet," I said, sitting on the edge

of her desk. The goofy, nervous feeling wouldn't leave me, no matter how hard I tried to calm down. "I've fixed things."

"Fixed things?" Sara glanced back up to look at me, a confused expression on her face. "What do you mean, you 'fixed' things?"

I smiled weakly. "I'm going out with Beau Russell tonight. Taking Rosie's place."

Sara's jaw dropped. "What? We're not allowed to date clients. We're *normal*, not paranormal. Neither one of us has the appropriate paperwork." Her voice lowered and she shook her head. "I think that's really sweet of you, sis, but Giselle will have a cow if she finds out."

"I won't tell if you won't," I said.

Sara shook her head, almost violently. Her fine hair flew about her shoulders and she turned back to her computer. "Don't be crazy, Bath. I can fix this—"

I grabbed her hand, leaning over her desk. "If you erase one file out of that database, I swear I'm going to pour water onto your motherboard at home. Understand me?" At her glare, I continued. "I'm the office manager. Let me manage this."

She stuck her tongue out at me in response, and I knew I'd won.

Was it wrong I was a little excited? I returned to my desk to help the man set up a profile, unable to get rid of the strange, goofy smile on my face.